Abigail's Window

Susan Lynn Solomon

For Eric,

Enjoy!

Susan Lynn Solomon

Publisher's Note:

This is a work of fiction. All names, characters, places, and events are the work of the author's imagination.

Any resemblance to real persons, places, or events is coincidental.

Solstice Publishing - www.solsticepublishing.com

For Charlie Ganim, a friend who introduced me to the Canadian bed & breakfast he once owned, and to Abigail Bender, the ghost that dwelled there.

Chapter One
Face in the Window

As I stepped from the rental car, I saw the lace curtains pulled aside in a second floor window. I felt eyes stare down at me. My jaw dropped. Had it followed me here?

Ronnie Hoffmann glanced at me over the roof of the car. "What's wrong *now*?" she said.

I stood, blinking.

With a shrug, she turned to Andrea O'Rourke, who popped the trunk and lifted out our suitcases.

When I looked again at the window I saw a woman, but not quite a woman. She appeared to be… transparent. Shuddering, I turned my back to the house.

"Yeah, I'm cold too, Katy. Get your suitcase." Ronnie took off her thick-rimmed glasses and brushed a strand of hair from her eyes. Though only in her early thirties, her long black hair showed streaks of gray.

I wrapped my heavy coat tight around my chest but didn't move. I hadn't wanted to come to Niagara-on-the-Lake, hadn't wanted to leave my apartment. After what I'd been through, I never wanted to venture out again. Ronnie had refused to let me become a hermit.

"You waiting for April when the snow melts?" she called to me.

I lifted my eyes to the window. The curtains were closed. Feeling as though the woman continued to watch me, I shrank back against the car door. "Somebody's… up there."

Andrea clicked her tongue.

"Another ghost?" Ronnie slammed the car trunk closed. "The Niagara Inn isn't any more haunted than your apartment."

My friend knew what haunted me. She had helped to pull me through a breakdown seven years ago. She didn't believe a ghost caused it then, and didn't believe one pushed me toward the edge this time.

I pointed to the window. "Don't you see her?"

Ronnie didn't bother to look. "Probably another guest."

The stiff Lake Ontario wind had turned Andrea's face almost as red as her hair. Looking around the empty parking lot, she said, "Can't be another guest. No one but us is stupid enough to travel in this weather." She hefted her suitcase. "Yap out here if you want. I'm going inside."

Shivering, I examined the bed and breakfast Ronnie had brought me to for a long, girls-only weekend. Pale behind the falling snow and surrounded by skeletons of azalea bushes and a row of evergreen hedges, the Niagara Inn rose two stories above what appeared to be an ancient brick foundation.

"Come on, come on. I'm about to turn into an icicle," Andrea complained.

"More like a cherry popsicle," Ronnie said.

"Yeah, whatever." Our redheaded friend turned and stomped off through the snow.

The wind rushed up to encircle me. In its howl, I heard a familiar laugh. This disembodied sound had chased me since my teenage years. I looked at our car, now coated with a thin layer of snow. I had an urgent desire to get in, drive back across the border to the Buffalo airport and fly home to Manhattan. Though the laughter also haunted me there, at least in familiar surroundings I could almost ignore it.

While I thought about fleeing, the lake wind pushed me toward the house. I held fast.

Ronnie grabbed the sleeve of my black faux-fur coat. "Come on!"

I pulled away. "I can't… the laugh."

"You're hearing it again?"

I nodded.

She took me by the shoulders. "You're not being haunted, Katy. What you hear is just in your head. How many times do I have to tell you that? Now get inside before we both get sick."

When I still resisted, she gave me a tight-lipped stare—her way of saying, Kaitlyn Novacs, get over yourself.

"Ken and I were here for our anniversary five years ago," she said. "This is a beautiful place, not some crappy dump with cobwebs your warped mind is turning it into. Now move!"

I gritted my teeth and took a deep breath. *Nothing in this house could be worse than what I've been through,* I thought.

The wind howled again, louder this time. It might have been telling me, *You think so?*

Ronnie's grin wrinkled her eyes. "What an expression. You look like an Eskimo searching for the nearest dogsled. Wanna rub noses?"

I grabbed a handful of snow from a bush and flung it at her. Then, feeling a rush of warmth for my best and sometimes only friend, I hugged her.

"Yeah, yeah, I love you too," she said. "Now can we get out of this storm?"

With her hand propelling me forward, I slogged through drifting snow from the parking lot to the Niagara Inn's door where Andrea O'Rourke waited.

Chapter Two
The Niagara Inn

A heavy-set, grandmotherly woman greeted us. "I'm Mrs. Hughes—Naomi Hughes, the innkeeper." She held the storm door open. "I must say, I'm glad you could make it in this blizzard."

The innkeeper rubbed her hands together. Her rouged cheeks rounding into a smile, she beckoned us into a hallway with a lacquered oak floor so highly polished it gleamed in the light of the chandelier. The walls were lined with flocked paper. A flight of stairs rose to a landing, turned, and rose again. At the foot of the staircase was an intricately carved newel post.

Always drawn to such ornate craftsmanship, I stepped toward the newel post. When I touched it, I felt a chill, then heard someone whisper. I glanced over my shoulder. Only the four of us were in the hall, none of the others had spoken.

Mrs. Hughes stared at me. "Uh… let me get you out of your coat," she said.

Doesn't she hear the whispering? I looked to Ronnie, then Andrea. It appeared as though they hadn't heard the voice, either.

The innkeeper touched my arm. "Your coat, dear?"

Behind me, a floorboard creaked. It sounded as though someone climbed the stairs. My head swung around.

"What?" Ronnie said.

The whispering stopped. I sucked in my lower lip.

Mrs. Hughes brushed snow from our coats onto the door stoop, then hung them on a rack. On a rubber mat, we struggled out of our wet boots. In our stocking feet, she introduced us to the house once owned by a man she called Old Tom Burke.

"A real entrepreneur, our Mr. Burke," the innkeeper explained. "He owned a number of businesses around here. Old money, I guess you'd say today, mined during the California gold rush."

"A history lesson," Andrea remarked. "We should take notes. Might be a quiz later."

Ronnie glared at her. "Hush!"

Mrs. Hughes led us to a room near the front door. "This is the Gentlemen's Parlor. Mr. Burke spent a good deal of time in here when the house reverted to him at the end of your American Civil War."

Lit only by gray sunlight that filtered through curtains over tall windows, the room seemed to be bathed in a mauve mist. A thick white beam ran up the wall and across the ceiling. Craning my neck to look into the room, I saw four plush armchairs and a sofa, all covered in fabrics reminiscent of a past age.

I sniffed. It smelled like I'd stepped into a bakery.

Again staring at me, Mrs. Hughes took my elbow and steered me to another room. "Your meals will be served in here."

"When?" Andrea asked.

Ronnie grinned at her.

"What? We haven't eaten since we got on the plane."

Andrea O'Rourke's hunger didn't surprise me. Well below average height, no matter how many hours she spent in the gym, she couldn't shed what she called her baby fat.

"Breakfast is at nine-thirty," Mrs. Hughes said. "That dining room table, by the way, is one of our very old pieces. It dates from the seventeen-nineties."

The oak table filled a modest interior, with walls painted a deep historic green. The window and cabinets were trimmed in white enamel. A brick fireplace filled one wall.

"I can imagine a lot of serious conversations taking place around that old table," Ronnie said. "Maybe even George Washington sat at it."

"I doubt that." Mrs. Hughes's voice had a defensive tinge. "This isn't the United States." With some pride, she added, "It's rumored Queen Victoria sat right there when she visited us in the eighteen-eighties."

Andrea giggled. "Hope the fire's not lit while we're eating. If it is, someone's ass is gonna get burnt."

Mrs. Hughes's grunt sounded like a comment on American manners. "Yes, well," she said. "We have a relaxing weekend planned for you ladies. Besides the breakfasts, there'll be catered dinners each night." With a glance at Andrea, she pointed through the open door to the kitchen. "If you get hungry in between, please feel free to raid the refrigerator."

Her face again lit with a smile, she completed her welcoming speech with, "I've picked out a number of movies I think you'll enjoy watching, so I hope you'll make yourselves at home here. If you choose, you won't have to get out of your pajamas all day. Of course, there's always the town to wander through if it stops snowing."

"Even if it doesn't," Ronnie responded with a laugh. "All this white stuff to run through, it could be like an old-fashioned winter at home. Mom and dad by the fire, holding hands, singing carols."

I had no memory of my parents doing anything of the kind. Those times they weren't arguing, my mother would read in the kitchen with a glass of scotch near at hand while my father watched television in his den. "Sounds like someone else's home," I muttered, lips pulled back as if I'd sucked on a lemon.

"Stop being a killjoy," Ronnie scolded.

"Stop? I thought you dragged me here because that's what I am."

"As usual, you've got things skewed, kiddo. I took you with us to keep you from thinking about—"

Everyone must have heard my sharp intake of breath. Our trek through the snowstorm had briefly knocked Richard Slattery from my mind. Ronnie's slip brought everything back. Richard. What he wanted. I tried to twist off the engagement ring he'd given me. It still wouldn't budge. Outside, the wind hissed with laughter.

Ronnie rushed to my side. "Hey, hey, none of that. It's gonna be okay, I promise. You're here to forget for a while."

"As if I could."

"Katy—"

"I'm… trying." I gave her a weak smile.

She stroked my arm. "Yeah, I know. Your imagination has you all wound up. A couple of days of being pampered, you'll get back to yourself. Then you can go home, marry Richard, and—"

"I won't do that! I… can't."

"Listen to me," Ronnie said. "Richard isn't your ex. He loves you and you love him. It shows in your face when you're together."

"What if I do? Doesn't matter. Not when—"

The windows shook. The laughing wind stopped me.

In the quiet that followed, I opened my mouth to continue the argument, but closed it when I heard footfalls on the second floor. My head bobbed up.

Mrs. Hughes peeked at me from the corner of her eye. "We… um, ought to get you ladies settled in. Leah," she called toward the kitchen, "would you come here please, show our guests to their rooms?" In a softer voice, she explained, "Leah Campbell is our housekeeper. If there's anything you need, ask her."

A very thin woman came through the kitchen door, drying her hands on a dish towel. Her black dress and sweater looked like old widow's weeds. She even wore a black apron. From the creases on her forehead and cheeks, I thought she must be in her late sixties.

While Leah Campbell approached, a stirring above again drew my attention. Not my imagination. I definitely heard someone pacing. The footsteps went back and forth. Constant, driven. But ours was the only car in the lot.

"Is there… another guest here this weekend?" I asked.

Mrs. Hughes's smile tightened. She rubbed her hands on her gray skirt. "Everyone else cancelled when they heard about the storm."

"Somebody's walking up there," I said. "Is it another staff member?"

Leah Campbell's head swiveled to me.

Mrs. Hughes's ample chest expanded with a deep intake of breath. As she slowly released it, her eyes flicked in the housekeeper's direction. "No. Only Miss Campbell and I work here."

The pacing continued. Leah Campbell looked toward the stairs.

I stared hard at her. The woman had her hair pulled back into a severe bun which emphasized a hawk-like nose and a sharply pointed chin. Her skin was so pale it might have been frostbitten. As the pacing became more persistent, she seemed to shrink back towards the kitchen.

She hears it, too.

Her head cocked, Andrea said, "I don't hear anything."

"Me either." From the way Ronnie's eyes narrowed, I knew she wondered if she'd been right to bring me to this place. When she glanced down to her purse, I thought she might be ready to pull out her cellphone and call Dr. Carver—the psychologist I'd seen during the seven years since my marriage fell apart, and then I did.

The footsteps came closer. They seemed to reach

the top of the stairs, then started to descend.

I backed away. "I don't want to go up there." I held my ears. When I released them, the footsteps had stopped. "I'm sure I heard—"

Andrea clapped her hands. "Maybe it's a ghost. I've always wanted to meet one."

Ronnie signaled her with an urgent shake of the head.

"It's her—the one that—" The housekeeper stopped abruptly when Mrs. Hughes shot a glance at her.

My hand went to my mouth.

"What you hear is just the house settling under the snow," Mrs. Hughes said. "You know how beams groan in these old places."

"See? Everything's explained if you're willing to be rational," Ronnie said.

"It's more fun to think it might really be a ghost. Is there one living here?" Andrea seemed so excited by the idea, she almost panted.

Ronnie smacked her arm.

The housekeeper opened her mouth. Before she could speak, Mrs. Hughes said, "Groaning beams. Of course that's what you heard." She turned her eyes briefly to me, then glanced at the ceiling. "Now, if you'll excuse me, ladies. I have to finalize the arrangements for dinner. Leah will show you to your rooms."

The housekeeper watched Mrs. Hughes's retreating back, as if she desperately wanted to follow her. Face pinched, lips tight, she muttered, "Only the old wood settling in the house… So she says."

Leah Campbell stood, unmoving, on the bottom step, gnawing at her lip. I'd have bet all I owned that she didn't want to go upstairs any more than I did. After a minute, she sighed. Pulling at the waist of her skirt, she said, "All right, then, follow me, please."

I backed further away. "I don't want to stay here,

Ronnie. Please. Let's go home."

"Roads are all closed 'cause of the snow," the housekeeper said. She grabbed for the banister, as if her arms might pull her in a direction her legs didn't want to go.

Ronnie pushed me toward the stairs. "We're staying!"

Lugging our bags, we climbed behind Leah Campbell to the second floor. Each stair tread groaned underfoot.

"Only an old house settling in the snow," I muttered, willing myself to believe it.

Chapter Three
Abigail's Room

Leah Campbell stopped on the second floor landing. "This is called Mr. Hughes's Room," she announced as she opened a door. "Ms. O'Rourke, you're in here."

"Mr. Hughes? Is he any relation to the innkeeper?" Andrea asked.

The housekeeper replied with what sounded like a lack of interest. "Maybe. Folks say she's a very distant relative to Benjamin Hughes. Built this house, he did, only but ten years after you Americans burned the town during the war."

"*We* burned the town?" Andrea seemed taken aback by the implication.

The housekeeper nodded. "Back in eighteen-twelve, that was."

Ronnie laughed. "You people have long memories."

"But we rebuilt. Always do." The housekeeper threw her chest out as if she claimed some of the credit.

"So, Mrs. Hughes's great, great, great—" Andrea counted back generations on her fingers until she seemed to be struck by another idea. "Hey, I wonder if his ghost wanders the halls at night."

Ronnie bumped her. "This was just somebody's home."

"An inn, actually. One of the oldest," the housekeeper said. "Records down at the History Society say Ben Hughes used it for other things, too. Most places here had more than one use in the beginning. Now, if you'll follow me."

Ronnie and I were led down the corridor to where

two closed doors faced each other.

"You're in here, Ms. Hoffmann. This one's called Mrs. Burke's Boudoir." The housekeeper opened the door to reveal a generous room, furnished with what looked like an antique bedroom set and a mirrored armoire. Two windows overlooked the street.

"And you're in there, Ms. Novacs. That's… Abigail's Room." The housekeeper pointed without opening the door, then did an abrupt about-face.

A floorboard inside creaked.

Only an old house settling in the snow, echoed again in my mind.

Before I could question why the housekeeper avoided this room, she mumbled what might have been, "Be careful of that one"—though I couldn't be sure—and retreated down the stairs. "Dinner's at seven. Find me if there's something you want."

Alone in the hall, I listened to my friends *ooh* and *ah* as they surveyed their accommodations. I stared at the closed door to my room, summoning the courage to open it. As I reached out, the latch clicked and the door opened a crack.

I gasped. I hadn't touched the doorknob.

A light breeze blew along the hall. The door moved another inch. *It wasn't latched. The wind's moving it,* I thought, although no windows were open. *Has to be the wind. Ronnie's right. I've got to get a grip.*

I pushed the door the rest of the way and poked my head inside.

With relief, I surveyed the interior. I didn't see the rundown gloomy chamber my imagination had built. This was a bright room, probably the lightest in the house. It had walls decorated with red and ivory floral paper. A rug of similar design ran across the floor. At the foot of the king-sized bed, I saw a fireplace. To the right of the bed, between two closets, was a window seat. I pictured myself snuggled cozily in that nook, a fire ablaze in the hearth behind me, quietly reading while the blizzard raged outside. I dropped my suitcase and went to sit on the window seat.

"What's this?" I asked the walls.

On the seat I saw what appeared to be a very old copy of Tolstoy's *Anna Karenina*. Open and turned down to mark a page, it seemed as if someone had been reading and left for a moment. I hadn't thought about *Anna Karenina* since I read the novel in college. A woman throws herself under a train after losing the great love of her life. As I stared down at the book, a similarity between the novel's story and mine struck me. Like Anna Karenina, I had lost a precious love. Unlike Anna, I hadn't been able to finish the job.

"Ronnie, why'd you do this?" I whispered.

My legal training—I'm a lawyer—taught me life abhors coincidence. My friend must have called ahead and asked that the book be left in my room as a not-so-subtle warning against where she feared I might be headed.

Clutching the volume, I stormed across the hall to Mrs. Burke's Boudoir. I threw the door open without knocking. Ronnie was sprawled on her bed. I crossed the room in two long strides and bounced down next to her.

She opened one eye. "What? Huh? Oh, it's you. Missed me already, did you?"

I glared at her.

"Aren't you glad you came now? It's so beautiful in here, I could stay forever." She yawned, then stretched like a contented cat.

I tossed the book on her stomach.

"Hey, what's that for?"

"How could you?" I said.

"What?" Ronnie sat up.

"You arranged everything so nicely. This trip, the rooms we'd be put in. You even had them leave that stupid book in my room." I slid away from her to the foot of the bed.

"What are you talking about? Have you gotten into somebody's bourbon?" She lifted the volume to read the spine.

"Don't play dumb, Ronnie Hoffmann. I know you too well."

She moved next to me. "Why would I ask someone to put a book in your room?"

"Oh, come on. You know the story."

"I don't."

"Now I know you're lying. Of course you do. We read it together, remember? Brooklyn College—our World Lit course."

She turned the book over. "I never read this."

"You did!"

She dropped the book on my lap. "World Lit was in our second year. I took a trip to San Francisco when *Anna Karenina* was assigned—"

My cheeks began to burn.

"—and you covered for me by writing my paper."

It *was* a coincidence. The realization caused my heart to do a slow twist. I picked up the book and held it tight against my chest, as if that would stop the fluttering I felt. "I'm sorry. I shouldn't have…" My voice caught.

As she always did when I couldn't find my way, Ronnie held me. "It's okay, Katy. You've been under a strain. Go unpack. Lie down until dinner. You'll feel much better after a nap."

I went back to my room and did as my friend suggested. But the way one thing invariably lead to another —like coming to the Niagara Inn, then finding the book—my nap started me down a path lined by trees overgrown with my past. And somebody else's.

Chapter Four
Sleepwalking

I tossed and turned in bed, arms flung in one direction, then another. I pounded the pillow, kicked at the comforter as if it were a rope binding my ankles. I knew how it felt to be bound, ankles and hands. Seven years ago, I'd been tied to a bed in a small room while white-clad figures peered through the reinforced window in the door. My wrists were bandaged—when pills hadn't worked, I'd torn them with my teeth.

I wrapped the pillow over my ears to mute the screams of memory. At home this helped. Here, though, the screams grew more intense and seemed to rattle the window. My hands clenched into fists. My abdomen tightened. My head felt as though it would explode. I prayed it would.

In the howl of the wind, I thought I heard someone say, "Not yet." Minutes later the pain began to abate. Exhausted, at last sleep overtook me, but not a dream-free sleep.

Under a winter sky, the world is dark. A lamp high overhead throws down a cone of light. A cement railroad station platform. I'm alone. Pacing. Large snowflakes fall. It's bitter cold. I pull my fringed wool wrap tight around my shoulders.

A steam locomotive hisses on the track. White puffs billow from the smokestack, mixing with the virgin snow. A square sign on a nearby pole reads West Fourth Street. *I blink. Can't be right. Steam engines don't pull New York City subway cars.*

I feel lost, anxious.

A loudspeaker blares, "Train for Moscow."

I cry out, "No, no, I can't leave yet. Not until he comes!"

Passengers rush by, boots clattering on the cement. Long skirts rustle over petticoats. A conductor leans from a car. Brass buttons gleam on his red and black uniform. He waves a lantern.

I rush to him. "Excuse me," I say, "I'm looking for—"

"Sorry, madam, these are First Class compartments." He points. "You have to board down there."

"Please, please, hold the train another minute," I beg. "He's promised to meet me."

"Yes, I know. But we have a schedule." The conductor pulls a large watch from his uniform jacket. Its tick tick *echoes like gunshots. "If your husband doesn't come soon, you'll have to wait for the next train."*

My husband is late, always late. Almost never there.

Annoyed, again I pace. The conductor's watch tick tick ticks.

A whistle shrills. Train cars thud, inch forward.

I groan. "Where is he? He swore he'd bring it."

Can't remember what he's supposed to bring, but it's important. Can't leave without it.

Nerves now raw, it's hard to breathe. Stupid maid, she's tied my corset too tight. All the times I've told her, she still can't get it right. I glance down. My crinoline afternoon gown is creased. Just below my stomach, a wet patch stains the skirt. Have I been pelted by snowballs? The stain turns crimson. I brush at it, cry out, every touch painful.

Tears well up. "No! The Count will never stay when he sees me this way." I brush again, cry again...

The dream image faded. I was sitting up in bed.

This isn't my bed, I thought. Panicked, eyes half closed, I gazed around. It took a moment to remember that

I was somewhere in Canada. I drew a hand along my cheek.

Why's my face wet? As I rubbed the moisture from my eyes, I felt overwhelmed by the sense of loss I'd lived with these past seven years. I rolled from the bed. As I stumbled to the bathroom, I smacked into the dresser.

"Ouch!" *That's gonna leave a bruise,* I thought. *People get bruised when they wake up in a strange bed.* Waking up in Richard's bed had left a bruise. Waking up in my ex-husband's bed had scarred me for life.

Before the toilet finished flushing, I got back in bed. In the quiet house I heard what sounded like the clatter of pans. I glanced down and saw an air vent low on the wall next to my bed. The sound came through that.

The kitchen must be just below.

Now I heard Mrs. Hughes's voice scolding, "You're not to say anything about footsteps. Do you understand me?"

"But—"

"Leah, it's your imagination."

My eyes shot open. The housekeeper knew about the pacing!

"It ain't," Leah Campbell insisted. "I hear her, all right. You do, too, if you was honest. And the blonde one, she heard her walking 'round. Saw it in her eyes. None of you believed her, but *I* know."

"You're being ridiculous."

"I know what I know—"

"*Shh*. Keep your voice down."

I leaned over the side of the bed, my ear close to the vent, straining to hear.

"—heard her stomping 'round up there first time I come into this place. Sounded like a parade on Queen Street. Hear it still when the house is quiet."

"Nobody's up there. I've looked," Mrs. Hughes said.

"Not no one a good Christian can see. But that devil has her ways. She was a Christian woman, she'd go away, leave God-fearin' people in peace."

"Enough! Whatever you think you hear, you'll keep to yourself."

"And the smell of bakin' bread—can't tell me that's not her doing. Old Ben Hughes may have built this house for a bakery, but now it's her manning the oven in the basement."

"Stop it!" Mrs. Hughes said. "I won't have your foolish imaginings scaring this group off."

"Cursed, this house is, after what she done. Wasn't I needed the money, I'd never set foot in here."

Mrs. Hughes's voice rose. "And I wouldn't have you here if anyone else in town would do the work."

"Someone ought to tell 'em afore she shakes the bed like she did to the last one what stayed in there. Didn't want *that* one messing up her room."

I gasped, certain Leah Campbell was talking about my room.

"Mrs. Davidson was a nervous, suggestible woman, Leah. She wouldn't have thought anything shook her bed if you hadn't put the notion in her head."

"Wasn't me what did it."

"You're a foolish biddy who's gotten worked up into a state. Take a moment to compose yourself before I say something we'll both regret."

A door slammed. The house again went quiet.

I swung my legs over the side of the bed. I had to tell Ronnie what I'd heard. I hadn't imagined the pacing. We had to get out of this house! I tried to rise. My legs wouldn't respond.

Frightened, I lay on my side, staring at the air vent for five minutes, maybe more, willing my body to flee from this room.

The window rattled. *Hush,* the wind seemed to say.

In another minute I grew weary, too tired to move. Too tired to recall why I wanted to. I yawned. My eyes closed. Soon sleep again overtook me. As if it were a DVD put on Hold, my dream picked up where I'd left it:

On a cement platform, under a cone of light. The engine chugs twice. The whistle blows. My stomach tightens. The crimson stain on my gown has spread.

A shout from down the platform: "Anna!"

I turn. Everyone else has boarded. Who's being called?

"Anna." A woman runs up, stops beside me. Black hair, thick-framed glasses. She looks like Ronnie Hoffmann.

"You've mistaken me for someone else." I peer past her.

"What are you saying? Anna, this is madness." Ronnie takes my arm. "You must come home with me before the other one shakes your bed."

"I'm sorry, but my name is..." I can't remember. Maybe I am Anna. Accepting it, I say, "Can't go back. Not ever. Not even if the world smells like bread. Dammit, where is he?"

Hiss, hiss, the engine's boiler sounds like the hissing wind.

Ronnie leans close, whispers, "The Count left a note. He's not coming. He said if you were a good Christian—"

"Not coming? And my child?"

"You'll never see your baby in this life."

Never see my baby? Shaking with spasms of grief, I turn to the moving train. "I've sacrificed everything, and for what? Love? What a fool I 've been!"

My laughter is manic.

The train lurches. How easy it would be to slide between the cars. How quickly the wheels would put an end to yesterday's sorrow. To fear of tomorrow.

"Anna, don't!" Ronnie yells.

The engine chugs, moves forward.

"Anna, Anna!" Ronnie's voice is muted, as if it's coming from behind a closed door.

The voice dissolved into knocking. I opened my eyes. I was in bed, the quilt pulled up to my chin.

The door to my room cracked open far enough for Ronnie to peek in. Andrea pushed her inside.

"You awake?" Ronnie said. "Hey, sleepyhead, it's dinner time."

"Yeah, get up. Can't you smell the food? Scrumptious." Andrea made a show of licking her lips.

I shivered, cold, as if I'd been outside. As if I'd been wrapped in a fringed shawl, standing in the snow. On a cement platform. I bolted upright, craned my neck toward the window. "No, no!"

Ronnie sat next to me on the bed. "What's the matter?"

Andrea stood in the doorway. There wasn't a door on the train platform, was there? And where had Andrea come from? I twisted toward her. "It's gone. It left without me."

"What's gone?" Ronnie asked.

She'd been there. She saw the train pull from the station. Did she think if she denied what happened, it would all go away? Frustrated, I said, "The… train," and twisted again to the window. "Have to catch it." I raised my hand to signal for the conductor.

Ronnie rubbed my shoulder. "Katy, you've gotta wake up."

"'M'awake!" I mumbled.

"You're not," Andrea said.

I peeked at the window. "'S'dark out."

"Has been for some time," Ronnie said. "Boy, you really did conk out."

I shivered.

"Are you all right?" Ronnie put a hand to my forehead.

I shoved it away. "'M'fine. Just a little cold."

"I'm not surprised. It's going down below zero tonight," Andrea said.

Ronnie reached for the lamp hanging on the wall next to my bed. Her movement shook the book, and *Anna Karenina* thumped on the floor. At the thud, my eyes snapped wide open. But I was still trapped in my dream.

"She jumped," someone shouts.

The iron rail. Cold. Sharp rocks between the ties. Gown torn. Flesh torn. Wheels screech. Too late. My body is shredded, yet I feel—

"Look at her," Andrea said. "She's staring like she doesn't see anything. She's still asleep."

—nothing. I let out a breath. I felt nothing. *Now I can tell the Count it's over, lose my baby, and feel... nothing.*

Ronnie shook me. "Katy, wake up."

I looked into a pair of hazel eyes. "It's you."

She laughed. "Who'd you expect?"

I slid my tongue across my lips and swung my feet over the side of the bed. I felt as though a weight had been lifted from my chest. My throat dry, I rasped, "I'm okay now."

"If you're sure... We'll meet you downstairs, then." At the doorway, Ronnie turned. "Don't go back to sleep."

I heard their footsteps descend the stairs.

"No, wait!" I shouted. "Give me a second to wash my face. I'll come with you." After a brief respite of calm—the calmness of my dreamed death—I panicked. I felt as though something in my room wanted to bring me back to life. If it did, I'd have to face Richard, and then endless years without him. "Wait for me!" I called to my friends.

As I passed through the door, from the nook of the window seat I heard a whispered, "Life's a hard, painful thing. More painful yet to flee it."

I froze in mid-step. Hesitantly, I turned back. No one was in my room, the only sound the wind howling in the street.

You really are losing it, girl, I thought as I rushed for the stairs.

Chapter Five
The Newel Post

I stumbled into the dining room, glancing nervously over my shoulder.

"Now what's the matter?" Ronnie asked.

Tell her! my mind shouted. *Tell her about the voice, about the argument Leah had with Mrs. Hughes. Tell her, then pack your bag and insist she take you home.*

I opened my mouth. My voice caught in my throat. It was as if something in the house seized my will and warned that if I spoke those words, it would spell disaster. For Ronnie. For me. I didn't know what put that idea in my head, had no thought as to what the disaster might be, but I felt its presence inches from me. Fighting to control my dread, I made my tone light. "What makes you think anything's wrong?"

Ronnie screwed up her face.

I didn't dare let her cross-examine me—my friend had a way of dragging from me all I tried to hide. I turned to the innkeeper. "What a lovely meal you've put out, Mrs. Hughes."

"Why, thank you, dear."

If I were hungry, the earthy smell of Camembert Cheese and the fruitiness of blueberries in pastry drizzled with rosemary wine syrup would have been a gastronomic delight. I saw the rest of the dinner laid out on the sideboard. Osso Buco and garlic mashed potatoes. For dessert, Molten Chocolate Cake with Brandied Cherries.

Mrs. Hughes joined us for the meal, and the four of us formed a semicircle at the near corner of the large antique table. A chair stood empty in front of a fifth place setting.

I looked at the closed kitchen door. "Where's Leah? Isn't she going to eat with us?"

"She's gone home," the innkeeper said. "Leah doesn't like to be out after dark."

Andrea gave a cruel laugh. "From the way she looks, I'd think that's just when she'd wanna be out—especially on Halloween."

Ronnie also laughed. "Yeah, Dracula's mother." She glanced at me over the lip of her wine glass, anticipating, I supposed, the catty remark I would make.

I slapped down my fork, scattering bits of my mostly untouched food on the placemat. "How can you guys make fun of someone you don't know?"

The others rolled their eyes.

Mrs. Hughes saved me from a comment Ronnie seemed about to make when she said to Andrea, "You're not so far wrong. People in this town think of Leah Campbell as something of a comic figure—the way she dresses and always worries her rosary beads like the Devil himself is breathing down her neck. She's a real throwback to Queen Victoria's time."

Andrea snickered. "Further back than that, I'll bet. Like maybe to Salem."

Ronnie nodded. "I can imagine her sitting on the jury during the witch trials, screaming 'Satan, get thee behind me!'"

I shoved away my plate. "Men didn't let women on juries in those days. They hanged us."

The innkeeper's eyes flicked in my direction.

Ronnie poured a fourth glass of wine. "Don't mind Kaitlyn, she's scared of men lately. That's why we brought old sourpuss with us—to get her over it." She turned to me. "Hey, kiddo, lighten up. We're on vacation and gonna be spoiled rotten for a few days. Get into the spirit."

Andrea flipped her shoulder-length red hair and

clapped. "*Hmmm*, spirits, that's it! Hey, Kaitlyn, drink some of this." She lifted a bottle of wine from the sideboard and put it in front of me.

"Yeah, drink up, girlfriend," Ronnie said. "The night's young and so are we. After dinner, we're gonna have a pajama party."

I sat back with my hands on my lap. Leah Campbell certainly seemed as strange as Mrs. Hughes said. Yet, as if I'd lost control of my thoughts, I rushed to defend her. "That's fine and good, but it doesn't give you a right to slander the woman. Just because she's different—"

Ronnie shot a look at me. "Lawyers. Wanna sue us, kiddo? Hey, Mrs. Hughes, give her Weird Leah's phone number. Katy's gonna get a new client."

"Gonna protect Weird Leah from us bullies?" Laughing, Andrea filled my glass to the brim. "Come on drink up. Gotta get in the mood for the japama marty... Oops." Her hand went to her mouth. A few drops of red wine ran down her chin.

I drank the entire glass of wine, hoping that would make my friends stop nattering like jay birds.

Mrs. Hughes's smile returned. "I took out a movie for you ladies to watch. There'll be a couple of big bowls of popcorn and more wine to wash it down with. Tomorrow I thought you might like to walk around town in the morning, have lunch out. I've arranged to have a woman from one of our local salons come in to give you facials and makeovers in the afternoon. How does that sound?"

"What could be wrong with that?" Though I tried to sound enthusiastic, there must have been a flat note in my tone.

From across the table, Ronnie took my hand. "Hey, these are the good times. Give it a chance. You'll see how fast it can take your mind off things."

"Of course it will," Mrs. Hughes said as she rose to clear our plates. "Our ladies who come for these girlfriend weekends can't wait to come back."

"See? So don't worry 'bout ol' Weird Leah," Andrea said. "She'd just scare the good times away."

"How about all of you going upstairs now, get into your PJ's?" With those words, Mrs. Hughes shooed us from the dining room as if we were teenagers.

***

I was last to return downstairs. Though it might have been the effect of three glasses of wine on a mostly empty stomach, by the time I got out of the shower and dried off, my room felt different. I felt safe there and welcomed the solitude. Without my friends' half-drunk twittering, I didn't feel pressed to pretend a lightness of spirit. Wrapped in a towel, I decided I would stay in the nook by the window and read.

Ronnie's voice broke into my musing. "Come on, Miss Slowpoke. We're waiting for you."

"Olly olly oxen free," Andrea sang.

"Time's a-wasting, girl. We're putting the movie in," Ronnie called from the foot of the stairs.

With a sigh, I pulled on my pajamas—the red and green striped ones Ronnie had given me for Christmas. Looking regretfully to where *Anna Karenina* lay open on the window seat, I left my room.

When I reached the bottom of the stairs, I rested my hand on the newel post. Instantly, I felt overcome by a wave of sorrow so deep and thick I thought I might choke. My grip on the post tightened. My hand stung. I pulled back, turned over my hand. I saw a red mark, almost a welt, in the center of my palm.

There's something about this block of wood.

When we first entered the Niagara Inn, I'd felt drawn to the newel post. Now when I bent to examine it I saw nothing peculiar about the post, just glued-together carved pieces of wood. Yet, when I again rested my fingers on it, I shuddered.

This newel post remembers something dreadful, flashed in my mind. I straightened up and laughed at such a ludicrous idea. *Knock it off, Kaitlyn,* I told myself. *It's just an inanimate object. Keep this up, girl, you'll start thinking you're psychic instead of psychotic.*

I again looked at my hand. The red welt was gone.

In the Gentlemen's Parlor, the shades had been drawn. Mrs. Hughes lounged in an armchair with her shoes off. Andrea had stretched out on the couch. Ronnie sat cross-legged on the floor next to her. Soft light from the table lamps spread a candle-like glow around them. Two large crystal bowls filled with popcorn were on the coffee table.

It wasn't the popcorn I smelled.

"Is someone baking bread?"

The innkeeper gave me the same look she had when I'd asked about the pacing upstairs.

I sniffed. After my father left when I was seventeen, my mother, brother and I had moved into a cramped apartment above a bakery. I knew the smell of bread fresh from the oven every bit as well as I knew the color of my hair.

"Maybe you're catching a cold," Ronnie suggested.

I glanced around the room, sniffed again. The aroma seemed to seep from the walls, the ceiling, the floor. "Yeah, a cold. Maybe."

"I told you to get out of the weather when we got here. But no, you had to stand in the snow, going on and on about someone staring at you."

I stuck out my tongue at her. "If I were sane, you wouldn't have had to drag me here."

Ronnie grunted. "Yeah, yeah. Come over here, snuggle under this blanket." She pushed a beautiful hand-knitted cover at me. "Pour yourself some of this wine. It'll cure what ails you."

Once I settled in, Mrs. Hughes raised the DVR remote and Tom Hanks and Meg Ryan came to life on a forty-inch screen. As they played their roles in a story in which she hears a voice on her car radio and falls impetuously in love with an architect who lives across the continent, the feeling of sorrow I'd picked up from the newel post faded. The first time I'd seen this movie it became one of my favorites. Barry, my ex, refused to see it with me. "Nothing but a silly chick-flick," he'd insisted.

I sat back, pleased to be years away from my life with him.

As I sipped my wine, I wondered whether Mrs. Hughes's choice of *Sleepless in Seattle* for our first night was a matter of chance, or whether she sensed something. I glanced over. Nothing in her expression suggested an answer.

I touched the engagement ring Richard had put on my finger and my heart sank. *Richard knows what I've been through. How could he have done this to me?*

Chapter Six
Richard

My affair with Richard Slattery had begun the year before.

After Barry and I divorced, I'd avoided relationships. Under other circumstances I would have avoided one with Richard, but I couldn't ignore an instruction from Cowen & Fine's senior partner.

The law firm's staff had gathered for our annual celebration on a cold Saturday evening. The office reception area had been draped in tinsel. *MERRY CHRISTMAS,* in large letters cut from cardboard and painted in red and green, hung over the receptionist's desk. Lights twinkled on the silver tree in a corner near the elevators. A bar had been set up in the adjoining glass-walled conference room, and canapé trays were spread across the polished table.

Off to the side with a glass of wine in my hand, I was talking with another lawyer when the elevator pinged to announce a new arrival. I took no notice of who came in until I heard Phillip Cowen say, "Richard, I'm glad you could make it. Let me introduce you to some of our associates."

I turned to see my firm's senior partner take a man's elbow and steer him in my direction.

Phillip's Santa hat barely covered his sparse white hair. A grin lit his round face. As he approached us, he said, "We have a modest size firm, only twenty lawyers. I like it this way, feels more like a family. Ah, here's someone for you to know. Kaitlyn Novacs, Gwen Porter, I'd like you to meet Professor Richard Slattery. Kaitlyn, Richard's the new client I spoke to you about."

Richard was quite tall. He had heavy brows and eyes as dark as his curly hair. He wore a light brown corduroy jacket with suede patches sewn at the elbows. His first novel having recently been accepted for publication, he'd retained Cowen & Fine to work on the contract. As he stood before me, I thought he fit the role of a Professor-of-Literature-turned-author.

"A pleasure." Gwen gave a brief smile.

I shook the professor's outstretched hand. "It's always nice to meet a new client."

Richard had a firm, warm grip. An amiable smile broke across his face and spread to his eyes when Phillip recited his background as if he were qualifying an expert witness. Still holding onto my hand, Richard said, "As Shakespeare wrote, ''T'is a pleasure known to us poor swains, all our merry meetings on the plains.'"

I patted my hair and smiled. "I read somewhere Shakespeare borrowed that line from Christopher Marlow. Now *you've* borrowed it from him."

Richard laughed. "Ah, well, I guess you've caught both Shakespeare and me out."

Phillip patted Richard's back. "As you can see, our Kaitlyn's quite straightforward—that's why I've given her your contract to look through. I wanted you to meet her first since you'll be working together. Now, let me introduce you to my partner."

Phillip took Richard's arm and led him to the conference room where Norman Fine, short and serious, was holding court.

Gwen stared after them. "Good looking man," she remarked as they passed out of hearing. "He might've stepped out of *Gentleman's Quarterly*. If I weren't married…"

"I didn't notice." I sipped my wine.

Richard glanced back. I felt his eyes settle on me.

"Professor Slattery seems to like what he sees," Gwen said.

"Don't be ridiculous. This is a law firm, not a dating service."

She gave me a look of exasperation.

I put Richard out of my mind until later, when I heard a rich voice say, "The lawyer you introduced me to when I came in—the blonde one with the laughing eyes—"

I turned in time to see Phillip Cowen glance in my direction. He pulled his glasses from his nose, wiped the lenses on his striped tie, and looked speculatively at Richard. "*Hmmm*, Kaitlyn Novacs," he said. "Thought you might find her interesting. She's been back with us five years now, and has become quite skilled in the area of law you're concerned with. In fact, it's one of her specialties."

I saw Richard look at me. "Yes, I understand that, but, um… what's her story? You said she's *back* with you? Did she take time off to have a baby?"

Baby echoed in my mind. My stomach churning, I quickly turned away. As a result, I didn't hear Phillip's reply. But I did hear Richard ask, "So, she's… available?"

"Told you so," Gwen said.

When I glanced back, I saw a quick smile cross Phillip's thin lips. "She's married to her work, but I don't suppose that's what you mean." He turned and beckoned, as if he were a king demanding the presence of a retainer.

I touched Gwen's arm. "We're being summoned."

She shook her head and stepped back. "Uh-uh, it's you they want. Have fun."

"Yeah, fun," I said. "That's all I need."

When we had talked for maybe fifteen minutes over another glass of wine, Richard asked, "Would you have dinner with me after the party? It would be nice to share Christmas Eve with someone."

"I prefer to share it with a TV movie and a cup of cocoa," I said. "Guess I'm a bit set in my ways."

I was about to say my good-nights, get my coat and head for my apartment, when Phillip's face creased.

"This year, Kaitlyn, why not do something different?" he said. "Have dinner with Richard. After all, you'll be negotiating his contract. It would be good for you to know each other. Maybe, Richard, Kaitlyn can answer some of those questions you asked me… about your publishing contract, that is."

I knew what Phillip was up to. He had tried to fix me up before—the son of his wife's cousin, a client's younger brother. I gave him a pinched-lips stare.

He leaned toward me. "I think working, uh, closely with Professor Slattery might be good for your career," he whispered. "Remember, you'll be up for a partnership soon. Having a successful author on your client list would certainly be a point in your favor."

Without phrasing it so bluntly, the sly old bastard had given me an ultimatum. My frown deepened. Trapped by the junior partnership Phillip dangled like a sprig of mistletoe over my head, I let Richard take my arm.

I suggested that we have dinner at SPQR, a restaurant in Little Italy. The corners of Richard's lips creased. Before he asked, I told him, yes, I knew that SPQR was the imprimatur of ancient Rome. He said he specialized in the Roman era. I told him I also knew that. A glint in his eyes, he said I had certainly done my research. I couldn't know that SPQR would be the place I'd later fall into another downward spiral.

***

My life would've been fine if I had gone home alone as I planned, I thought. *But no, I wanted to be a partner of Phil Cowan and Norm Fine.*

Embarrassed laughter came from the television's speakers, and my mind returned to the Niagara Inn. I was in the Gentlemen's Parlor, watching a movie with my friends.

I had no difficulty picking up what was happening. I'd only missed a couple scenes while I wandered in the past. Soon, between the few kernels of popcorn I chewed to a pulp and glasses of good wine I needed to wash them down, I joined my friends in tossing around memorized lines from the movie.

Ronnie twisted toward me and stroked my knee. "See? You're feeling better, aren't you? Told you this would happen if you gave it a chance."

I nodded and forced some popcorn into my mouth. "*Sh.* I want to see this. It's my favorite part."

The movie neared its dénouement in which the lead characters, having nearly lost their chance at true love, meet on the observation deck of the Empire State Building. I always got a bit teary at this point in the movie. Richard had smiled when I teared up as we watched this film together. *He'd never say it, but he loves the fact that I'm like this.*

As soon as I thought this, my ring finger started to burn.

On the screen, the hero and heroine looked deep into each other's eyes. An adorable child took their hands—

All at once the Gentlemen's Parlor became filled with the same choking despondency I'd felt when I touched the newel post. My shoulders slumped, I began to bawl.

Her voice heavy with concern, Ronnie asked, "Katy, what's wrong?"

I covered my face with both hands. "I don't… I…. Leave me alone!" My eyes burning, I ran from the Gentlemen's Parlor and tore up the stairs.

***

In the dark in Abigail's Room, I curled up on the edge of the king-sized bed. Moments later, Ronnie opened the door and tiptoed in.

"Hey, kiddo, you wanna talk?" She pushed me over so she could sit beside me.

I couldn't stop whimpering.

"Come on, it's only our first day away. It's gonna get better, I promise."

I gulped back tears. "Uh-huh."

"Look, you were having a good time tonight, so I know you can put this thing with Richard out of your mind for a while."

"Uh-huh."

"Sure you can. Do it for me, okay, honey?"

"Uh-huh."

"Better still, do it for you. And for Richard—for the wonderful life I know you two will have once you get your head straight. You're a perfect couple. Just like the people in the movie, you're fated to be together."

I sat up and knuckled the tears from my eyes. "I'd like to believe that, but I've gotten too old for fairytales."

Ronnie held me while I trembled. "You haven't. I know you better than that."

"No, you don't! No one does." Tears streamed down my cheeks. I tasted the saltiness when I licked my lips.

My friend wiped my eyes with her sleeve. "Okay, I can see you need to cry this out. Come to my room when you're ready to talk, even if it's the middle of the night."

She rose and padded out as quietly as she had entered. She didn't, however, completely close the door.

"Kaitlyn gonna be okay?" I heard Andrea ask in the hallway.

"Yeah, I think it's coming to a head," Ronnie said. "She should be more herself in the morning."

Andrea sighed. "I'm doing what I can to lighten her spirits, take her mind off—"

"Yeah," Ronnie said. "I know you are. Keep doing it."

When I heard the doors to their rooms close, I twisted the switch of the bedside light. *Anna Karenina* was at the foot of my bed. I stared at the book, certain I'd left it on the window seat when I went downstairs for the movie. Holding my breath, I glanced around. Everything else was in its place: my necklace and bracelets on the dresser next to my hairbrush, my overnight bag in the corner. Maybe I *had* left the book on my bed. When the past snuck up on me, I sometimes forgot where I put things.

Hesitantly, I reached for the book, as if I were afraid I would get another palm-stinging shock if I touched it. With a sigh and the book in my hands, I settled back against the headboard. I figured it would be easier not to think so much about Richard if I immersed myself in Anna's life.

In a short while my tears stopped and I no longer needed to read the same paragraph three times in order to take in the words. Not too many pages later, I heard a clock somewhere in the house strike midnight. Shortly afterwards, I fell asleep sitting up with the book in my hands. I didn't know what time it happened, but at some point I felt the book lifted. Gentle hands helped me settle down on the pillows.

"Thanks, Ronnie. It's nice to know you're always here when I need you," I murmured without opening my eyes.

"Sure and why shouldn't I be?" was the reply.

Almost asleep again, I didn't react to hearing a voice other than my friend's.

I awoke several hours later, stirred by something. I sat up, listened.

Pacing. In my room. At the foot of my bed. The steps moved back and forth from the far wall to the window. My eyes accustomed to the darkness, I saw no one there. This was *not* the sound of an old house settling.

I cringed back against the antique wood headboard.

Was this the laughing ghost? Had it followed me from Manhattan? My mouth opened as wide as my eyes. I wanted to scream. Tried to scream. My voice caught in my throat. I tried to swing my legs from the bed so I could run from the room. I felt frozen in place.

The pacing stopped. A voice said, *"Shh."*

As with the aroma of baking bread, the voice was in the room but at the same time it wasn't. It could have come from anywhere.

"No, no, no!" I managed to whisper.

"Shh," the voice said again.

Tears welled in my eyes.

Someone touched my wrist. *"Shh."*

In spurts, I sucked in breaths.

Now I felt my hair being stroked.

I groaned.

"Hush," the voice whispered, "You've nothing to fear."

The stroking stopped. The voice fell silent. The room was still. Whatever presence filled it a moment before seemed to be gone.

For five minutes, ten minutes, I sat panting. At last, into the darkness, I said, "W-who… are you?"

No answer.

I closed my eyes. *It isn't the laughing ghost*, I told myself. *Whatever that was could have hurt me. It didn't. I've nothing to fear, it said.*

My breathing slowed. Maybe there hadn't been a ghost in my room. Maybe I'd dreamt it.

I switched on the light, slipped from beneath the covers, and plodded to the bathroom. At the sink, I held tight to my bottle of sleeping pills. As I stared longingly at the bottle, I knew what I needed to do, what I'd tried to do seven years ago when I lost—

I stopped when I heard Dr. Carver's voice speak in my mind. One minute at a time, one day at a time, he'd tell me at the end of each of my sessions.

I took a deep breath. *Not yet, maybe tomorrow.*

I put down the bottle of pills. Settled again in bed, I reached for the book so I could read myself back to sleep. It wasn't on my bed. I peered around and saw it on the window seat with the page turned down. I remembered that Ronnie had come back to take it from my hands.

"I'm glad you're my friend," I said, willing the words to float through the house and find her ears.

"Sure," came the whispered reply.

Right then, I knew Ronnie Hoffmann hadn't been the one who earlier settled me down to sleep. My body tensed, then relaxed. Whatever roamed my room wasn't an evil, taunting presence—not at all like the laughing ghost. If *this* ghost had sought me out, I might have a conversation with it. Maybe learn what waited beyond, whether *he* was happy—

I forced that thought into the past, as I always did when I thought of him.

Chapter Seven
Morning

The idea of a benign presence with which I might speak kept me awake the rest of the night. As morning fought to break through the dark gray cloud cover, I settled on the window seat with the book resting on my knees. Instead of reading, I gazed through the window to where shadows played like children in the snow.

A ghost in my room?

How else could I explain the footsteps, the voice? What other explanation could I find for a book I felt connected to being left on the window seat? Maybe the spirit saw *me* as a ghost. Such an idea might have been a metaphor of my life. No family to speak of—mother and father gone, brother estranged—I felt as though I were destined to float through time, until one day I would just… dissipate.

Lost in these thoughts, I didn't react to a gentle tap on my bedroom door.

"Hey," Ronnie called from the hallway.

I rested my head against a windowpane, gazing down the block. *Where is he?* I had no idea where that thought came from.

The door opened.

"You still asleep?" Ronnie asked the crumpled quilt on my bed. When I didn't respond, she bounced down on the bed and threw back the covers. Then she craned her neck to look into the bathroom. "You in there?" she said.

I snickered.

She glanced around. When her eyes found me snuggled in a corner of the window nook, she jumped and grabbed her mouth. Her glasses slipped from her face.

"What on earth?" she said. "You nearly scared me to death, hiding there like that."

I laughed. "If I wanted to scare you, I would have jumped out of the closet. Maybe next time I will."

"Wiseass." Black curls fell across her face as she stooped to retrieve her eyeglasses. "You nearly turned the rest of my hair gray. At least you're in a better mood this morning. Have a good night's sleep?"

"Didn't sleep much at all."

"I can see you didn't. Your eyes are all red. So how come you're not cranky and snapping at me?"

"Have I been snapping?"

"Yeah, you have."

"Sorry." I tried to sound contrite.

"You're forgiven. Seeing your stupid smile makes up for it." She stroked my arm. "Listen, Andi's already eating breakfast. I'm going down to get some before only crumbs are left. Hurry up, get dressed. The snow's tapered off some. This beautiful town's calling for us."

I didn't move. "Be there in a minute. Just want to finish this page."

Halfway out the door, Ronnie turned back. "Are you sure you don't mind being by yourself in here?"

"What do you mean?"

From her puzzled expression, she might have sensed something was slightly off-kilter. "Last evening you didn't want to be up here alone."

What an understatement. I recalled the fear I felt when I woke from my nap yesterday, recalled my fear when I heard footsteps in the middle of the night. How foolish I'd been to feel frightened of a spirit that seemed to mean me no harm.

I turned to the window. "Yeah, I guess I didn't."

"So what's changed?"

I knew if I told her what I'd experienced during the

night, my friend would pull out her cellphone—she probably had Dr. Carver's number on automatic dial. And if I lied, she would surely read it on my face. Same result. Only one way I could climb out of this barrel of pickle brine.

"You're beginning to sound like a prosecutor cross-examining me!" I turned again to the window so she wouldn't see the deception in my eyes. "Nothing's changed. Yesterday I was just worn out."

My friend wouldn't let up. "If you didn't sleep, you must be exhausted."

"Stop mothering me!"

I twisted to see down the block. *Where can he be?* I felt anxious.

Ronnie came to the window and hovered over me. "What are you looking at?"

"Huh? Uh, nothing really. I, um… just wondered what was out there."

How could I explain I was looking for somebody, but didn't know who? I shifted my entire body toward the street.

As if the windowpane were a mirror, I saw spots of red appear on my cheeks. It felt like a sign I'd been caught doing something shameful. As I watched, the spots spread across my face until I appeared to glow. I bounced back in the nook. When I turned again to the window, I saw no glow, no red spots. Not even the reflection of my face in the glass. I gasped.

"You sure you're all right?" Her brows knitted, Ronnie looked me up and down, as if trying to diagnose some mysterious ailment.

"I'm fine. Really."

"I don't know… Maybe I should call—"

I grabbed her hand. "I said I'm okay! Something moved out there. It startled me."

She leaned over me to look through the window.

"You're sure that's all it was?"

"Guess I'm just jumpy from lack of sleep. Go eat. I'll be there in a minute."

The smile I forced seemed to take the edge off Ronnie's concern. After some hesitation, she headed for the hall.

While I watched the door close behind her, I thought, *Gotta get hold of yourself, Kaitlyn.* If I failed to, sooner or later my friend would make the call to Dr. Carver.

***

A breakfast array greeted me when I finally wandered into the dining room. On the sideboard, muffins were stacked on a platter while fruit crepes and oatmeal steamed. The aroma of fresh-baked bread permeated the house. Because I'd barely touched my dinner last night, I should have been ravenous, but my stomach tightened at the sight of the food. I just poured myself a cup of coffee, then sat at the far end of the table with my book.

My friends, dressed like twins in matching pink and white striped turtleneck sweaters and blue jeans, huddled over brightly colored brochures spread before them.

"This is a good place to go." Mrs. Hughes sounded like a tour guide as she leaned over Ronnie's shoulder to tap one of the pamphlets. "See here? Antiques of Niagara-on-the-Lake. The building has more than thirty vendors who sell everything you could think of: china, glassware, quilts, jewelry. It's just down there." She pointed, as if the street could be seen through the wall.

"Sounds like fun," Andrea said. "I could kill a whole day in a place like that. You up for it, Katy?"

Mrs. Hughes placed another glossy tri-fold over the rest. "And of course, Bartlett House is right nearby. See? All kinds of wonderful old furniture."

"Cool." Andrea beamed.

Ronnie appeared doubtful. "I don't think we should

drive around just yet. I peeked outside. There's a snow drift where we left the car."

"Oh, you big baby," Andrea said. "Between the three of us, we can clear the car in no time." I knew she liked the idea of two large stores in which to spend a portion of her ample salary.

"Uh-uh, the roads are still all covered," Ronnie said. "Let's give the snowplows time to do their work. We'll save antiquing for tomorrow."

"Absolutely," Mrs. Hughes agreed. "With the roads like this, it's best to wait. Better to be safe, I always say. For lunch, you can walk to the Angel Inn. It's one of our oldest buildings." She looked up from the brochures. "They say there's a ghost in their basement."

Andrea instantly brightened. "Now you're talking."

Ronnie glanced at me. Mumbling, "That's all I need," she folded the brochures and rose from the table.

"Don't forget to be back before three," Mrs. Hughes said. "That's when Mary from the salon is coming over to give you ladies facials."

More might have been said about what we could see and do, but sipping coffee while I read about Anna Karenina's suffering, I missed it. The next thing I knew, Ronnie poked me.

"Hey, dreamer, wake up."

The coffee mug slipped from my hand. A swirl of brown liquid spilled on the tablecloth. I glanced nervously at Mrs. Hughes and my eyes filled with tears. "I'm s-so sorry."

Ronnie muttered, "Not again. I thought you cried yourself out last night." She elbowed me aside, and patted at the spill with my napkin.

Andrea peered at me. I was sure she wondered, not for the first time since we left home, if I had again slipped into a black hole. I wondered, too. Spilled coffee was no cause for tears.

"Don't worry about it, dear. Spills happen all the time." Mrs. Hughes took the napkin from Ronnie's hand. "This old thing will launder just fine."

Still at the edge of tears, I followed my friends to the door.

The innkeeper poked her face outside. "Bundle up, ladies. It's cold. Going to snow again, I think."

As if it were a security blanket, I clutched the volume of *Anna Karenina* while I struggled into my coat.

Ronnie teased, "Do you plan on carrying that book with you everywhere for the rest of your life?"

"Why don't you give that to me, dear?" Mrs. Hughes reached for it. "That looks like a very old book you've brought with you. It might be better to let it stay here. I'll have Leah put it in your room."

"Brought with me? I-I didn't." My cheeks burning, I looked around.

"You must have. It isn't ours," the innkeeper said.

"I didn't bring this!"

Ronnie touched my arm. "Hey, it's okay. Someone who stayed in the room before you must have left it behind."

"Yeah, that's probably it." Andrea opened the door, ready to start our excursion.

As if to herself, Mrs. Hughes said, "I'd have known if that book was left here. Leah looks through the rooms when guests checkout. She'd have given it to me."

Her words buzzed like wasps in my ears. *She never saw this before?* Confused, I turned to follow the others through the front door.

At least, I thought I followed them.

Under oath, I would swear my feet moved toward the door, yet I hadn't taken a single step. When I tried to move, it was as if strong hands grabbed my shoulders. They held me in place. I felt them tighten until it hurt. I visualized welts growing where invisible fingers gripped.

Oh my God, oh my God! I heard myself scream, but no sound came out.

Now the hands covered my mouth. I was being smothered. I struggled to inhale air. For what might have been an hour, I squirmed within that vise-grip. If I didn't break free I would slowly die, and no one would see, or hear… This wasn't how I wanted to die! I gasped and tried to twist away. Now, a sea of red liquid rose to engulf me. I was drowning—

"Have you forgotten something, dear?"

At the sound of Mrs. Hughes's voice, the red ocean receded. The air smelled sweet, breathable. Whatever had held me no longer did. As if from a distance, I heard myself say, "What?"

"I asked if you'd forgotten something. You were standing very still with a puzzled expression. It was only a moment, but I thought—"

I looked nervously at Mrs. Hughes. "What would I have forgotten?" I tore at my coat to pull it off.

I'd had a similar experience once before. A memory of the first time it happened rushed back. Panicked, I thought, *Oh God, no! Not again. After all these years*— Eyes wide, I stood in front of the innkeeper, my coat in one hand, tugging on my sweater with the other.

By this time Ronnie must have reached the bottom of the front steps and noticed I wasn't behind her. She called to me.

My eyes darted from room to room, from the floor to the ceiling. I heard the ghost pacing again. Through the jumble in my mind, I clung to a single thought: I had to fight my way back from the past in order to disentangle myself from what just happened.

"Aren't you going with your friends?" Mrs. Hughes asked.

I strained to smile. "Uh, no… I-I don't think—" I felt my smile melt.

"I'm sure you'll enjoy the sights in town." If Mrs. Hughes noticed my odd behavior, she hid it.

"Well, maybe," I said in voice I barely recognized as my own. "Yes, the town. The Angel Inn." *Did the ghost in my room try to strangle me?* It couldn't be. That ghost seemed kind, caring. It must be the other one, then—the ghost with the cruel laugh. I shuddered. I had to get out of this house.

Again I turned to leave. My feet wouldn't obey. *The house doesn't want me to go*, flashed through my mind. Not a rational thought, but at the moment rationality might have been an arcane word in a long-dead language. *Ronnie,* I called. Terrified, I cried, *Help me!* Though my lips moved, the house seemed to swallow my words.

My friend poked her face in the door. "What's holding you up?"

"The house—" I caught my breath.

"What about it?"

I imagined telling her what just happened, then watching her face fill with empathy while she dialed Dr. Carver's number. *Maybe I ought to let her call him.* That thought got immediately shoved aside by another rush of panic. *No! Can't go back to that place!* Fighting for control, I composed my face. "The house is so quiet. I'd like to stay here this morning. Just relax." I faked a yawn. "Reading all night's finally caught up with me."

A stiff wind off the lake yanked the storm door from Ronnie's hand.

I shivered.

"What's the matter?" My friend took off a glove and felt my forehead.

"Must be the cold air got to me, made me realize how tired I really am. Like I said, I'll stay here and rest this morning." I yawned again to cover the lie.

Ronnie began to strip off her coat. "Then Andi and I will stay to keep you company. Heck, tomorrow's soon enough to go wandering."

On the stoop outside, Andrea nodded. "Of course we'll stay with you."

There was something I couldn't read in Mrs. Hughes's expression. I recalled the argument she'd had with Leah Campbell. Did she think the housekeeper had gotten the wind up my skirt over some imaginary spirit?

"You guys go on," I insisted. "I'd feel awful if I kept you here. You've got it all planned. Don't worry about me. I just need a little rest."

Ronnie and Andrea looked at each other.

"I'll keep an eye on her," Mrs. Hughes said.

So they went, and I stayed—just me and *Anna Karenina* in a house that didn't want me to leave.

Chapter Eight
The Past In Context

Dr. Carver would have told me I needed to relate what I'd just experienced to how I felt about my parents' constant battles, how I felt when my father had finally had enough of mom's drinking and left her... us... me. He would have patiently explained that through this self-examination, I would come to understand in context the choking I felt. Right. He wasn't there the first time I felt choked by ghostly hands when my marriage to Barry failed, and the life I'd so carefully planned flew apart as if it were churned up by a tornado. By the time Dr. Carver arrived, the only thing left was to sweep the aftermath under some psychological rug. Hysteria, he called it. He told me the ghost I heard laughing was only a metaphor for my past. But I *knew* the laughing ghost was real, and if it lived in my past, there was no way I would stroll back there to have a cup of tea and a chat with it. Likewise, after what just happened, I couldn't go for a lark through historic Niagara-on-the-Lake with my friends, couldn't listen to them imagine what this town had been like way back when. I needed time by myself—quiet time alone to build another wall. So, as soon as Ronnie and Andrea were out of sight, I took my book from Mrs. Hughes and climbed the stairs.

The room they called Abigail's felt like a sanctuary. In this room a gentle hand had stroked my wrist and hair. Outside this room rough hands had tried to kill me. Though I welcomed the idea of oblivion, I had no desire to be dragged painfully into it.

Leah Campbell had just finished straightening up when I walked in. "Thought you and your friends are going out this morning," she said, her hands fluttering nervously.

Alone with the housekeeper, I had my chance to ask her about the pacing and the voice. Afraid I might scare her off if I approached the subject directly, I sniffed the air.

"Are you baking in the kitchen?"

As if she wanted only to get out of Abigail's Room, Leah Campbell looked to the door. "Kitchen's closed. Nothin' being made in there." She took a step back from me.

I persisted. "I know I smell something delicious—"

"Don't smell nothin'."

"—and I thought, if you're baking, maybe I could watch—"

"Told you, no one's doing nothin' of the kind." She grabbed her cleaning supplies.

I reached for her arm. "Since we're the only ones here, how about if you stay and talk to me awhile? I want to ask you about—"

She stared at the window seat. "Can't waste time. Got a lot to do."

Rags, bucket, cleaner held tight in one hand, she used the other to twist the beads of her rosary. I was certain that if I took a single step toward her, she would hold out her crucifix and hiss as if I were a demon.

"Get out of my room, you old biddy!" a voice said.

Not even a whisper, it might have been nothing more than a gust of wind rattling the window. In fact, a moment afterward, I couldn't be sure I'd heard anything. But I must have, because it appeared as though Leah also heard it. She gasped and her gray eyes grew large. Clutching her bucket, she ran from the room, dropping a few rags as she almost flew through the door.

"Go on, scat!" The voice trailed like a breeze after her.

I turned in a circle. "Who are you?" I demanded of the empty room, not frightened by the disembodied voice.

Whatever or whoever it was, had only shooed Leah from its presence. I seemed to be welcome.

"Who are you?" I asked again.

A rattling window was the only reply.

***

When Ronnie and Andrea returned shortly after two o'clock, I was in my pajamas and robe, reading on the window seat. From the second floor window, I saw them bounce down the street. Laughing like children, throwing snow at each other, they giggled their way into the house. I made no effort to rush downstairs so they could regale me with their adventures. After what I'd experienced that morning—hands on my neck, being frozen in place—I wanted to stay in Abigail's Room where I felt safe.

I heard Mrs. Hughes greet my friends at the door. She positively gushed when she said, "Well, well, the rose in your cheeks tells me you ladies had a *grand* time."

"Sure did," Andrea said. "You were right about everything. Look what I bought."

A rustle of paper suggested she displayed a new treasure.

"Did you eat at our Angel Inn and hear the ghost walk around?"

"Nope. Guess the ghost was somewhere else," Ronnie said. After a momentary hesitation, she asked, "How's Kaitlyn doing?"

"Been up in her room most of the day," the inn-keeper answered in the tone of a worried parent reporting on her ill child.

"Has she eaten anything?" Ronnie asked.

"I made her a cheese sandwich and some tea. She drank the tea, but only nibbled on the sandwich."

"We'd better go up, see how she is," Andrea said.

I heard them work their way out of their coats and boots. Then I heard footsteps ascend the stairs.

"Okay, you hermit, I hope you've gotten some rest, 'cause we're gonna rock this old place this afternoon," Ronnie announced when she threw my door open.

"Sounds good." I didn't look up from my book.

She rested a hand on my shoulder. "Mary's gonna be here for our spa treatment soon." With a sigh, she said, "Your eyes are bloodshot and sunken. Come on and get dressed. Gonna take all the magic Mary knows to make you look human."

I stared past her, half-expecting the voice to tell my friends to get out. I heard nothing. Since it had chased the housekeeper from the room hours before, the voice had been silent. Still, all day I had sensed a presence sitting quietly nearby.

At Ronnie's urging and with Andrea's assistance, I got dressed. Soon, inside the laughter and small talk that rose above rock music, I felt myself come back to life. During the next two hours, the three of us behaved like children who had gotten into our mother's makeup. By the time Mary's magic had been woven and she collected payment for the cosmetics we couldn't wait to buy, we were such a beautiful trio I thought it a pity no one was around to see us.

"Ah." The whispered word floated through the Gentlemen's Parlor door.

My head snapped around. It seemed someone who could be heard but not seen watched my every move.

Chapter Nine
Life's Lost & Found

Dinner. Spinach salad, roast salmon with a creamy dill sauce, fruit and cheese for dessert. As good as the food looked, I still had no appetite. While the others ate, my mind drifted to what started me tumbling down the slope.

I should have said no when Richard invited me to dine with him again, I thought, and snuck a glance at Ronnie. She smiled at me, sipped her wine and laughed at something Andrea said. With a twinge of resentment, I thought my friend could have—should have—discouraged me from letting a relationship with Richard become more than a casual night out. Ronnie knew me better than anyone. How could she not know what would happen?

My thoughts slipped back to last year.

January fourth was the first workday after the holidays. Richard phoned me at my office; he had just opened his mail and learned that Cowen and Fine billed him for the time we spent at SPQR. He sounded shocked.

"What did you expect, Richard? You spent half the night picking my brain for legal advice."

"Yes, but I spent the other half trying to impress you."

My legs crossed, I leaned back in my large chair. "If you look carefully at our bill, you'll notice we didn't charge you for those hours."

"Or for the goodnight kiss at your door," he pointed out.

Had I been looking in a mirror, I would have seen my face turn as crimson as my dress. I ran a hand through my hair and swiveled my chair to stare at the Manhattan skyline beyond my office window. I couldn't believe I'd let him—even kissed him back. When he had leaned down to whisper how much he enjoyed our dinner, I knew what he wanted. I'd offered him my cheek. Somehow, though, my lips got in the way.

With my hand over the phone's mouthpiece, I whispered, "That's what I get for drinking too much wine."

Back in control of my thoughts, I swung around to my desk. "No, the firm wouldn't charge you for the kiss." I laughed. "Unless, that is, you were actually kissing Phillip Cowen and Norman Fine."

"Oh, Please!" He sounded as though he'd choked on the idea.

"Thinking about it now," I said, "maybe I should have told the billing department about the kiss. If I had, they would've charged you for it at twice my usual fee."

"All right, Kaitlyn, I surrender." I pictured Richard raising his hands.

"Is there anything else I can help you with?" The phone tucked on my shoulder, I picked up a pen to strike a line from the document in front of me.

After a brief silence, he said, "No… uh, yes."

I sensed he was working up the courage to bargain over what I had charged him. I thought about his kiss—it happened just before I closed the door and climbed the stairs to my apartment. Alone. Again I felt the touch of his lips. It had been a while since I'd been kissed by a good looking man, so I'd responded. Hell, who wouldn't? Maybe I *would* shave a little off his bill.

Instead of talking about money, Richard said, "Um… to paraphrase Shakespeare, might I try to o'erperch your walls with love's wings?"

"Excuse me?" I held out the phone and stared at it.

His laughter was deep, rich. I enjoyed the sound of it. "Don't tell me Shakespeare stole that line from Christopher Marlowe. I looked it up, he didn't." Again he hesitated, then said, "Kaitlyn, I've been thinking about this for a week—"

A baby cried. I froze, as I always did when I heard that sound.

"Excuse me a second," I said into the phone.

I set the receiver down, opened my office door and peeked nervously down the hall. I saw two secretaries cooing over the newborn a client had brought with her. I settled again into my chair and picked up the phone. "I'm sorry, Professor Slattery, what were you saying?"

He took a deep breath. "Professor Slattery? I'd hoped we'd gotten past such formalities. Look, Kaitlyn, in my clumsy way I'm asking you to have dinner with me again—this time, off the clock."

I should have held firm to my determination. No dating. No relationships. Not ever again...

Ronnie's voice brought me back to the Niagara Inn's dining room. "This salmon is so good, it ought to be illegal. Isn't it good, Katy?"

"Huh?" I looked up.

Her myopic stare riveted on me, she twirled her eyeglasses. "I said everything tastes so good."

"Oh, uh, yeah. It does."

"So why aren't you eating?"

"I am." My cheeks feeling warm, I took a bit on my fork, then sipped some wine to force it down. The rest I moved around my plate. After half an hour of this charade, I leaned back in the chair, and said, "This was wonderful, Mrs. Hughes. Thank you. I'm absolutely stuffed."

Ronnie gave a heaven-help-me sigh. "You've hardly touched a thing. And thinking about it, you haven't eaten since we got here."

I felt as though I would cry.

"You've got to eat," my friend persisted.

"I've had more than enough." In the best Middle-Eastern tradition, I pushed up a small belch. "Can't expect me to finish all my food—not when the women in Los Angeles are so skinny. I'm training to fit in out there."

A week ago, when Richard changed the rules of our relationship, I knew I had to break it off. But there were so many places we had gone in Manhattan—my favorite places—I would be tortured by memories. Knowing I couldn't live with those memories, I decided to transfer to Cowan and Fine's new Los Angeles office. When I calmly told my best friend what I planned to do and why, she went nuts, locked me in my apartment and stayed there with me. Then she kidnapped me to Niagara-on-the-Lake.

Ronnie gasped. "You haven't taken the transfer?"

I patted my hair.

"When? I didn't leave you alone once this past week."

I looked straight at her without blinking. "Didn't you think I might have Phil Cowen's home number, and that I might call him after you fell asleep?"

While I'd spoken with my boss about the west coast transfer, I hadn't yet requested it. Still, I wanted Ronnie to believe I had. This was a lawyer's trick, a little mis-direction, done so my friend would stop nagging me to eat.

"I knew I shouldn't have trusted you," she said. "Does Richard know?"

"He would if you'd let me call him."

I could almost see Ronnie kick herself. "Not a chance! Not while I still have time to talk you out of this stupidity." She turned away, muttering something indiscernible.

***

Dinner concluded, I spent a second evening in the Gentlemen's Parlor, where my friends and I laughed and talked over the soundtrack of another romantic comedy. After the movie, while the others bounded happily up the stairs, my movements were slow, lethargic. I felt as though sitting through the film had sapped all of my energy.

Alone in Abigail's Room, the veneer of a smile slipped from my face. Wrapped in the heavy comforter from my bed, I settled on the window seat with *Anna Karenina* on my lap. When I opened the book, a sheet of paper fluttered to the floor.

I picked it up. The page looked to be quite old and felt brittle. How had it gotten into the book? I turned the page over. It seemed to be part of a letter. The faded words were hard to decipher, but still I made out some of what was written:

> *...sleep is difficult, my love, without you curled up beside... I try to stay busy. That helps for only a short while... too soon evening comes... I go off by myself to think of you... I pray... again be warm in your embrace... Until that happy day...*

Who had written this? I felt love in each word, longing and an overwhelming sadness that was palpable when I touched the page. I'd felt the same sadness when I touched the newel post. I held the letter to my breast, wondering whether Richard would feel such sadness when I'd gone.

After reading it again, I placed the letter on the dresser. In the morning I would show it to Mrs. Hughes and ask her if it might be a clue as to what was going on in the Niagara Inn. Would she believe this piece of paper had appeared from nowhere the same way as the book it fell from had? Would she insist it had been left by someone who had stayed in Abigail's Room before me? What would Ronnie do when I showed it to her? What would she say if I told her what I felt when I touched it? Those wonderings led my thoughts to Dr. Carver and then to the asylum where I'd met him.

I brushed my hand across the folded letter. I refused to think about the asylum and why I had been there.

I found forgetting hard, though. Again on the window seat with the book open on my lap and my head against a chilled glass pane, my mind returned to the words on the old page: *I go off by myself to think of you.*

I stared down the street, thinking about Richard…

Why had I agreed to have dinner with him again? When I met Ronnie for lunch the afternoon after our second date, I told her it was just a release of the panic I felt when I heard the baby's cries.

"I thought you were past that," she told me.

I gave her a crooked grin, then glanced through the Burger King's window at the noontime bustle in Times Square. "Don't think I'll ever be."

"I don't care why you went out with him," she said. "I'm glad you're seeing someone."

"I had dinner with the man twice. I'm not *seeing* him." I waved my hand as if brushing away the idea.

"Yeah, right. You're smiling like a cat. This is happier than I've seen you in years. In fact, you're absolutely glowing."

My face grew warm.

Ronnie caught her breath. "My God—you slept with him, didn't you?"

"I didn't. H-how could you even think for a minute I'd— It was just a second date."

"Uh-huh," she said.

"Come on, you know me better."

"Yeah, I know you. When you start fidgeting with the hem of your dress—"

"I-I… didn't."

Ronnie laughed. "Hey, kiddo, you can't kid a kidder."

"Well…" I wrinkled my nose. "What if I did?"

She raised her hands. "Praise the Lord! What is it, seven years since you and that guy who'll remain nameless got divorced? It's about time. You must've been getting green and moldy down there. Ugh." She screwed up her lips.

"*Shhh*. People are staring."

Ronnie leaned close. "I'll be quiet if you tell me all about it."

"There isn't much to tell. We had a few drinks and dinner—"

"Where? Don't leave anything out."

When I told her where Richard had taken me, her eyes went wide. "Le Cirque? This guy doesn't fool around!"

"Hey, you said you'd behave if I told you. Besides, it was just—"

"Yeah, yeah. And afterward?"

"We went back to his place. Ronnie, you ought to see it. Overlooks the East River. I didn't know Manhattan had such big apartments." I shook my head.

"Speaking of big—" She let the word hang.

Feeling my face again flush, I told her it was more than adequate.

"Ohmigod! No wonder you're glowing."

"Don't get excited. It was a just a dinner date with a happy ending."

"Yeah, I get it. You had good sex with someone who has a brain and who took you to Le Cirque. When will you see him again?"

The Times Square burger joint had grown crowded. People hovered around us, trays in hand, waiting for a place to sit.

I glanced at my watch, then started to slide from the plastic bench. "It's late. I've gotta get back to work."

Right then my friend could have stopped me. She should have told me I had a great date, so now I could get on with my life. She should have told me there are hundreds of guys like Richard Slattery in New York City, that fate intended me to sleep with every one of them. Those words might have changed everything. Instead of rushing to protect me from myself, Ronnie said, "You *are* gonna to see him again? Please tell me I didn't get this excited for nothing."

Through the plate glass window I saw a driver throw a finger at a city bus caught in the intersection.

"*Katy!*" She drew out my name.

"Uh… tonight, actually," I said. "We're going to the opening of a Monet exhibit at the Modern."

Chapter Ten
A Woman in Blue

The cold wind off Lake Ontario battered the window. Rumbling gusts brought my mind back to my perch on the window seat. The quilt no longer warmed me. I closed the book and slid from my nook. Tired as I was, sleep didn't come quickly. The room had become frigid. Even with a blanket and comforter, I couldn't stop shaking.

I dozed off eventually, but not for long. My eyes opened at 3:17. I knew the time because I looked at my watch on the bedside table. No longer shivering, I now felt overly hot and must have been for a while. I'd kicked off the covers in my sleep. My skin felt tight where perspire-ation had dried on my forehead, neck and chest. The crackle of wood and yellow flickers at the foot of my bed told me why. A fire burned in the hearth. I leaned over to look.

How could someone have built a fire without waking me?

Split logs and kindling were heaped in a copper bin on the floor next to the fireplace. It looked to be enough fuel to keep the blaze raging for days. *That's going to leave sawdust and ashes all over the carpet*, I thought, shocked that Mrs. Hughes would permit such a breach of clean-liness.

I leaned further over to assess the damage already done. My bed now rested on polished wood slats—the beautiful rug that matched the room's wallpaper no longer covered the floor. "How'd they get the rug rolled up without moving everything in here?" I mumbled.

"You're awake," a soft Irish brogue said from

somewhere nearby.

I sat up, gasping. Who had spoken to me?

The voice sighed.

It's one thing to sense an invisible person is watching you. It's another thing entirely when that invisible someone addresses you directly. I pushed back hard against the bed's headboard. "W-who's there?"

No one answered.

I released my breath. My eyes panned the darkness like a movie camera until they reached the window. There I saw a figure perched in the nook—a woman in an old-fashioned blue gown with a scoop-neck and puffed sleeves secured by a row of buttons at each wrist. She had long red hair—I could see that in the firelight. Red curls cascaded around a thin, pale neck that, in profile, arched swan-like forward while she read a book propped against her bent knees. As clear as everything about her was, she seemed almost transparent.

Sweat broke across my forehead. I pushed further back against the headboard.

"I like it warm," she said without looking up from her book.

The woman speaking didn't cause me to cower—by now I could almost deal with a disembodied voice. I shook because I *saw* the body the voice belonged to. Fighting for breath, I stammered, "W-what are you d-doing in my room?"

"Indeed," the woman said, as if I were an after-thought. "Isn't this my room you're in, and aren't I being kind enough to let you stay here awhile?"

I lurched forward, rubbing my eyes. *This isn't real!* my mind screamed.

I peered toward the window, praying the image was something my imagination had dredged from the shadows. If it wasn't— Tears in my eyes, I yanked the bed covers up to my chest.

Her head still turned down to her book, the woman said, "I'm not a shadow—though some might call me a shade. Nor am I a dream."

This is *a dream. It must be. Please, please, let it be!* My heart beat so rapidly it seemed to echo off the walls. I willed myself to wake up.

The woman sighed.

This is insane. Maybe I do belong locked away in some asylum. The way I've been feeling... and now this!

"You'll not be getting hysterical on me now?" The woman said.

Tears running down my cheeks, I said, "You're a... Y-you really are? Oh God, I've gone totally—"

The ghost *tsked.* "A bit daft maybe, from all I've seen."

Blinking rapidly, I whispered, "Was that you I heard in here this morning?"

"And why shouldn't it be?" she said. "I keep myself up here and don't bother a soul."

"And it's been you pacing around?"

The ghost continued to read.

I inched to the edge of my bed, swung my legs over the side and gazed deeper into the shadows. I couldn't deny what I saw. A ghost perched by the window was talking to me! Frightened for my sanity, I whispered, "Not bothering anyone? The way you've been stomping around like there's an army marching in here?"

The ghost chuckled. "It isn't everyone that can hear me."

Whoever this ghost was, she looked and sounded... human. The fact that she did was almost calming. I reached out a hesitant hand, then quickly pulled back.

"Fewer yet can see me," she said.

Ronnie, Andrea, and Mrs. Hughes had stared at me when I asked about the footsteps. I closed my eyes and opened them again. The specter still sat there, quietly reading. One finger twisted a long red curl.

Whoever this is, she doesn't seem to mean me any harm. I thought, and eased down on the bed.

"I *am* the only one who can—" I began. Then I remembered. "Hold on now. Leah Campbell can hear you. You nearly scared the poor old woman to death, snarling at her yesterday morning."

I stopped abruptly, struck by another thought. This woman seemed too inoffensive to have done that. *What if she isn't the only ghost haunting this place? Maybe there's another... angry one.* I glanced nervously around. "That was you, w-wasn't it?"

"Who else would it be? I'm the only spirit living here, aren't I?"

"I... don't know. What about the smell of baking bread? Tell me who's doing that."

"Bread baking, is it now?" the ghost asked as if she had no idea.

"I can smell it all over the house," I insisted. "It's so prevalent I've completely lost my appetite."

"There's no spirit baking anything here. What you smell is just a memory of when this was Ben Hughes's bakeshop."

"Memory?" I asked.

The ghost turned to me. "Of course, memory. Houses have them just as people do. And Ben Hughes's house remembers very well the way he and his missus worked through the night at their brick oven in the basement."

"But—"

"Not believing me, are you? Would you care to have me conjure up Ben to tell you himself?" The ghost laughed.

I failed to see any humor in the idea of another spirit in my room.

She shook her head. "Don't be making such a face.

Old Ben had no reason to stay around, so his baking's not to blame for you losing your appetite. That you did very nicely by yourself."

I pushed down the bedcovers. "I didn't!"

The ghost shrugged. "Have it your own way, then. There's no point quarreling with someone who won't listen. Go back to sleep. Leave me to read in peace."

"Oh, no, you don't!" I sputtered.

"Don't want to sleep?" The ghost sighed and closed her book. "All right then, what other nonsense are you about bothering me with?"

Questions tumbled one on another in my mind. All I could get out was, "How come no one else but me… What about poor Leah?"

"Poor old Leah," the ghost mimicked me. "Sneaking around like an insane person with a crucifix in front of her face, trying to use it like some exorcizing priest to chase me from my own house. Poor old soul, indeed!"

"But… why can *I* hear you, and… and see you?" I brushed mussed blonde hair from my face to reassure myself I really did see the ghost. "Why can't the others?"

"There's a good question." She unfolded her legs from the window seat and turned toward the bed. "I've been wondering about that for years, why one does and not another. I suppose it's something to do with some needing me."

"Needing you?"

"That's what I said."

"But I don't… I-I mean… what could I possibly need you for?"

I pulled back my hair with both hands. It felt like the sheerest lunacy to calmly discuss with a ghost why she manifested, yet here I was in the middle of the night, engaged in just such a conversation.

"You were going to say, any more than you need the thing that's been laughing at you?" she said. "Only you can answer that. I can just tell you what should be obvious. You do. Why else would fate have brought you here?"

Forgetting for a moment that I was speaking to a spirit, I said, "It wasn't fate. My friend dragged to this place so I could be baby-sat for. I don't want to be here."

"Baby-sat? Indeed." The ghost looked through the window and softly crooned, "Yes, baby-sat." She turned back. "Do you not understand wanting has nothing to do with it? It's the *need* that bought you here. Now leave me to my reading."

She leaned back in the nook and began to fade.

I don't know why, but I felt an urgent need to stop her. "But, what about—"

"Leah?" Fully present again, the ghost smiled.

My hands on my cheeks, I said, "I can't believe I'm sitting in the dark, listening to a ghost complain about Leah Campbell."

"Then turn up the lamp if it's the dark bothering you," she said. "I can make fun of the hag when it's light, too."

When I went to bed an electric light hung on the wall. In its place I saw an old-fashioned gas lamp with a flame turned down low. Given everything else going on in the Niagara Inn, I didn't question it being there. With little effort I turned up the flame. Now I could see the woman clearly. Beneath her red tresses, she had delicate features and wide green eyes. I gasped when I looked at her.

Again the ghost *tsked*. "What's bothering you now?"

"You're real. I mean… you're not all misty. I can't see through you." I reached for her. "And your hand—mine doesn't pass through it."

The ghost laughed again. "Of course I'm real. What did you expect? Maybe it's something out of a book by somebody who never saw one of us you're looking for. No, I'm as real as you *need* me to be."

I pulled back my hand. "Real is good. At least this

way, I won't feel as though I've gone entirely crazy."

The ghost patted my arm. "There's no need to be worrying about that. Seeing me doesn't mean you belong shut away again."

I gasped. How could this ghost possibly know I'd been confined?

As if to cut off the question, she said, "Besides, crazy's not half bad if you're nice about it. We're all a bit daft now and then." Book still in hand, she moved to the bed. I felt the mattress depress slightly when she sat.

At last I felt at ease—well, as much at ease as a person could feel when being calmed by a spirit. "What are you reading?" I asked.

"It's a wonderful story of a great love found, then lost. *Anna Karenina,* it's called. I'm sorry this Leo Tolstoy who knows women so well didn't write it while I lived. I'm thinking it would've helped to read of a lass whose pain is as great as mine. If I'd known of her, I wouldn't have—Och, it's a lonely thing when no one understands what you're feeling."

Her words, moaned longingly, struck a chord. I watched while the ghost wiped tears from her cheek. Then I asked what should have been my first questions. "Who are you? How did you come to be here?"

"Abigail Bender's my name. Abbie, folks called me." The ghost smiled so wistfully that she might have recalled a long-ago time when people had been pleased to speak her name. "I was Abbie Kirby by birth. And as to why I'm here, it's my punishment. I'm condemned to remain in this house forever till I learn to regret what I did."

"Condemned? I don't understand."

She dropped her eyes to where my hand held hers. "No, you wouldn't, would you? Not without knowing how these things work. And as you're sitting here alive on this fine bed, you couldn't be knowing such things."

"Knowing what?"

"Ah, that's just it, isn't it? I don't know, either. No one ever told me, so I've been here a long time trying to learn for myself."

I leaned against the headboard. "Learn what? You're talking in riddles."

The ghost groaned, "Och, you'll not understand anything without knowing what happened here."

I'm asleep and dreaming, I thought—in a dream, what makes no sense is perfectly logical. I fluffed my pillow and put it behind my back. In the tone I used to get information from a new client, I said, "If I know, I might be able to help." I flipped my watch on the night table so the face didn't show. "Tell me. I've got time to listen."

"*Have* you now?" The ghost's tone worried me a little. "Well, then, we'll see."

Leaning back next to me, Abigail Bender told me she'd been born in the section of Niagara-on-the-Lake called the Dock. Her father was a fisherman who plied Lake Ontario's waters and her darling brother fished with him. She said, "I didn't live in this fine place, then. Ours was a cottage down there." She pointed through the window toward the Niagara River. "I became a Bender and moved here when I was wed."

As the ghost spoke, I thought, *She needs to tell her story, needs me to hear and remember.*

Abigail gave me a strange look. Her soft voice mixing into the crackle of the hearth flames, she said, "Yes, remembrance is why you're here."

She turned the light low and we sat in the large bed, watching the glow of the fire.

Chapter Eleven
Yesterday in the Window

"Some things need remembering," the ghost repeated.

I heard the bed frame creak as she pulled a pillow behind her back. I felt the mattress sink. Do you hear and feel such things in a dream?

She patted my arm. "You're not dreaming. Haven't I told you that?"

I cringed. It seemed that this ghost could read my mind.

She pinched my hand.

"Ow!"

"Will you believe it now?" she said.

I *was* awake. A ghost sat beside me! Why didn't I run, screaming from my room? A normal person would have, but then, I hadn't been normal for years. Besides, she didn't moan or howl the way ghosts do in horror stories. No, this was a woman. Like me. Except she could vanish if she chose. And...well, I just didn't feel threatened by her.

"Do you need more convincing?"

I rubbed my hand where she'd pinched. "I'll take your word for it."

Nodding, she laid aside her book, then began to tell of things I needed to hear, though I didn't yet know it.

Abigail said, "My Will was a gentle, loving soul. Not many with him in those last terrible days saw it. They didn't know him as I did before the unthinkable horrors he saw changed him. I'm thinking maybe it was better I hadn't been there when he started to change, though I didn't feel that way when I heard what happened."

"I thought you're going to tell me about you," I

said.

Her eyebrows pinched down. "And you an intelligent woman. Do you not understand Will *is* my story? Not everything was about me—not when we had so much love."

"Wait a minute." I leaned forward, twisting to look at her face. "You're telling me your life had no meaning outside a man?"

The ghost sighed. "Och, if you can ask such a question you've never known—" She shot me a look. "That's why you're here."

I sat back. "I told you, I'm only here because—"

"I heard what you said. Still, in your heart you must know God doesn't mean us to be alone."

"I'm not! I have friends."

She patted my hand. "You do—fine ones, from what I've seen of them. But I'm thinking that even with a hundred friends, you'd still be alone." When I opened my mouth to protest, the ghost raised a hand. "I can tell your life's built on arguing even when you aren't right. But time's short. I fear for you if you won't listen."

I caught my breath. "Fear for me?"

She looked pensive. "You—" She shook her head. "I can only say the answer to what ails you lies in what happened in this house, and everything began with Will. I was just a part of it—and you are too."

My head snapped around. "I'm part of it? How *can* I be?"

The ghost again raised her hand to silence me. "Don't ask me to explain. You'll not believe me till you've heard it all." She looked away so quickly I couldn't read her face.

"Yeah, right!"

"Stubborn." She faded into the shadows.

She'd hinted that my life was tied to hers, to this house in some way. She had my attention. "Don't go!" I said.

The ghost was back. "You'll listen?"

I nodded.

From the way her eyes roamed over my face, I thought she might be assessing whether I meant it. "Well, then, we'll see how true your word is."

Once more settled against the headboard, she tucked her skirt around her legs. He eyes closed as if to bring back a memory, she said, "Will's and my story began in eighteen fifty-seven, though we didn't know of each other. What started him toward me was a fear Father Bender felt while living in a fine house in Erie, Pennsylvania. You see, he saw what was coming."

"How could you know of this if you hadn't met Will yet?" My words were a knee-jerk reaction. Catching story tellers in a lie is instinctive with lawyers who have questioned witnesses in court.

The ghost gave me a less than cordial smile. "Still arguing? Some of it Mother Bender told of while Will and me were courting."

"And the rest? Did you imagine it?"

Abigail's green eyes flared. Instead of shooting a sharp reply, she gazed at the window with a puzzled expression.

"What is it?"

"Nothing… and everything," she said. "I know what I know, because looking through my window…"

When she fell silent, I urged, "What?"

"I see…" Again she faded into the darkness.

I reached for her hand.

As if held there by my touch, the ghost was once more solid. She brushed at her tears. "Remembering is hard. I've grown used to doing it alone."

Finally, she'd said something I understood.

She away wiped her tears with a quick motion, then lifted the edge of the sheet. "Here. Dry your eyes."

I hadn't realized I'd started to cry.

"I expect you've been crying without knowing it for a long time," she said. "And I expect you know why."

She touched my shoulder and a memory rushed up. *'He hasn't been to see her even once since she lost it,'* one white-clad figure said to another. *'Is it any wonder she—'*

I waved my hand to sweep away the past, then used the bed sheet to dry my tears. "I know my story!" My voice was harsh. "The window—you said you see things through it."

Light from the streetlamp reflected off the heavy snow once again falling like sugar from the bowl of the sky. As if the flakes were prisms, they cast an eerie blue glow on the window seat.

Abigail's expression held both longing and dread. "Yes, my window. Through it I see things done by people I cared for, even if I wasn't there when those things happened. I hear them talk, too. And before you ask, I don't know why it is. I'm thinking that living these things over and over this way is part of my punishment."

My brow creased. *Punishment?* As the word formed in my mind, I felt as though I'd been stabbed in my chest. I winced, bent over.

The ghost's face held an expression I can only describe as satisfied. I wondered whether she had caused my pain. Could a ghost do that?

She must have read my thought again. It wasn't her, she said. As with my loss of appetite, I did this to myself.

I didn't believe her. Using very unladylike words, I told her to make the damn pain stop. Now! She said she would if she could, but I had to cure myself. The way she said it, she might have regretted she had so little power. Or maybe the empathy in her voice hid a dark promise she might make things worse for me—at the moment, I was in no condition to unravel the ghost's motive. Nearly doubled over, I cried out.

"You know what you must do," she said.

Damned if I will! I made my mind a blank slate. "Your story," I moaned. "You said everything I need to know is in it. Tell me." Another sharp pain left me almost breathless. "Please!"

Abigail seemed to take pity on me. Or maybe she thought of a different way she might convince me to face the memories I'd buried. Whatever her reason, the pain subsided enough for me to sit up. When I did, she said, "It seems to me there's a better way for you to know my story." She glanced again at the glowing snow. "Through my window I've seen my days and all that happened in them."

She took my hand and helped me to the window seat. As she settled beside me in the nook, she pointed toward the lake as if reaching out to a distant past. "If you look hard, you also might see it."

I peered through the window. "It's just the street out there—and the snow."

"Look harder," the ghost insisted.

"This is silly. All I see is—"

"Can you not see what's before your eyes?" Abigail Bender sounded frustrated. She took my face with both hands, and turned me to the window.

I gasped. Instead of a white landscape, I saw a small town. It was as if I floated above it. A wide avenue cut through the town's center. On one side, houses—some brick, most large—lined streets laid out in a neat grid. On the other side of the avenue, narrow lanes twisted down to the lake. Houses along these narrow streets were small, made of wood with sharply sloped roofs. To the right, railroad tracks ran by a pier. I saw coal heaped near the tracks. Wagons, heavy with crates, sacks and barrels, bounced along the roads. A fleet of small boats sailed on the water. Men leaned far over the sides to draw in nets. Closer in, large ships sat at anchor offshore. Rafts loaded with coal and lumber were tied to them.

"Can you see it now?" Abigail asked.

Stunned, I could only nod.

"What you see is this town when I was a lass," she said. "Back then it was made of four parts—the Dock, the Town where the wealth was, Irishtown, and the Colored Section." She pointed first in one direction, then another. "Yes, the Colored Section," she repeated, as if that section had some special meaning. "I once knew every part of this town. You might think there was wide gulf between people who lived in the different sections—maybe broad as the river you see flowing into Lake Ontario. There wasn't a gulf, though, because old Tom Burke lived in the Town and owned half the Dock and businesses, from Prideaux Street down to the beach. If you look hard, you'll see me there on the beach watching while Mr. Burke's good pine lumber is loaded onto shallow boats afloat near the great schooners. Those wee boats were used to row Tom Burke's wood over the sand shoals to shore. Old Mr. Burke brought together folks from all the sections to do his work, and everyone said his lumber built a bridge between them."

She pointed to a tree-lined path. "Over there—that's the Dock, Ricardo Street, the house I was born in." Each time she pointed I floated nearer to the landmark. "I was born in eighteen forty-one, so as you see me there I'm all of sixteen, though if you'd asked me then I'd have told you I was a grown woman."

"Didn't we all feel that way at sixteen?" I said.

When she smiled, I felt a connection between us.

After a moment she turned back to the window. "Our house was small, no more than a bungalow. But it was fine for a fisherman's family. I lived there with Ma, Da and my older brother. Brian, his name was, though I called him Brinny from the first time I spoke it."

As I watched, a younger Abigail strolled into one of the houses. With those alert green eyes, swanlike neck and long red hair draped across her shoulders, I would have known her anywhere. As if a camera followed her through the door, I now saw inside the Kirbys' cottage.

The ghost said, "You're seeing the kitchen—most of our living was done there. Those two doors at the end go to small bedrooms—one Ma and Da's, the other, Brinny's. I had a bunk behind the curtain across the far wall. I slept there after growing too old to share a bed with my brother. That was all right, I suppose, except in the early morning when tiny red bedbugs crawled across the wall." She shuddered. "I still hate the sight of those wee reds running."

At a table in the kitchen, Abigail and a woman floured biscuit dough. Each wore an apron tied over a long dress. From the older woman's red hair, high cheek bones and the delicate cast of her face, I knew she must be Abigail's mother. Behind the women I saw an open brick fireplace. A rude iron stove stood next to it.

"That's me and Ma—Mary's her Christian name," the ghost said. "In the kitchen it's eighteen fifty-seven, and will remain so as long I think of us on that day."

I couldn't comprehend how I saw all this. If I were dreaming it was in Technicolor. And there was Surround Sound. "I hear you and your mother talking, and—" I turned to the ghost, mouth open. "I even—"

"What?"

"I hear—no, it can't be."

The ghost grinned at my confusion. "Some things seem impossible but aren't, though you don't know it yet. Other things…. For now, tell me what you hear."

"I-I hear what you and your mother are thinking. It's like I'm inside your heads. This can't be right. I feel like a voyeur." Feeling my face flush, I averted my eyes.

Her smile became a laugh. "It's like that, looking through my window. But I'm thinking there's nothing wrong in it if these things remind me of my time in the light." She pointed. "Now watch."

As if forced, my eyes turned to the scene playing out beyond Abigail's window.

"Ma, why do *I* have to sleep with the wee red ones?" the young Abigail complained. "Brinny's about early and out to the boats. Why can't he sleep there?"

"And do you not think the wee ones run in your brother's room as well?" Mary Kirby sounded annoyed. A long tendril of red hair escaped its tie. She brushed it from her face. The movement left a white streak on her cheek.

The sixteen-year-old Abigail frowned. With a towel taken from the table, she wiped the flour from her mother's face. "But there's nights Brinny comes home late, and—"

"Aye, late." As Mary stood, hands on her hips glaring at her daughter, I heard—and felt—her mind race. *Aye, late—* She dreaded what those words meant. Though I couldn't pick up what lay behind her fear, I felt acid bloat her stomach. Twisting the hem of her apron, she snapped, "Sure, and maybe you should've been born to a fine lady of the Town instead of folks in the Dock! Then you'd have a grand room of your own. And maybe then I wouldn't be knowing how you sneak out at night to wait after your brother at the beach."

"But, Ma—"

"Lass, you're after bothering me now," Mary Kirby scolded. "Get you down to the beach. Your father's boat'll be putting in. He'll need you to tend his nets." She snatched a broom and swept her daughter from the house along with dust from the rough wood floor.

As if I were watching a movie, through the window I saw Abigail skip down the three steps from the house. After looking once over her shoulder at the closed door, she strolled along a narrow lane, hands held carelessly behind her. It appeared to be high summer—watching from behind the window, I felt the heat of the day. As she walked, dry dirt from the unpaved road made her cough. I smelled the dust the lake-breeze swirled around her. This was too much! I not only heard what those people said and thought, I felt and smelled what they did.

While the teenage Abigail walked, I heard her think how much better summer was than spring, when rain turned the ground to a lake of mud.

The ghost tapped my shoulder and pointed to the street where her cottage once stood. "My house was just there, close to the Coal and Lumber Works Tom Burke built near the beach," she said. "You might still see it today if you were to walk down that way.

She pointed in another direction. "Ah, there I am, just getting to the beach. Like most girls of the Dock, now my morning chores were done, I went there to help with the day's catch."

Chapter Twelve
A Day in the Life of the Dock

Through the window I now saw an expanse of pebbly sand. Beyond it, Lake Ontario glittered. Up and down the shore-line, men hauled shallow-draft craft ashore with heavy ropes. Then they climbed aboard and tossed out fish. Others knelt near their boats, scraping the sides. Between the beached craft, girls sat on nets spread across the ground, their fingers patching holes with string tied to long needles.

As Abbie made her way to what the ghost told me was a double-ended cedar hull Mackinaw, a deep voice called, “Daughter, take these here fish from the boat. Crate ’em and stack the crates so’s me and Brian can run ’em up to the Town.”

Tall and sturdy, the man was dressed in water-stained overalls buttoned over a red and black jersey. Above a dark, curly beard, the deep tan of his face ran up to a slightly receding hairline. Where they protruded from rolled-up sleeves, his forearms seemed muscular. Next to him I saw another man, not much more than twenty, if that, I thought. Instead of a full beard, his face had what appeared to be a two-day stubble.

“It looks a good catch, Da,” I heard the young Abbie say as she began to sort the fish.

The older man shaded his eyes with a hand and looked to the sky. “Aye, God’s been good to us this day.”

While Sean—the ghost told me her father’s name—and Brian Kirby secured the Mackinaw’s rig, Abbie separated perch, lake herring and shad. That done, she stretched the nets flat to dry and began to sew the torn places.

Two barefoot girls, skirts gathered and tucked in at their waists, dragged nets behind them. They spread their nets on the ground nearby.

"Fine day," one of the girls remarked. Dark curls fell around her broad shoulders when she squinted up at the sun.

"Aye, it is that, Tilda Riley," Abbie said.

Tilda jabbed an elbow at the third girl's ribs. "And all the better for watching those fine lads at work, ay? What're you looking so intent at, Annie Stark?"

This girl pointed to a young man. A giggle in her voice, she said, "The Morgan lad." She ran her fingers through sun-bleached hair, arched out her ample chest and posed for a long moment.

Abbie laughed. "Chasing after Dick Morgan now, are you? Done so soon with Bob Wright?"

"More like Bob Wright's done with her, now he's had his way," Tilda Riley teased.

Annie Stark blushed. "Never did." With another giggle, she added, "But not for lack of trying."

Dick Morgan, the boy they were admiring, strutted up. He nodded once to the girls, then moved off to flirt with a newcomer. He was a hunk—no other way to describe him. Square jaw, sharp features, intense eyes. I understood why the thought of him knocked everyone else from Annie Stark's mind.

"Ah, but that lad's a sight to see," Tilda said.

Abbie returned to sewing her nets. "Too full of himself for my taste."

Annie poked her. "Got no taste for any lads here, ay, Abbie Kirby? Too good for 'em, are you?"

As she rapidly shoved her needle through the heavy mesh, Abbie grumbled. "What is there about any of them worth dreaming of?"

"Keep on this way, you'll die an old maid," Tilda said. "They'll write 'ne'er been kissed' on your gravestone."

Abbie gazed across the lake. I heard her think her friends were right. She'd yet to meet a boy interesting enough to give more than a passing thought to. She doubted she ever would.

Sean Kirby hefted a crate and called, "Enough of this gossip. Get you gone, lass, up to the house. Lend your Ma a hand fixing dinner."

On my side of the window, the ghost sat back, smiling. "There's times I wish those days had never ended."

I felt a chill when her smile faded.

The scene shifted. Abigail said, "It's evening of the same day now. We've had our meal, and the kitchen's been straightened up." She pointed. "There I am at the table, writing on a slate in candlelight. I'm doing a lesson Ma prepared for me."

Her voice took on a melancholy tinge. When she glanced away from the window she caught me looking speculatively at her. "It was a good life we made here," she said. "Och, but everything changes so fast. What counts is what's brought to those changes."

She looked now through the window at her mother. "Before a potato famine drove her from Ireland, Ma learned to read, write and do sums. Those were things she wanted me and Brinny to know. She always told us if we did, we'd find an easier life than she and Da had. She never complained of her life, mind you. Fate smiled on her enough to bring her a strong, hardworking man who made sure we had a warm home, cloth for decent clothes and a full table no matter the change in seasons. Ma wouldn't have dared to ask fate for more. Because she didn't, fate gave her much more.

"While other husbands rushed through silent suppers, then betook themselves to the Angel Inn for a night of drinking with friends—and maybe some debauchery with women of easy virtue who hung about there—Da took his pleasure in Ma's company." As if in wonder of so fine a love, the ghost's face glowed.

I felt an itch of jealousy.

Beyond Abigail's window, I now saw a kitchen lit by a small hearth-fire and two candles on the long table. Mary's hair hung loose to her waist.

"You look fine tonight, wife," Sean Kirby said. He pulled a pipe from his shirt pocket. With what looked to be a contented smile, he settled down next to Mary at the table. His dark eyes watched her help Abbie with the lesson. When he stroked his wife's hand, I felt her skin tingle in response. "It isn't every man on the lake can look forward to coming home to such a sight," he said.

Abbie glanced up from her slate, grinning at this show of affection.

"No, that sum's wrong. You know better!" Mary said. "What's wrong with you, child?"

"Nothing, Ma."

"Well, if there ain't nothing wrong, do the problem again."

Sean nuzzled his wife.

Again Abbie looked up.

"Your lesson's on the slate, not on my forehead or your Da's," Mary said.

Abbie dropped her gaze to her slate.

Sean glanced from his daughter to his wife and knocked the ashes from his pipe. "The candle's burnt low, wife. I'm thinking it's time we're in bed. Morning comes fast these days."

Abbie pushed aside her slate and kissed her parents. With a knowing look, she slid behind the curtain of her bunk.

"And just what do you find so amusing, child?" Mary called after her.

"Nothing, Ma."

"Goodnight, then."

"Sleep tight, daughter." Sean took Mary's hand and

led her to their small bedroom.

***

As the door closed behind them, Abigail told me, "When they were in bed, Da held Ma safe from the night and touched her until she thrilled in ways she thanked God for—albeit she never confessed *that* in church." She turned her eyes from the window and laughed. "No, Ma couldn't complain of her life. But she wanted more for me and Brinny. Knowing of the fine homes in the Town, she hoped we'd use the small education she gave us to make our way in the world. If we did, she always told us, maybe one day one of those grand places could be ours.

"Over time, she gave up her dream for Brinny. Like Da, he had no patience for learning letters and numbers. 'The lake's where I wanna be, Ma,' he'd tell her. I can still hear him say, 'Out there with the sky and water and nothing between them, that's heaven sent down to this earth. That's freedom. Don't need no book learning to ride the lake.' Brinny always talked of one day sailing off to the west in one of the great schooners.

"Ma feared his dream. You see, Kaitlyn, danger lurked out on the Great Lakes. Ma knew many women whose sons were lost in shipwrecks out there. Still, in time she came to believe that if that was fate's plan for Brinny, she could do naught for it.

"I was different. Early on, I easily understood how letters were made into words. They painted pictures in my mind. From those pictures I built *my* dreams. Ma was so proud of me she'd often trade a fat fish to the woman at the lending library so she could bring me home a book to keep for a week."

While Abigail spoke, the image of the Kirbys' warm kitchen receded into the twenty-first century winter landscape. Intent on telling me about her childhood, she didn't seem to notice.

"It was the way men and women loved truly in my books," she said, "and the way Ma and Da looked at each other that taught me what I wanted from life. I know stubbornness was as much one of my sins as it is yours, Kaitlyn. And like you, I didn't care to change. So it wasn't till Will—" She stopped, sighed and leaned back in the nook.

I scrunched up my face.

"What lemon are you sucking on now?" the ghost said.

"The kind of romance you described only happens in authors' minds," I said. "Sure it's nice to read about, maybe even dream of. In real life—" I shook my head. "Romance, love? Those things are writer's lies, invented so they can sell their books."

Abigail's green eyes went soft. "Och, it's sorry I'd be for you if you believed what you say. I'm thinking the only lying is in what you're telling yourself."

"I'm a realist is all."

Now the ghost shook her head. "Realist, is it? How can you be that if you'll not face the truth standing bold as day before you? Though my world and I might be naught but mist now, betwixt us it's me who knows what's real and what truly matters."

Chapter Thirteen
Fate Laughs

Abigail touched a windowpane. "I'll show you what matters," she said.

"Is it about you and Will Bender you're going to tell? You said everything started and ended with him."

"I'll be getting to that, won't I?" The ghost sounded peeved that I'd interrupted her. "Just now I'm remembering a time our minister, Mr. Cox, told me it wasn't Christian to believe Will's life and mine were torn asunder because fate would have it so—"

The ghost stopped in mid-breath. After a minute her eyes seemed to focus on me. "I was sitting, pining right by this window when Mr. Cox came to call," she said. "He told me God gave people freewill so we'd choose to do His work, and I was failing Him if I didn't get myself up right then and go about it. The why of things isn't for us to know, Mr. Cox said, and I had to accept what happened because the whole of history was written on the first day. He said that to me soon after I lost my Will. I was hurting and so angry with God over it that I wouldn't listen. Now I'm thinking that's the truth of it. We're all tied to our parts in the history God wrote. Why else would it be Will came to Niagara-on-the-Lake and I fell in love with him? And why couldn't my loving him with the whole of my heart stop him from doing what he would have done if he hadn't come here? Now *you've* come to hear of it because you're also hurting from having known such a loss. Yes, you have. Don't deny it. I feel it in you. And I know what you did to run from it."

"I've never run from anything!"

"Never run, have you? We'll see."

As the ghost said this, a cloying weariness crept over me and total darkness lowered like a curtain across the room. The cadenced crackle of the hearth fire sighed like a lullaby. It sang of my teenage years—the time a girl fights to break free of her mother's grasp yet fears what life might hold. It sang of the first time I heard the rasping, disembodied laughter. That evening came back like in a dream:

A two-story attached house in the New York borough of Queens. My parents arguing.

"Damn ballgames. You gonna watch it all night?" Mom calls out. Annoyed. She always sounds annoyed.

"Aw, hell, what now?" Dad grumbles.

A cabinet door opens, slams shut. Ice cubes clink in a glass. "I could use help here," she whines, her words slurred.

"In a minute," Dad says.

"I work my tail off, and with him it's always 'in a minute,'" Mom says loud enough for the neighborhood to hear.

I run up the stairs, slam my bedroom door. Lean against it. Hold my breath. Seventeen, I don't want to hear them go at it again. Mine is a small room, sparsely furnished. A bed, a desk by the single window covered by a blind with broken slats, a dresser, stained carpeting.

Downstairs, my parents' tempers flare. A fire out of control. Behind my closed door, I can almost ignore them.

Laughter seeps under the door.

"Who's there?"

No one answers.

I crack open the door, peek into the hall. It's empty. My brother's room is empty. I'm imagining things. Damn my mother, my father, they're the reason. I turn up the volume of my stereo. Through the speakers, Bonnie Raitt wails, I can't make you love me—

Mom's voice is shrill, cutting through the closed door as if the wood is cardboard. It rises over the music. "Every day it's the same damn thing. You shovel dinner down your throat like you can't wait to get outta here. Then you plop down like a lump of lard in front of the damn TV!"

Dad shouts, "I work my ass off at the lot all day! Is it too much to want peace when I get home?"

"My dream man," Mom snarls. "Instead of a prince, I got a used car salesman and a pile of bills we can't pay."

The laughter again. I crawl onto my bed, hold a pillow around my ears. Doesn't help.

Mom again: "You might as well not be here, Lou. You hear me?"

Dad again: "Aw, hell, why do I try?"

Heavy footsteps move toward the front door.

"You don't *try, that's your problem! Sure, go ahead, leave. You're not here when you're here. What difference does it make?"*

The screen door squeaks.

"Go on, run off to your friends in that greasy bar!" Mom shouts.

He doesn't answer.

From the front stoop, she yells, "You'll be back!"

His voice comes through my bedroom window. "Not this time!"

A car door slams.

Hahahaa.

"Stop it, stop it!" I scream at whatever is laughing. "Stop it!" I scream at my parents. I want to run from the house, not stop until I'm with my boyfriend. I can't. Barry's a waiter at summer camp.

"Why aren't you here when I need you?" I cry to the thought of him. I'm trapped in my room, in my life.

Hahahaa.

It's night now. Dad hasn't come home. Mom's at the kitchen table crying into a glass of scotch. At my desk, bent over my diary, I write a life-plan. Bulleted points: Go to Harvard Law School; Marry Barry (wedding reception at the Plaza); Work for a Wall Street firm that pays lots of money; Have a baby; Buy a house in the suburbs; Another baby; Spend my life surrounded by my husband and children.

"I won't be like my mother," I mumble through my tears. "Barry will never leave me."

The laughter comes again, loud, long.

I jump into bed, pull the covers over my head. I'll run away, that's what I'll do.

That dream ended as quickly as it began. It was replaced by a stark landscape of sand, sage brush and a cliff with nothing beyond it. The end of the world. The end of everything. I raced toward the precipice—

"Not so soon, Kaitlyn Novacs!" Abigail's voice tore me from the dream. "There's more for you to know before you decide again to go *there*."

A breeze rushed through the room. My eyes now open, I saw the fire flare in the hearth. The dark curtain rose. In a flash of understanding I knew the ghost held a line firmly tied to my awareness, to everything that had happened in my life. Before I could grasp the implications, she said to me, "It's time I tell you of when Will and his family came here. When I do, you'll know of the lute fate carries in its bag and plays on while it sings its lies."

She pointed out the window. Another scene appeared among the snowflakes.

"It's autumn now," Abigail said. "See there? Will and his family are stepping down from the train."

On the track near the beach, half a dozen Pullman coaches stood along the station platform. Beyond the train, a scow with square bilges and two schooners lay at anchor in the harbor. Rafts ferried goods back and forth between the ships and the beach. A fleet of sixteen-foot Mackinaws and smaller fishing skiffs rode the horizon. Horses pulling open wagons loaded with cargo clopped along the rutted road from the pier. Three people climbed down from the train.

“That’s Will and his Ma and Da—Elizabeth and George Bender, they were,” Abigail told me.

On the platform, George gazed into the distance. “This is fine,” he said with a nod.

Elizabeth brushed dust from her skirt and took his arm. She looked doubtful.

“Doesn’t seem to be much commerce here, Father,” the fair-haired Will said. “Certainly not the kind we’re used to seeing in Erie.”

George gave him an indulgent smile. “It’ll do, son. It’ll do just fine. This is the future. Now, look to our luggage while I secure a carriage.”

From the station, crammed on the seat of a one horse chaise, the Benders drove along a wide avenue. “This is Queen Street. Our new home is just down there.” George pointed.

“Queen, indeed,” Elizabeth muttered. “That Victoria person will never be *my* queen.”

George laughed. “I suppose you won’t invite her to tea anytime soon.”

The street bulged with shoppers meandering in and out of stores, arms filled with baskets and bundles. Three long blocks further on the Benders turned onto what a sign said was Victoria Street. Moments later, George tied the carriage horse in front of a brick house.

While I watched the scenes rapidly flash on one windowpane then another, I saw Elizabeth Bender arranging and rearranging the furniture in her new home. I saw George and Will setting up a haberdashery on the ground floor. Of the three Benders, it appeared that only George took pleasure in this work. I was certain of this when I heard Will complain, "Why did you bother sending me to college if my future's only to clerk in a store? Father, there are important things I should be doing."

The young man was as tall as his father, though not as broad. He had the same light hair and ruddy complexion.

George Bender stopped counting the inventory he carefully laid on newly constructed shelves and dropped his hands to his hips. "How many times must I explain this to you?"

"As many as it takes me to understand why I was pulled from everything I know for what feels like a whim. You were doing fine in Erie. I was doing fine at Allegheny College."

"I ran a successful shop," George said. "But I couldn't build a future for you on it. What with the port at Cleveland coming into its own and railroads set up to haul freight instead of risking it on ships that keep sinking, a port city like Erie cannot last. In a few years most of the businesses there will have moved elsewhere."

As if he sensed his father held something back, Will pressed. "If what you say is so, then what's the purpose of moving to a backwater town such as this?"

"It won't always be. Niagara-on-the-Lake is growing into a center of commerce."

"But even Mother says—"

"That's enough, Will!" George said. "Come over here. Help me move this display case."

The young man gritted his teeth, but did as he was instructed.

I turned to Abigail. "Will's stubborn. I can see it in the set of his jaw."

She grinned at me. "You know him, then, do you? Stubborn, yes—in that we were a good match. He wasn't so easily strapped into Father Bender's harness. In those early days he kept his eyes turned south to the place he still thought of as home and continued to question Father

Bender's judgment during the months it took their shop to take hold. Now, hush. Look!" When she pointed to the window the scene changed. "There are Mother and Father Bender walking in the garden behind their fine house. She's questioning his judgment just as Will did."

"It's hard for our son, Mr. Bender," Elizabeth said. "Maybe if he had friends…" She turned away.

The garden looked rough, untamed. Grass and weeds threatened to overrun the brick path running through it. Hedges grew wild.

George took his wife's arm. "I know it's difficult here for you with all *your* friends still in Erie. Have patience, dear. Soon we'll be as much a part of this place as we were there."

"Still, to have to start over…" Elizabeth sniffed. "At our age, and just at a time we were about to be accepted by society."

George grumbled. "Don't fool yourself. Those high society people were never going to accept us. We don't have enough money, and what we have isn't nearly old enough."

She dabbed at her eyes with the handkerchief she pulled from her sleeve. "Still, George, what kind of society is there in this place? Fishermen and laborers wander into any shop. And there are no grand balls, only church dances to which just *anyone* comes." She touched his wrist. "Remember the Spring Cotillion in the Arbor back home?" She glanced around the rude plot of earth she now walked on. "And our own ball at Christmas time? Women in fashions from Paris and New York, men in their finest—What would my mother have said if she saw me living among such rabble as this?"

George turned her to face him. "My dear, your mother would have reminded you that she too was such rabble when as a young bride her husband brought her to a small port town called Erie."

***

I waved a hand to dismiss Elizabeth Bender. "That woman's far too stand-offish for my taste. Small woman, small mind. You must have had quite a time with her."

Abigail threw me a stern look. "You mustn't be so quick to judge. There's none of us is just one thing. Foolish Mother Bender may have been in many ways, but a good heart beat in her breast. You'll see that once you know her."

Not convinced, I said, "I can imagine what the townspeople thought of her. What they must have thought of Will. And poor George—it looks as though he's trying hard to hold everything together."

Abigail smiled at the memory. Folks were polite, she told me, but they held their distance. While she spoke the room seemed to fill with voices. I heard snippets of conversations.

"That Will Bender, he's too quiet," A man's voice said.

"Aye, he is that," another voice agreed. "The boy looks right past you like his mind is somewhere in a London mews."

Next I heard women speaking. "I stopped to talk to Missus Bender on Queen Street this morning," one said.

Another said, "I saw you and that… person. Her nose in the air and all gotten up like a duchess at Queen Victoria's Court."

Now a third woman's voice: "Ah, and did you see her standin' by herself at the church social Saturday night?"

"Lookin' to the door all the time like she couldn't wait to leave."

"See," I told the ghost. "It's as I said. You mother-in-law was a snob."

Abigail clicked her tongue. "And it's like I said, Kaitlyn Novacs, none of us is just one thing. Listen, will you?"

She pointed, and I heard, "Good day to ye, Molly Patterson."

"Ah, and a fine day it is, Mary Kirby."

A laugh, then, "Fine, indeed. I hear you've taken a post cleaning and cooking for that Bender woman. Must be hard being around her."

"At times it is, but there's other times the woman's real down-to-earth. Generous, too. Always says to me, Molly, whyn't you set, have lunch with me. Lonesome's all she is, just plain lonesome. And knowing as how my Burt got hurt on the Linnie Powell and can't work, she says to me, Molly Patterson, you just take this here roast to cook for his dinner. Yes, underneath them fancy manners, I think there just may be something real."

The voices went silent. This time, when Abigail pointed, George Bender's image appeared on a window-pane. As if caressing his face, she stroked the glass. The motion told me how much she cared for the man. I appreciated that. Yet, at the same time I felt envy. She'd had two fathers. I barely remembered having one.

"Father Bender was a salesman and a good one," Abigail said. "He went out of his way to greet his neighbors. 'How's the boy, Bob?' he'd always say. 'Strange weather we're having, isn't it? Too bad about the Linnie Powell going down. Heard some of the crew was from here. Anything we can do to help?'"

"'Aye, a regular Joe that Bender fellow is,' folks said of him."

Again the ghost looked through her window. "That was at the very beginning. People always feel strange around newcomers. But everyone was a newcomer here one time and another, and old Mr. Burke made sure they didn't stay that way long. I should tell you something of him before you see how he went about it—it's only right that I do, since this is his fine house keeping us from the blizzard outside.

"In those days Mr. Burke was in his sixties, hefty with a full gray beard. People said he visited this town after stopping for a while in New York City and liked what he saw so much he stayed till the end of his days.

"The week after he first climbed down from the train, Mr. Burke bought the old Methodist Church and hired men from the Dock, Irishtown and the Colored Section to help him move it to the corner of Prideaux and Gate Streets. He opened a pork factory in it, and when his factory started to make money, he hired more folks, opened other businesses—including the Coal and Lumber Works that fate used to bring Will and me together."

Abigail leaned over and pointed down the street. "There he is now, the most important man in Niagara-on-the-Lake."

Outside, the image of a man who could only be Tom Burke appeared. He stood on a plank walk beneath a sign that read BENDER HABERDASHERY. On that sultry afternoon, he was sweating while he gazed past the gilt-letters on the shop's window. After a few moments he brushed dust from his sleeve and strolled in.

George Bender greeted him, jacket off, waistcoat unbuttoned, sleeves rolled up. "Good day to you, Mr. Burke. July already, I never realized it could be quite so hot this far north. How are you holding up in this heat?"

Burke nodded and glanced around as if he had never seen the like of Bender's shop. Hands clasped behind his back, he silently inspected the neatly stacked shelves. Then he moved on to a display case filled with men's accessories. Every so often he glanced to the back where Will worked to fit a fidgety customer with new suit. After several minutes, he said, "I stopped in to find something or other for a gift."

George all but bowed. "We carry some fine gift items. Look here in this case. Maybe a stick pin? A set of studs? Or would you prefer one of these embroidered silk smoking jackets?" He reached toward a shelf. "They're just in from London."

Burke fingered a few of the items while he listened to the sales patter. When George stopped for breath, Burke said, "I heard as how you sold Jack Connolly a new suit of clothes a few weeks back. Also heard that after wearing it, he found a tear in the material."

"I was sorry to hear that." George frowned. I heard him worry about how quickly a reputation for selling faulty merchandise could travel from lip to lip. "But my son—Will over there—took it back and refunded Mr. Connelly's money."

"Jack told me that, too." Burke sucked in his lower lip. "There are some as would've insisted the material was fine when he took it home, and wearing it, it must have gotten torn. But your boy took it right back without a question."

George hooked his thumbs in his belt. "That's the way we conduct business at Bender's."

"Surprising, though." Burke cocked his head in Will's direction. "He seems a fine young man, but he's not very sociable."

George glanced at his son. "All this is new to him. He misses his friends back in Erie… and in college."

"College?" Burke's eyes were now alert.

"The boy studied for three years in Allegheny. He was reading the law before we came north."

Burke stroked his beard. "I see. Then why's he doing tailor's work if he's smart enough to study the law?"

"My son's always done what's needed of him," George replied. "Just now we haven't enough business for me to hire a tailor."

"I've a feeling your shop might not be slow much longer." Burke's face wore an enigmatic smile. "It also occurs to me there might be a position available that's more suited to young Will's talents. Something where he'd get to know people his own age around here."

George turned his eyes to his son.

Burke nodded at the young man. "I'm thinking that with my Coal and Lumber Works growing, I could use an honest young fellow with his skills to read and write contracts and to help in running it. I've got other businesses to look after. Even with the help of my son, young Tom, it's gotten to be more than I can handle." He laughed and leaned an elbow on the counter. "Hell's bells, I guess I'm not so young as I used to be."

George smiled. "Who among us is? But, as to Will—" He glanced at the back of his shop. "I don't know."

"It might be good for everyone concerned—especially for your boy. Make him feel more a part of things." Burke's tone was suggestive.

George Bender's eyes clicked back and forth, as if he calculated the cost of losing his son's labor against the benefit of the offered link to the town. At last he said, "Well, all right then," and reached across the counter to shake Tom Burke's hand.

"Have the boy stop by tomorrow morning. I'll talk to him about it."

"Thank you, Mr. Burke."

The old man took George's hand. "Call me Tom—there's too much to do around here to worry about formalities. In fact, you might mention that to your wife. I hear as how she can be regular people when she lets her hair down."

George pulled back. "Elizabeth's a fine woman, and a good helpmate. I won't hear anyone say different."

Burke's face broke into a smile and he relaxed against the display case. "I certainly understand. I was also a newcomer here once, with the rough manners I learned out west. Haven't forgotten how I felt being different in a new place. By the way, George, you might want to stop by our Town Council meetings. We usually get together on Monday nights. Meantime, show me that stick pin again if you would."

I couldn't tell the true reason Mr. Burke had come into the shop. Unlike the others, I found his thoughts difficult to hear. I could only wonder if, as he said, he'd stopped to buy something or if his sole purpose was to hire Will. Whatever his reason, he paid George for the stick pin and with a wave, walked out into the July heat.

Chapter Fourteen
Comparative Love

The ghost turned from her window. Twisting a red curl around her finger, she peered into a dark corner of the room. "So many steps led me to Will," she said. "The lads in the Dock weren't near as interesting as the men I met in books. Father Bender moved his family here. Old Mr. Burke brought him to the Coal and Lumber Works. If any of that didn't happen— Och, but fate wouldn't have it another way."

Her hands dropped onto her lap.

Fate called the shots? Rubbish! I didn't say it, though, for fear the remark might lead to an argument. Or worse, to my being doubled over by another stomach ache. From what I'd experienced earlier, the ghost seemed capable of causing me pain.

Still, she seemed to expect me to say something. I settled on a neutral topic. "Your parents—I wish mine had been more like them. Maybe if they were…" I shrugged. When she didn't respond, I added, "You must miss them terribly." *More than I've ever missed anyone.* I looked down at my hands, wondering whether the purpose of all I'd been shown was to make me realize I'd become emotionally crippled.

The ghost stroked my arm.

My thoughts turned dark. *If there's no one I'd miss, am I happier for it? No commitments, no disappointments. No pain.* My stomach fluttered. *No one to hold me when the past sneaks up in the middle of a cold night.*

I heard Abigail's voice in my mind: *Do you truly think so?*

Instantly, a memory of a night spent with Richard leapt forward.

***

In the year I'd known Richard we'd gone to operas, to performances of Shakespeare in the Park and to movies. Now he took me to see *A River Runs Through It* at the Cinema near Columbus Circle. Certain moments dog-eared a page in my life. That night what it meant to spend time with him changed. *Had* to change. I'd been around, seen enough relationships implode. I should have known what that change would lead to. Dammit, I did know! I was an idiot for not ending our relationship right then.

When we left the theater he wanted to discuss the movie's underlying meaning.

I laughed. "What underlying meaning? It was a story about trout fishing."

"Oh, come on now," he said.

"Come on what? Richard, it was just a big fish story."

The more I resisted, the more insistent he became. Finally, he wore me down—but not until he agreed to buy me dinner at the Ginger Man, the nearby bistro where Marsha Mason ate in *The Goodbye Girl*. *That* film really had an underlying meaning. It was about a woman with strength and determination.

In the restaurant, claustrophobically packed against the crowded bar, we waited for a table. Richard turned to me holding two glasses of red wine above his dark, curly hair. A few inches taller than most men, he managed to break free of the human herd without spilling a drop.

Polished brass rails circled the restaurant's sections much the way, he observed, they might separate the outer levels of Dante's Hell. The walls were draped with crimson paper, a color that tied perfectly to his metaphor. I heard laughter at the far end of the bar. Then somebody wheezed.

It sounded like hoarse laughter. Nervously, I glanced around.

"What's wrong?" Richard asked.

"Nothing," I said quickly, and shook my head. "I thought I heard… Uh, nothing."

He rested his glass on the slightly less crowded sideboard, took my arm and looked into my eyes. "You were reminded of something?"

"No. I… um… You mentioned Dante. What's he got to do with the movie we saw?" It wasn't the first time I'd flitted to another subject when he got uncomfortably close to my past. I'd never told him what hid there, no matter how hard he pressed.

He continued to look at me. Sounding uncertain, he answered, "Well, if you think about the themes—the father was a minister, you'll recall—"

"Richard, the movie was nothing but a story about trout fishing," I still insisted while the maître d' led us to a table next to a large window overlooking Broadway and Lincoln Center.

He wouldn't let go of the idea. "No, don't you see? It's metaphoric of forging family bonds?"

"Forging bonds?" My face lit with the impish grin I put on when I was about to give him a difficult time. "Forgery's a Federal crime. We ought to call the Treasury Department. Maybe there's a reward."

"Please, Kaitlyn, you know exactly what I mean."

I leaned forward. My eyes narrow, I whispered, "It's a story about trout fishing, Richard. That's all."

"No. It has a deeper meaning. That's what makes it so attractive."

"Yeah, and what's the meaning?"

Apparently my challenge left the opening he sought. "Love, that's what. The most universal and deep seated of all human needs. Tolstoy called it—"

I laughed. "Yes, Richard, I know. I've crawled

along that bookshelf with you. Tolstoy's Prince Andrei said, 'Love is life and all, everything that I understand, I understand only because I love.' So I suppose if I'm not in love, I don't know anything. Just a stupid kid from Queens, I guess—" Realizing where he'd led me, how cleverly he'd done it, I stopped and stared through the window.

It had begun to rain, a sudden downpour. Heads bowed, pedestrians huddled under umbrellas as they rushed along the sidewalk. Puddles on Broadway reflected light from the streetlamps. Rushing cars splashed past. Raindrops slowly crept down the window.

"You're far from stupid," Richard said. "Does that mean you're in love?"

I glanced at him, then again turned my eyes to the street. "Look, the ballet is just letting out. Do you think we could go to a performance there sometime?"

He reached for me across the table. His large, well-manicured hands turned my face to his. "You're avoiding the question."

I caught my breath. Moisture in Richard's eyes said he both craved and dreaded my answer. Like the raindrops slipping down the window, tears worked their way down my cheeks. "Oh, Richard," I said, "'Love is too young to know what conscience is.'"

"Don't!" He raised a hand to ward off an unwanted answer. "Please, Kaitlyn, don't hide behind Shakespeare. That's my trick, and right now I don't like it." Richard's voice shook as he asked, "Are… you in love… with me?"

My hand went to my mouth. I nodded. An unintended response. Richard's face broke into a broad smile that quickly faded when I said, "And it scares me to death."

He glanced at the ceiling as if he saw Damocles' sword up there, ready slash his hopes.

I looked away.

He took my hand. I pulled it back. The scars on my

wrists described what love led to. I had lied about how my wrists got scarred when he asked about them early in our relationship. Afraid? Ashamed? It was easy to keep mournful memories boxed up if I put makeup over the scars they left.

He stroked tears from my eyes with his thumb. "What frightens you about it? Love can be joy and laughter. It's the purest of emotions. It's—"

My lips tight, I shook my head. "Love is a terrible, hurtful thing, Richard. Can't it be enough that I care a great deal for you?" I laughed then wiped my eyes and showed him the napkin. "Look at this. My mascara's running. I must look a mess."

He took the napkin from me and carefully patted away my tears. "You could never be that."

I kissed his hand.

"So you love me?" he asked.

I released a slow breath. "I suppose so." Flustered, I rushed on. "As for the rest of it, that's something I have to work out."

"Or not?" he asked.

I answered with a dull smile.

He leaned close and took my hand. "I don't know what's holding you back. Maybe if you told me—"

A catch in my voice, I said, "Richard, please. I need—"

Reaching again for me, he sighed, "Time. I know. But Kaitlyn, I'm here for you."

I didn't answer. The past was supposed to be just that—past. It never really was.

***

He swore he'd hold me for as long as it took to shake off the past—even if he didn't know what needed shaking or how long it would take to be free of its grip. Even if it took a lifetime? Such a promise can't be trusted! Tears worked loose from my eyes. *Richard...* If my heart had had hands, it would have reached out for him.

Abigail gave me a stern look. "You don't miss any-one, ay?"

Her words snapped me back to my perch on the window seat. The ghost had forced me to face another memory. I sniffed. "I'm not crying, I'm catching a cold." I wiped my nose with my wrist.

She looked disgusted. "You can tell me anything you choose. It won't change the truth."

"I'm not lying. I don't—"

"So you say." Her head tilted, she sighed.

I took a breath. In a more reasonable tone, I said, "I know people love each other— Most people do. I'm not one of them. If you knew—"

"Yes, if I knew." Something in the way she said it made me uncomfortable. I glanced longingly at my bed. If I climbed into bed and closed my eyes tight, this torture might end.

The ghost seemed to relent. "Since you asked, I do miss Ma and Da," she said. "And I miss Father and Mother Bender, also. But fate's been kind to me in a small way. I can see them all through this window whenever I've a need to remember. Still, I can't touch them."

It wasn't difficult to figure out what she meant: *I* was able to touch someone, but refused. A pang of loss stabbed my chest.

Her smile was that of an innocent child, yet the smile gripped my heart with strong fingers.

"Damn you, stop this!"

"Haven't I told you, only you can stop your tears? You know what you must do." I grimaced. She rolled her eyes. "And Will, I miss him most of all," she said.

A trickle of tears ran down Abigail's cheeks. Though her words hid another accusation, I didn't react with anger. It's difficult for a *living* human to be harsh when faced with another woman's tears. Especially since I sensed I was to blame for them. What she'd done to make me think of Richard obviously forced her to think of Will Bender. Though I didn't yet know why, I saw the memory of him hurt her deeply. For some reason this woman wanted me to face my pain, and because I refused to, she was facing hers. I wanted to explain that her heartache could have been avoided—might still be—if she refused to feel anything. Like I refused. The words stuck in my throat when I realized it would be cold comfort, given what emotional numbness had cost me.

The edges of Abigail's mouth creased slightly. "My Will—" She shook her head as if to shed her sorrow. "I knew him almost from when he began working at Burke's." She bit on corner of her lip. "No, that's not right. I knew *of* him because Brinny would come home talking about the new lad who'd taken a place at Burke's. My brother met Will before I did because his friend Charlie Bolton worked at Burke's."

She took my hands in hers. Holding tight to me, she leaned back and closed her eyes. "Charlie was a strapping nineteen year old. He had brown wavy hair that hung loose across a long face and skin rough from the wind and wet of the lake. He used to ferry lumber over the sand bars from the great schooners to the beach behind Burke's. Other times he shoveled coal hauled up from the Pennsylvania mines. When a schooner was ready to weigh anchor he piled the coal onto his raft, and ferried it out to be loaded for shipment to the west.

"It was hard labor, and he loved it. But he loved fishing more. Fishing is why he and Brinny got to be friends. And there were other things they did together—more dangerous things across the Niagara River. We'll talk of those things later. Right now you need to see how I first learned of Will."

Abigail turned to the window. I followed her glance.

Chapter Fifteen
A Fish Story

Beyond the glass panes, I now saw a small room crowded by a desk and two chairs. Will Bender sat at the desk with his head in his hands and his eyes turned down to study something on a page set before him. An iron safe stood in a corner, its door open. A shelf over the safe held a few leather-bound volumes. A narrow window overlooked the activity in the lumber yard.

A young man with long brown hair and a pock-marked face strolled through the door. "I'm here for my pay," he announced.

Will raised his eyes, then swiveled to the safe and took out some coins.

"Thanks. It'll be good to have this in my pocket come Saturday night." The young man turned and started for the door.

"Not so fast, Charlie Bolton," Will said. "You've got to sign here in the pay book. You know that." He ran a finger down the list of names. Some were followed by crude signatures, most by marks.

While the other man printed his name, Will leaned back in his chair, "Sitting in this office all the time's no way to live. You know, Charlie, I sometimes think I'd rather be out working the lumber and coal with you boys, doing something that—" He dropped his eyes to the sheaf of pages neatly piled on his desk. "I don't know."

"If it's backbreaking work you're after, come ahead. We'll be glad to have you." Charlie laughed and pulled up a chair. "But it seems to me there's better places a man could pass his time than hauling lumber summer and winter."

"Like what?"

Charlie pointed through the door. "Like being out there, fishing."

"I've seen you pushing your boat into the lake some evenings like you can't wait to get to it," Will said, and glanced at Charlie. "I also like fishing. Used to go all the time with friends back home. When we lived in Pennsylvania, I mean. We weren't far from the Lake Erie shore. Some nights we'd row out and stay until dawn with our lines in the water."

"Catch anything?"

"Nah, but you should have seen the one—"

"Yeah, I know," Charlie said. "I nearly snagged a couple that big."

The two boys were lost in fish stories when Tom Burke walked in. "What's going on here?" The old man's tone sounded stern. "Charlie Bolton, are you getting in young Will's way?"

Charlie stood up so quickly his chair toppled to the floor. "No, sir. I was just on my way out."

"We were talking about fishing, Mr. Burke," Will rushed to explain. "I haven't done any since we moved here, so I asked Charlie to stay and tell me what it's like on the lake."

Burke's smile pushed through his thick beard. "Seems to me fishing may be the one topic Charlie here knows something about. There've been days I had to send someone out in a boat to chase after him, get him back to his work in the yard."

Charlie's face turned bright red. "Aw, Mr. Burke, you don't have to do it all that much."

"No, I don't," the old man conceded. "But maybe next time you might take Bender out with you." He turned to Will. "In the meantime, young man, how're you doing with my coal shipment contract?"

When Tom Burke leaned over the desk to examine something Will pointed to in the document, Charlie started to leave. In the doorway, he turned back, and said, "Going out tonight 'bout eight o'clock. I'll bring some extra gear in case you're needing it. Wear dark clothes."

Without looking up, Tom Burke said, "Afraid the fish will recognize you boys? In that case, Charlie, better bring something to cover your ugly face so you don't frighten them off."

Will stretched his neck around his boss's wide body. "Thanks, I'll be there."

Abigail shifted on the window seat and said to me, "If Will knew what that night of fishing would lead to, his smile would've been twice as big."

I wanted to know what it led to, of course. Had it changed Abigail's life the way my dinner at the Ginger Man had changed mine? The woman sitting next to me on the window seat—it had become more and more difficult to think of her as a ghost—seemed to share some of my experiences. Perhaps something in her past actually might help reconcile me with mine, but what I wanted more at that moment was to go back to my bed. I felt exhausted, needed to sleep. I twisted from my place by the window.

Abigail clutched my shoulders and held me in place. "Not yet, Kaitlyn. I want you to see this." Her soft voice belied the strength of her grip.

"Tired," I groaned.

"You'll sleep a long time when we're done."

A flock of butterflies swirled in my stomach. What did she mean? Before I could ask, she took my hand and whispered, "Please."

I didn't know whether the ache in her voice awoke empathy I couldn't control or her touch stripped away my will. Whatever power Abigail Bender employed was like sunshine on snow: it caused my weariness to melt.

***

When Abigail settled me back in my corner of the window nook, the scene outside her window shifted. The sun had dropped from the sky. I now saw the beach wrapped in a navy velvet blanket. No sails billowed on the lake. The large ships at anchor appeared to be deserted. The shore looked empty of life except for two fishermen a hundred yards up the beach who stood across from the promontory at the Niagara River's mouth. Abigail told me to watch the way those men cast and reeled in their lines. Maybe they were angling for shallow water fish, she said. My brow creased with curiosity, I asked why they fished with rifles slung across their shoulders. She smiled at me but didn't explain.

In the foreground small boats huddled on the shore, their masts unstepped for the night. Moon-cast shadows crept between their hulls and along the coarse sand to a grassy, tree-lined rise. Beyond the trees, sleeping bungalows looked like black boxes.

Dressed in dungarees and boots, Will Bender ran along the shore to a break in the line of skiffs. In the shadow of two boats, Charlie Bolton and another man pushed an eighteen-foot cat-ketch toward the water.

Earlier, I'd seen the young man who was with Charlie Bolton. A smaller version of Sean Kirby, he had his father's oval face and dark, curly hair. His muscular arms were taut as he leaned into the effort of moving the boat.

When Will came up to them, Charlie said, "This here's Brian Kirby. He's a fisherman by trade, but what he really wants is to stow away on one of those schooners out there."

"Pleased to meet you," Brian said in a raspy voice. He didn't sound pleased.

Will nodded to him.

"And this is Will Bender," Charlie said.

Now we all know each other, Charlie Bolton," Brian said, "can we get this leaky wreck of yours into the water?"

Charlie stopped pushing. With a grin that narrowed his eyes, he peered across the boat. "What's the hurry? Fish ain't going nowheres. Got all night to catch us some."

"What about—" Brian said.

With no change in his smile, Charlie said, "When I'm with you, ain't you always where you need to be when you need to be there?"

Will glanced from one to the other, then bent to help shove the boat from the shore. At last clear of the pebbly beach, Brian raised the single sail. Charlie took the tiller and steered them toward the Niagara River channel. All the while he kept up a running commentary on the differences between lake and river fishing.

"Out there's perch and shad, mostly," he said. "Other kinds closer in and down the river. Me and Brian been fishing both places since we was kids. Found some pretty good spots where fish can't wait but to jump into your boat."

"Have you ever tried casting for trout?" Will asked. "I've fished Lake Erie and the Allegheny River, but I never knew what it could be like until I took a trip with my friend Nathan. There's this stream he knew where cold water goes white over the rocks and the trout jump to hurdle them. There I was this one time, standing knee-deep in the middle of the stream, trying to figure out how to cast a line without getting tangled in it. Then I thought, why bother? The next time a trout leapt to clear the rocks, I held out my net and let him fall into it. A ten-pounder, as I recall. Made a fine dinner."

For the first time a smile crossed Brian's face. "Never knew anyone afore could go word for word and lie for lie with old Charlie."

Will laughed. "That wasn't a lie."

Brian shook his head.

"At least not much of one," Will admitted.

Charlie patted his back. "Sounds like gospel to me. I do believe it must've happened just the way you told it."

"Liars, both of you, and one bigger than the other." Brian laughed too.

After what might have been thirty minutes of talking their way upriver, Brian stood and gazed into the darkness. "This is the place." He trimmed the sail.

"Like as not," Charlie said. While he worked the tiller to hold them steady against the river's current, he told Will, "There's a whirlpool a bit further up. Small boat comes too close, it gets sucked into the spin and pulled down. Heard tell some who got caught up in it ain't never been seen alive since. 'Course, folks say some nights you see their ghosts sailing down the river."

"Hey, Will, throw the anchor over the side afore Charlie gets lost inside his yarn," Brian said. "*We* don't wanna wind up sucked down in the whirlpool."

They were in a deep green gulch. A high rise guarded either side. The shadow of the far bank hid them from moonlight bursting like fireworks on the choppy water. They baited their hooks, dropped their lines and leaned back. But Brian didn't settle down. Every so often he stood and stared across the river, as if he were watching for something. Just past ten o'clock two flashes showed midway up the rise. It might have been a signal from a lantern opened briefly, then quickly shuttered.

Will's eyes flicked.

"Some camper in the hills must be stoking his fire," Charlie remarked. "Oughta watch out afore it gets away from him, ay?"

Brian Kirby continued to watch.

The flashes came again. Two more, evenly spaced, then nothing.

At last Brian relaxed. As he pulled at his line, he

said, "Looks like we're out here again, day after tomorrow…"

Will's thoughts crawled into my mind: he believed he understood what this night of fishing was really about. If he were right, it was one of those more important things he'd done before he'd been forced to move here. He reached for a sense of the men with him, trying to decide how much to say and how to say it. If he were wrong—

Never tell anyone what we're doing, his friend Nathan had warned the first time they were out together. *Spies are everywhere. Jail waits if we're caught—or worse.* Nathan, with the swept-back black hair and eyes that rarely smiled, had been his roommate at Allegany. It was he who introduced Will to the dangerous activity Charlie and Brian might be engaged in. *Don't go about it unless you're armed*, Nathan always said. Will had never fired a gun before he met Nathan. Did he dare risk telling these two why he'd learned to shoot straight?

After what might have been five minutes, Will asked, "Couple of packages coming across Sunday night?"

Brian caught his breath.

Charlie coiled both his fishing line and his body. "Got no idea what you're talking 'bout."

In a voice as hushed as the river and the hills around them, Will said, "Sure you do. I figure you came out here tonight to wait for that signal. Seems to me it's one of two things. Either you're smugglers running goods or maybe whisky across from New York—"

Charlie leaned close to Will.

"I don't think so, though. Not enough room in this tub to make smuggling worth doing for anything but the excitement of it, and you boys don't strike me as looking for that kind of excitement. Besides, what could you bring across that you can't get in Canada at much less risk? No, I don't think you're smuggling. Which leaves just one thing."

"Yeah?" Charlie's body tensed further. His

expression changed from concern, to annoyance, to fear. He wondered why he'd he been foolish enough to bring this newcomer along tonight. To please Mr. Burke, certainly. But he could have pleased the old man by taking Will fishing some other time—in an afternoon, maybe. Faced with he and Brian having been found out, he had to decide what to do. "Yeah?" he asked again, allowing a threat to hang in his voice.

Will's mind churned. His excitement grew. *I'm right about this,* he thought. With his lip sucked in, he said, "What makes you boys think you're the only ones who've ever worked the Railroad?"

Brian's breath escaped in a long hiss.

Charlie sat back, laughing. "Well, who'da thunk it?"

A smile grew on Will's face.

Chapter Sixteen
A Mother's Fear

Again the scene outside Abigail's window faded. This time a series of new ones flashed like a collage on the windowpanes. In one, I saw Brian eating breakfast in the Kirbys' kitchen. As soon as Mary turned her back, he glanced at his sister across the table. "Met an interesting fella out fishing last night," he said. "Town boy—works over by Burke's."

"Did you, now?" Abbie didn't show much interest.

"Yeah, new boy old man Burke brought into the office. Think he might be spending some time with me and old Charlie."

She glanced at him.

"Knows a thing or two about… fishing."

"Fishing!" Mary snorted at the porridge in her pot.

While this scene played, the ghost said to me, "Ma used to wonder why Brinny couldn't wait to set out again after fishing with Da on the lake from before sunup, most times till near dark. Just him and Charlie Bolton. A wise woman, Ma knew the ways of young men. She figured they were out for some mischief, blowing off steam the way lads will. She kept believing that till one day when she was going to the market. On the street she stopped to console a friend whose husband had been lost on the Linnie Powell. Look now, there they are."

When she pointed to the window, a second scene played on a different pane.

Mary Kirby and another woman stood on a corner. A frail black woman walked up and stopped a few feet away, fidgeting with her calico dress.

Mary shifted her basket from one arm to the other, smoothed her skirt, then patted her red hair to be sure it hadn't slipped from its bun. "Is there something you'd be wanting?" she asked.

The black woman came close. "You bein' Brian Kirby's ma'am, aincha?" she whispered, and glanced around. "'Cept for the color of 'is hair, ya boy lookin' jes like ya. Wonder if you'd tell 'im, Manda say thanks. Tell 'im my boy gone up to Toronto, git 'im some steady work up there. Be doin' good now."

Mary stared at the woman.

"Jes' want 'im to know he done a good thing, bringin' my boy 'cross that big river."

Again Abigail broke in. "After that, Ma knew what Brinny and Charlie did those nights on the river, and it frightened her. Look there." Abigail pointed to a third windowpane.

This scene seemed to be late in the afternoon. Mary Kirby knelt to place more wood on the fire in the hearth.

Rising from his seat at the table, Brian cleared his throat. "Be back later, Ma. Me and Charlie are gonna do some fishing 'fore it gets too dark.

"Fishing, indeed!" Mary said. Wringing her hands, she turned on him, "They've got laws over there against helping slaves run off."

Facing his mother, without blinking, Brian said, "Bad laws."

Mary grabbed a dish towel and ran it hard across the kitchen table. "There are men as make a living at stopping people from doing it. If you're caught—"

She told him she'd heard of a man caught by fugitive slave-hunters and soldiers as he shoved off from the shore above Lewiston. The man refused to give up the Negroes in his boat and was shot where he stood. By a slave-hunter or soldier, no one knew. They called it self-defense, though the man didn't have a gun or a knife.

"Don't go worrying 'bout the like of that happening to me, Ma," Brian said, and kissed her cheek. "Charlie and me, we take care."

"But why? Why do *you* have to do it?" Mary cried. "You don't know those people you bring across."

"Because it needs doing," Brian said.

This windowpane went dark. Abigail leaned back in the nook and said, "When Brinny told me he'd met someone new who liked to fish, Ma knew what he meant."

The ghost pointed again to the pane on which played that first scene with her, Brian and Mary in the Kirby's kitchen.

Mary slammed a wooden spoon around the cast-iron pot she worked at. After a minute, she sighed. "If fate'll have it this way—"

Abbie's face showed interest. "*Does* he fish now? And how would you be knowing that?"

"He was out with us last night. Told us as how he'd go fishing down in Pennsylvania. Pulled some big ones out, he says."

Abbie raised an eyebrow.

Brian looked slyly at her. With a wink he added, "Good looking lad, too."

"And what makes you think he would interest me?" The way she tilted her head signaled it might.

Again Mary slammed her spoon. "I'll at least keep *one* child safe in this world." She turned from the stove. "Your sister has enough to do without knowing another troublemaker!" She took half a dozen rapid steps and dropped Brian's wooden bowl on the table.

"Girl's getting to be an old spinster, Ma. She'll soon be dried up like old Miz Carpenter. Won't be no one interested in marrying her then."

"Indeed!" Abbie said. "As if I'd be needing help from the likes of you to find someone worth knowing." She pushed her brother's bowl into his lap.

Brian laughed while he scooped up what remained of his breakfast. "I'm thinking you might. I'm thinking this one could be interesting."

Abbie turned her back.

Brian continued to talk of Will. "A light-haired lad, and educated," he said. "Walks 'cross the Common to Burke's every morning. Surprised you ain't seen him."

"Enough of this!" Mary threw down her spoon. "I'll not have your sister seeing a man she has to worry about nights the way I worry after you. So you'll kindly be keeping your friends to yourself."

Abbie's skirt swirled as she spun away from her mother. "Who says I'll be seeing anyone?"

"Don't know 'bout this lad," Brian said. "Makes a good living from old man Burke."

A deep frown furrowed Mary Kirby's brow. "Stop dawdling here with such nonsense. Get you down to the beach—your Da's waiting." She shooed her son with a towel.

Chuckling, Brian let his mother push him out the door.

Abbie stuck her tongue out at his back. "As if I'd find anyone interesting who'd even think of talking to Brinny Kirby," she muttered.

As the scenes on the different windowpanes progressed through days, I saw Brian continue to talk about Will Bender. Each morning after Charlie, Will and he had been on one of their excursions, he teased Abbie with Will Bender said this, and Will Bender did that.

"Smart lad, that Will Bender. Charlie says old man Burke can't get on without him," Brian started one morning. When Mary stormed from the kitchen, he lowered his voice. "Fearless, too, Will is. I wish, Abbie, you would've seen him last night when this barge sailed up to shine a lantern on us. We had a Negro wrapped in sail cloth in the ketch's hull. 'Row over to the eastern shore,' one of the men says, and shows us a rifle barrel. Ol' Will, he stands up in the boat, looks the slave-hunter in the eye, and says, 'Don't think we'll be doing that.' So the man says, 'We'll board you right here and take off what you got in your boat.' Will, he just stares the man down. 'Nothing but fish in here,' he says. ''Sides, you should've checked the charts afore sailing out. New York's boundary ends middle of the river. We're well past there. Taking our catch is piracy in Canadian waters. The men watching for us through a telescope over there on the western shore'll testify to that when we haul you into court.'" Brian paused, shaking his head. "Never thought afore 'bout where Canada begins in the river."

Her eyes wide, Abbie said, "Brinny, what would you have done if they'd tried to force you over?"

He leaned across the table. "Don't know what I would've done, but I know Will Bender was ready to make a fight of it."

"How do you know?" From the way her eyes grew wider still, Abbie seemed to be lost in the drama of her brother's narrow escape.

His voice low, Brian said, "'Cause he'd been holding a rifle against his side from the time we first saw the barge come at us. When one of the men in it threatened to come closer, Will showed it to 'im. Said he'd shoot 'im dead without a second thought, defending himself against river pirates. The way he said it—kind of soft and cold like—sure had *me* convinced. Convinced them fellas too." For a while, Brian seemed lost in the recollection. When he spoke again, it sounded as though he mused to himself, "Gotta care a lot 'bout what we're doing to face that kind of trouble."

The scenes on all the panes faded, and I saw only the street outside. Deep ruts in the snow showed where someone must have driven past while I watched what went on in the Kirbys' kitchen. Was it a car or a horse cart? At the moment I found it difficult to separate the ghost's time from mine.

Abigail turned to me with a shy smile. "After hearing what Will did, I stood outside each morning to watch him come across the Common. I asked for news of him after each of Brinny's fishing trips. I also paid more attention those nights I waited in the shadows to lead the boys' cargo to the church in the Colored Section."

My jaw dropped. "You were part of it?"

She laughed. "Ma might've known I snuck out some nights to wait after Brinny by the beach. She didn't know it was me as took their cargo to where it was safe. I waited in the shadows of the trees up where the beach and the grass met, face hidden inside the cowl of a dark cape, till I saw their boat loom black against the night sky. Then I flashed a lantern to signal the beach was empty and all was clear. It wasn't as dangerous as what Brinny and the others were about. Still, there was always a chance some slave-hunter would be waiting by the shore, looking like he was angling after shallow water fish. Or maybe one of those from the Dock or Town or Irishtown who sided with your South—there were plenty of those. And others who just didn't want us bringing the Negroes here. Muddying our clean waters, *they* called it. So, you see, I also had to take care in what I was about. I would've liked to go with Brinny in the boat, but he said I had to stay where I was and be satisfied. If I didn't, he'd tell Ma and she'd make sure I couldn't do even that."

Her smile fading, Abigail turned to look out her window. "I did what he said so I could at least be of some use, and I never let Will see I was part of it. Leastwise, not till the night the Devil himself burst through the woods down from Tryon's Folly."

Chapter Seventeen
The Morning After

The night was nearly gone. Heavy snow still fell.

Abigail put out her hand. "You need to rest now."

I did. I felt more exhausted than I could ever recall being. Why? I'd stayed awake through entire nights while working on big cases and had never been so bone-weary. Could the ghost have tapped into my strength in order to manifest? I'd read somewhere that ghosts steal the energy of the living. Could showing me her life through the window be a ruse to rob me of *mine*?

That thought slipped away as soon as I settled in bed. Covered by only a soft linen sheet, I rolled onto my side. If Abigail's motives were dark, if it were really my life force she sought, she was clever in the way she went about taking it. I had become fascinated by the story she showed me. It certainly played like the kind of romantic movie my friends and I liked so much: Will, the handsome hero and Abbie, the damsel I was sure would soon be in distress. I wanted to see what would happen next.

"The Devil walking out of the woods—tell me about him," I said like a child begging her mother to finish reading a fable.

"Hush now," Abigail said, and pulled the comforter over me.

My eyes half closed, I said, "Don't need that. It's hot in here."

She smiled and sat beside me on the bed. While gently stroking my forehead, she began to sing.

I don't know how long I slept. Alone in the room, I opened my eyes and saw gray daylight poke through the louvered shutter now closed over the window. I shivered.

The fire's gone out. I leaned on an elbow to look at the hearth. I saw no ashes in the grate, no wood piled in the bin. Nothing showed the fireplace had been recently used. I looked down and saw the rug again on the floor. *Had I been dreaming?* I wondered.

I felt for the place on the bed where Abigail had been. The cover and sheets were rumpled, the pillow pushed in. *Anna Karenina* lay open beside me.

"Abigail?" I called. "Abbie?" The effort of those few words took all my strength. I fell back on my pillow.

She didn't answer. I no longer sensed her presence.

"Where are you?" I croaked, then thought, *From the place between sleep and awake, or maybe between alive and... dead?*

Through the depth of last night, Abigail Bender showed me how she fell in love with a man she hadn't yet met. Then she left me to dangle without knowing what the story was supposed to mean to me. *She said at the start there was a connection.*

"Abbie..." I called again. The single word left me short of breath. "Abbie?"

There has to be something in her story she wants me to know. If there isn't, why did she show herself to me? She said I could see her because I needed to. Why do I?

"Abbie..."

I found sitting up to be a struggle, almost more than I could manage. The movement left me short of breath. *What's wrong with me?* "Abbie... where are you?" I needed to find her.

With the little strength I could muster, I slid my legs over the side of the bed and pushed up. *She must have gone to the cottage on Ricardo Street,* I thought. *I'll follow her there, that's what I'll do. Get her to finish the story. Tell me what it means.*

I remember holding tight to the banister, forcing

one foot after the other to inch my way downstairs on wobbly legs. I remember thinking, *I can find her house. I know I can. She told me where it is, described it in detail—a small, gray cottage with shutters tied by fish twine. It's at the end of the street near Burke's Coal and Lumber*. I felt certain that if I went outside, I would find all the landmarks I'd seen through Abigail's window.

I remember staggering to the front door, struggling for each step, for each breath. This time no invisible hands prevented my passage through the door. At the bottom of the stoop, I looked up, turned in a circle. Snow fell steadily from a dappled gray sky. The temperature felt well below freezing. My shivers came in quakes. After that I only remember things in spots.

***

Weeks later, while I tried to piece together what happened, this is what Ronnie told me about that morning: She and Andrea were in the dining room. It was just past nine-thirty. Over coffee, they talked of visiting the antique shops Mrs. Hughes had told them of.

"Aren't we gonna wake Katy to go with us?" Andrea asked.

"The way she's been feeling?" Ronnie said. "She may be coming down with a cold or something. It'll be better to let her sleep it out of her system."

They heard the front door open, then close.

"Mrs. Hughes must be going out to brush the snow off the stoop," Ronnie said. She had just poured a second cup of coffee and settled back to read the antique shop brochures, when she heard a gasp in the hallway. Leah Campbell stumbled in a moment later. Her face gray, her eyes were so wide they seemed ready to pop out.

Andrea snickered. "What's the matter, Leah? Seen a ghost?"

Leah tried to speak, but her words broke into sobs.

She pulled at her black apron, stammered and pointed.

"What is it?" Ronnie said.

The housekeeper clutched the doorknob, as if she needed it to maintain her footing. She craned her neck around the doorframe. Her hand shaking, she pointed at the stairs. "It's… it's…" She gasped, sank to her knees.

"What's wrong with her?" Andrea said.

"Talk to me, Leah." Ronnie knelt to cradle the old woman.

Terror in her eyes, the housekeeper said, "I saw… she was… But it can't be, she's… dead." She threw her head back, howled, "Noooo!"

"What did you see?" Ronnie demanded.

Leah tore the chain from her neck and held out the crucifix. "He walks beside me in the valley of the shadow of death—"

Andrea leaned from the dining room and peered up the stairs.

"She's got your friend!" Leah said. "The one that lives up there's got her now."

"Katy's been so depressed," Ronnie said. "The way she's been looking all drawn and wasted… Andi, you don't think she tried to… She has sleeping pills. I saw them in her overnight bag." A sob burst from her throat. "Go make sure Katy's okay!"

Andrea went, while Ronnie stayed downstairs trying to make sense of Leah Campbell's yammering.

The housekeeper knelt against the door, trembling. She said the same thing over and over. She might have talked in tongues for all the sense Ronnie could make of her words. At last my friend took her arm and helped her cross the hall to the Gentlemen's Parlor. When the woman collapsed onto the sofa, Ronnie went to the front door. "Mrs. Hughes!" she called outside.

The innkeeper rushed from her office behind the kitchen. "What's going on here?"

Ronnie did a double-take.

"What is it?" the innkeeper asked.

Ronnie led her to the Gentlemen's Parlor. She dropped onto the sofa beside Leah, and tried to calm her. The housekeeper cringed and pulled away from each touch.

Mrs. Hughes said gently, "Tell me what's happened."

When Leah still couldn't answer, Mrs. Hughes poured a glass of brandy from a decanter on one of the bookshelves. She forced a few drops through the woman's trembling lips.

Andrea ran down the stairs. She looked bewildered, is the way Ronnie described it to me. "Kaitlyn's not in her room," Andrea said. "She's not anywhere up there."

Leah clutched the crucifix to her breast. "No, she wouldn't be up there. Not when I saw her ghost float down them stairs and pass right through the front door."

"Nonsense," Mrs. Hughes said. "Have you been drinking?" She held Leah by the shoulders and peered into her eyes.

Leah shivered. "Only what you just give me. It was her ghost, I tell you. She was all white!" She cowered against the sofa's cushions.

"Come on, this is way out of hand," Ronnie said. "There's no such thing as ghosts."

A floorboard creaked. Ronnie's head snapped around.

"It's her, I tell you—the one haunting this place," the housekeeper cried. "If your friend ain't with her, where is she?" She started to babble again.

Ronnie and Andrea rushed for the stairs.

"There's got to be an explanation," Ronnie said as she started up. "Maybe she got confused in a strange house, fell sleep in another room."

On the first step, Andrea grabbed her arm. "The front door's open. Maybe Kaitlyn *did* go out."

When Ronnie turned to the door she saw my black coat on the rack and my boots on the rubber mat. "Leah must have opened it," she said. "It's freezing outside. Katy wouldn't have left without her coat and boots."

"She's not anyplace upstairs. I looked," Andrea said. "Where else could she be?"

Though doubtful, Ronnie poked her face out the door and saw something stir down the block. "Could be her—with all the snow, I'm not sure." She flung her coat over her sweater and jeans and started out.

Andrea also grabbed her coat. "It has to be. She's nowhere else."

They saw me as soon as they got down the front steps. Andrea pointed. Ronnie still wasn't sure. It might have been a person bent over, or could have been a pile of snow by the curb halfway down the block. Then the snow pile turned its head.

"Katy!" Ronnie shouted.

She and Andrea half-ran, half-skidded through more than a foot of snow.

I was sitting on a high drift in my pajamas. My face was white, my eyes red. My pajamas and my hair were drenched. I shook uncontrollably. I had apparently wandered this far, then unable to go any further, sat down.

Ronnie wrapped her coat around me. "What're you doing out here with no shoes or coat on? You're gonna catch pneumonia!"

"I can't find it," I mumbled. The effort to speak started another shivering fit.

"What're you looking for?" Ronnie asked through chattering teeth.

"It has to be around here someplace."

Andrea's head swiveled in each direction. "What has to be?"

"It has to," I moaned. "She was so clear about it." I rolled to my knees and tried to stand then fell back onto the snowdrift.

Ronnie grabbed at me. "Who was clear about what,

Katy? Come inside and tell me."

I pulled away. "Don't understand."

Ronnie brushed the snow from my hair. "I want to understand, but first you have to come back inside."

"She's practically naked and cold as ice," Andrea said. She rubbed my hands, then took my arm and tried to lift me. "There isn't time for this. She'll die of exposure if we don't get her to move."

Together, my friends yanked me to my feet and steered me toward the house. They slipped in the snow each time I twisted to go back to where they found me.

"Have to find out," I said over and over.

"Find out what, honey?" Ronnie asked.

"Have to."

"She doesn't know where she is," Andrea said when they finally dragged me up the stoop.

Mrs. Hughes held the storm door open. "Get her right upstairs and into a warm shower—not too hot or it'll burn her. I'll call a doctor."

I remember saying, "No, no! I've got to get to Ricardo Street!" but I'm not sure if I just said it in my mind.

Halfway up the stairs, I turned, latched onto the banister and fought to go back down. Ronnie held tight to my arm. Andrea pried my fingers loose.

I flopped down on a step. "I've got to. I… I've got to."

It took the two of them to drag me to my room and strip off the pajamas that clung stubbornly to my shaking body. Andrea went to turn on the water in the bathroom. "Here," she said, handing a bath sheet through the door.

Ronnie let go of me long enough to reach for the towel. By the time she turned back, I was nearly through the bedroom door. Naked.

"Oh, no, you don't!" She grabbed me.

I remember thinking, *Voices. Is someone here?*

Then I moaned, "Abbie?" and collapsed on the floor.

While she wrapped me in the towel, Ronnie said, "Andi, hold onto her while I get undressed. She won't be able to stand up in the shower on her own."

Under the stream of warm water, I stopped shivering. Ronnie and Andrea dried me off and got me into the flannel nightgown the innkeeper must have brought up. Then they sat me on the edge of my bed.

"Tell me, Katy, what's going on?" Ronnie said very softly.

I turned to the window, thinking, *Mrs. Kirby, is Abbie home?* After a minute or two, my eyes focused. My friends stood in front of me. "Ronnie?" I coughed. "Andi?" Another cough. "What are you doing in Abigail's house?"

"What are we doing here?" Ronnie sounded as though she were scolding a child. "What are we doing here?" Her voice went up an octave. "We found you sitting half-naked in the snow, and you ask *us* what *we're* doing!"

"Did you? I'm… sorry," I said, fighting for every breath.

"Were you trying to kill yourself?" Andrea said.

Ronnie shot her a sharp look, and mouthed, "I'll call Dr. Carver when we get home."

"What if she tries again before then?" Andrea asked.

I glanced from one to the other, annoyed. "I'm… right here, you know. And no, I wasn't trying to—" I took a rasping breath, then barely whispered, "Do you know where Abbie is? She'll explain everything."

Ronnie stroked my hair. "Who's Abbie? Where can we find her?"

"She lives on… Ricardo Street. I… have to go to her there." I yawned. "I'll go later. I'm very tired."

"Good idea." Ronnie helped me slide under the covers and tucked the quilted comforter under my chin.

Warm again, I closed my eyes.

As I drifted into a semi-sleep, I heard Ronnie say, "She's so weak. I don't think she could have gotten into bed by herself."

Mrs. Hughes came into the room just when Ronnie switched off the light.

"Should we keep her awake until the doctor gets here?" Andrea asked.

"Dr. Early said sleep's the best thing. He told me to give her something if she didn't want to sleep."

"Isn't he coming?"

"I reached him on his cellphone," Mrs. Hughes said. "He's seeing someone in St. Davids. He said the roads are awful, but he promised to get here when he could."

"You told him what happened?" Andrea whispered.

"Yes."

"Go downstairs and wait for the doctor," Ronnie said. "I'm staying here in case she wakes up."

I heard Ronnie settle on the window seat. I heard footsteps move past my bed toward the door. I heard them descend the stairs. I heard nothing else for a long while.

***

I remember some of what followed. The rest I've put together from things I heard Ronnie and Andrea talking about during the next few days.

The doctor finally arrived at the Niagara Inn just before noon. As he handed his heavy overcoat to Mrs. Hughes, he said, "Good to be inside where it's warm. It's a beast out there." He leaned back through the door to shake snow from his hat. "Always the way, isn't it?" He sniffed and rubbed his hands together. "Folks seem to get sick at times it's near impossible to get to them. Where's the patient? How's she doing?"

Mrs. Hughes pointed up the stairs. "There hasn't been a peep from her since I called you. Her friend's sitting with her."

"Good, good," the doctor said. When he entered my room, he said to Ronnie. "What seems to be the trouble? Tell me everything."

"She's been very depressed since we got here," Ronnie told him. "It started before that, really, though I'm not sure it has anything to do with—"

The doctor interrupted her. "I mean her physical condition. What symptoms do we seem to have?"

I groaned. My breathing was labored.

Ronnie's crying woke me.

"Oh, my God, oh, my God," she said. "Her lips— T-they're blue."

Dr. Early had thick gray hair. Wire-frame glasses rested high on his nose. His cheeks were red, obviously from being pelted by wind-blown snow in the few yards he'd slogged from his car to the house. "I see," he said. He lifted my lids and shined a light into my eyes. "Uh-huh, yes, I do see. Help me sit her up." While Ronnie held me, he pounded on my back. "Okay, miss, I need you to cough for me." He held a tissue to my mouth. "Yes, yes. That's good. Get it all up."

He shooed Ronnie, Andrea and the innkeeper out of his way, then pulled down the covers to continue the examination. When he finished, I settled back down.

Before I fell asleep again, I heard the doctor say, "She's quite ill. It may be pneumonia. Bacterial. There's a lot of this going around. Yes, yes, um, I'm sure that's it." He took a small vial from his bag, stuck a hypodermic into it, then flicked a finger at the needle's tip. "This antibiotic should help."

He stuck it in my arm. I didn't feel a thing.

"Isn't there anything else you can do for her?" Ronnie sounded as if she were pleading.

"Nothing else to be done for pneumonia." The doctor pulled the glasses down his nose and glanced at the window. "Can't be sure of anything, though. Wish I could get her to the hospital, run a few tests. I'll take a blood sample, just to be sure."

"That's not enough," Ronnie said. "Take her to the hospital!"

"Can't, miss. Have you seen the roads? Nothing's moving. I nearly couldn't make it here. In fact, I'd better be going before this storm gets any worse."

"But—"

Again the doctor cut Ronnie off. "The roads should be clearer tomorrow. Call me if she hasn't improved any, we'll take her in then. Right now it's best to give the antibiotic time to work."

Ronnie followed the doctor downstairs. When he reached for his coat and hat, he said to her, "You saw what I did? If she has trouble breathing, lift her, make her cough. Make sure she drinks plenty of liquids—broth and hot tea with honey is best. Keep her as comfortable as you can."

A boreal wind pounded the door as it closed behind Dr. Early, so it was hard for Ronnie hear anything but the howling from outside. Still, as she muttered, "Keep her comfortable, he says," she heard a soft voice reply, "That I will."

At least she *said* she heard that.

Chapter Eighteen
Memory, the Thief

I slept fitfully through most of the day. A few times I awoke to what sounded like an infant crying in the street. *What kind of mother would leave her baby outside when it's so cold?* I thought, distressed by the idea. I would never have risked the health of my baby. I would have been a good mother. My baby… I dozed into a dream.

On the third-floor of a walkup, in a dim hallway, I stumble against a blue baby carriage. Cobwebs stretch from the wall to the wheels. I look into the carriage bed, see a blanket in plastic packaging, the price tag still on it. The apartment door creaks open a crack. Behind the door, a woman wails. I push my way inside, past the rubble of someone's days, to see who she is, ask why she's crying. She sits by a window with no blinds or curtains, her face in her hands, her head bowed. When she glances up, I see. She's... me—

I woke, shaking my head from side to side. Outside, the baby cried louder. I had to get out of bed, take the poor child from its uncaring mother, raise it the way I would have raised my child. I couldn't move. I again drifted off, whimpering.

This time I woke to the sound of pacing at the foot of my bed. Abigail had returned. I had no strength to call to her. *She'll talk to me when she's ready,* I thought, *tell me about that devil, how Will saved her from it.* I closed my eyes and tried to imagine how the story would go: *Will and Abbie... and me, and...*

Memory is a wily second-story man: it sneaks into your dream, robs you of sleep. Just when I began to drift off again, I snapped awake as memory showed me Richard's face on a night when Ronnie and her husband Ken had had us over for dinner at their co-op in Manhattan's re-gentrified Tenderloin District.

Ronnie had finally convinced me to introduce Richard to them. Halfway through the evening, she pulled me away to work with her in the kitchen. Richard and Ken strolled onto the balcony.

"You planned this, didn't you?" I said to her. "Is your husband interrogating him?"

The kitchen was square, large enough for two people to work comfortably. New appliances gleamed under florescent lights. A louvered folding door opened onto a dining nook. I leaned from the kitchen to look through the open balcony door. The guys appeared to be in a serious conversation.

My friend pulled a roast from the oven and shoved a meat thermometer into it. "Another ten minutes, I think, until it's done," she said. "Would you sauté the mushrooms so I can make a pan sauce? They're already cut up in the refrigerator."

I turned her around. "Ronnie, is Ken interrogating him?"

"What a silly thing to say. You're the lawyer, not Ken."

"Ronnie?"

"Well…" She looked away.

I turned and took a step toward the balcony.

She grabbed my arm. "Things have gotten serious between you and Richard—"

"They haven't," I insisted.

She pulled her thick black-rimmed glasses to the tip of her nose and looked at me. "They have. And Ken—he loves you almost as much as I do, you know? After what you've been through, he wants to make sure you don't get hurt again."

"I'm not a china doll. I won't break—" I stiffened as a baby's cry came through the open balcony door. My head snapped around.

Ronnie reached for me. "See. That's what I mean, kiddo. Seven years and you're still not over it." Holding my arm, she moved with me to the bifold kitchen door. "Listen to them—it might do you some good." She yanked me back. "Hey, just listen, I said. And don't let them see you."

My head resting against the doorframe, I looked to the balcony where Ken and Richard seemed to be gazing at the lights across the Hudson. The distance between us was small enough for me to hear all they said.

"Beautiful night." Richard leaned over the railing. "The kind of night that poets write about."

Ken was a successful musician with a scruffy blond beard and an easy, informal personality. On the road, when he wasn't performing, he spent his time lost in books. As a result, he was almost as well-read as Richard. "Must be the Romantics," he said. "Do you teach poetry?"

Richard laughed. "I read poetry, but I don't know it well enough to teach it." He stared across the river for a minute. "Ken, I've grown to care a great deal for Kaitlyn, but…" He ran his hand through his hair. "Something she said a while back has been bothering me."

"Oh?"

"She told me love is a hurtful thing. Do you know what she meant?"

Ken glanced over his shoulder in the direction of the kitchen, then steered Richard to a corner of the balcony. "To understand half the things Katy says—and most of what she doesn't—you need to know that her marriage to Barry Novacs was never very good. It ended when he took off with another woman. Happened pretty soon after Katy lost the baby." He shook his head. "To run out on someone like Katy— But then, I don't think they were ever in love. Ronnie says they got married because all their friends were doing it." He shrugged.

I glared at Ronnie. "You said that?"

"*Shh.*" She turned me back to face the balcony in time to hear Richard say, "I know her. She'd never do something like that."

I snickered. "Listen to him—my knight's defending my honor."

Ronnie punched my arm. "You'll never have a knight if you're sarcastic when he shows up."

On the balcony, Ken gave a soft laugh. "Our Katy was much younger then. In those days, she had her whole life carefully mapped out. Barry once told me that getting married was part of her life-plan."

"Life-plan?" Richard repeated with a shake of his head. "Still, just because things didn't work out as she wanted once, it shouldn't be enough to make her cringe at the thought of falling in love now. Even if the divorce was difficult—"

"Hasn't Katy told you what happened in the end?" Ken asked.

Richard turned his back on the river. "She said she had a miscarriage, but not much more."

Ken slid next to him. "It wasn't a miscarriage. She carried the baby to full term. Katy could have died while she was losing it—might have if Ron hadn't gotten to her in time and called for an ambulance."

"Where was her husband?"

"Good old Barry?" Ken slapped the railing. "The SOB was in a meeting. He couldn't be bothered when Katy phoned him. Took a long time for her to get past it." He chewed on his lip. "Have you ever taken a good look at her wrists?"

Richard glanced north to where lights flickered over the George Washington Bridge. "She told me she scalded them in boiling water, learning to cook when she was a kid. She laughed about it."

Ken shook his head at the lie I'd concocted.

Richard's face took on an expression I'd never seen before. "I wish I could get my hands on that bastard she was married to."

I laughed. "I can picture Richard and Barry fighting over me—one a pacifist, and the other a coward. They'd probably argue all day about why they shouldn't take a swing at each other."

Again Ronnie punched my arm.

"Hey, that's gonna leave a bruise."

"Yeah, well, you deserve it." She hit me a third time.

Ken moved closer to Richard and lowered his voice. "Katy would kill me if she found out I told you this—"

Enough was enough. I pulled free from Ronnie's grip and stormed out to the balcony. "Hey, you two, don't get too comfortable out here. Dinner's almost ready."

Ken cleared his throat. "Uh… as I was saying, Richard, that's something you'll have to ask her about."

Ronnie caught up with me. "Where are you going? You're supposed to be giving me a hand." She leaned past me. "Guys, come to the table. It'll just be another minute." She yanked me back to the kitchen.

As he and Ken came inside, Richard said, "It's not easy to get to the bottom of Kaitlyn."

Ken chuckled. "That's for sure. But keep trying. It'll be worth it."

Richard took Ken's advice. He did keep trying. But what he tried was why I wound up in a bed in the Niagara Inn.

Chapter Nineteen
Across the Common

When I again opened my eyes, Abigail was on my bed. Just as Ronnie had earlier insisted on sitting nearby, the ghost now appeared to be my wakeful guardian. From her posture, I thought she must have been sitting beside me for a while. Her back against the headboard, her knees bent, she looked to be absorbed in the volume of *Anna Karenina* resting against her thighs. For a minute I watched her chew absently on a strand of red hair.

"This is such a touching story," she said when I stirred. When she set the book aside, I noticed she marked her place with a folded sheet of paper. Though it now showed less age, I thought it might be the letter I'd set on the dresser—the one I intended to show to Mrs. Hughes. I remembered a line written on it: *Sleep is difficult, my love, without you curled up beside me—*

Abigail must have heard my thought. "Will wrote that to me," she said.

Looking toward her window, she brushed away a few tears. It was a long moment before she spoke again. When she did, her words conveyed a connection to Anna Karenina's story. "The mistakes people make by thinking they can't live, having lost all they loved. It's something I truly wish I'd known before."

I watched her face crumble with sorrow. She didn't appear to be the dark presence I'd made of her last night. She looked like a woman in pain.

I reached for her hand. "Before what, Abbie?"

She sniffed back her tears. "Isn't that what I was going to show you when you went and fell asleep?"

I rolled toward her. "I didn't want to sleep. You decided I had to—even sang me a lullaby."

"Och, must you always quibble so?"

I sighed. "Okay, it doesn't matter. Where'd you go?"

Abigail pushed the blonde hair from my face. "It's nothing for you to fret over. For now, we should go on from where we were before. If I remember right, you saw how I fell in love with my Will without ever having met him. After that, I watched for him mornings on the Common and down at the beach nights when he, Brinny and Charlie put in with their… *cargo*. Then one morning while I hung laundry outside, as fate would have it, I chanced to meet him." She blushed. "I was so brazen in going about it, I can scarcely repeat it." She covered her face with her hands. "It's better, I think, that you see for yourself." She slid from the bed and took my hand. "Hold tight. It'll be only a minute till you're strong enough to rise."

With slow backward steps, she led the way to the window seat and wrapped me in the quilted comforter. When I had settled, she pointed down the street. "See there? Will's coming across the Common to his job at Burke's."

Through Abigail's window, I saw the light-haired young man step gingerly around the milling cows, horses and geese feasting on the numerous mushrooms that filled the Common's gentle grassy slopes.

A broad smile on her face, Abigail leaned forward to watch. "It wasn't the cattle turned out to graze that made him take such care walking across there," she said. "No, it was what they did after eating that made for such slippery footing that he feared his fine shoes would slide on the grass. It was bound to happen sooner than later. See, there he goes, bottom over top to the ground." She laughed and slapped my arm.

I saw the teenage Abigail walk lightly onto the

Common, her skirts swaying. Will sat on his rear, brushing grass, mud and animal feces from his knees. She stood above him, giggling. The sound of her laughter seemed as light as the flutter of birds' wings, yet from the expression on Will's face, it might have been the squawk of geese.

"Excuse me, but snickering at another's misery is quite impolite." He rolled to his feet.

Between giggles, Abbie Kirby replied, "That's as it may be. But if you'd seen yourself…" Her hands mimed his tumble.

While he scowled at her, I heard the growing annoyance of his thoughts. He intended to chastise this rude girl for her provincial ill manners, then retreat home for a cleanup and change of clothes. When at last on his feet, he looked at her and froze. *Her eyes—they're greener than a sparkling spring day's reflection on Lake Ontario,* he thought. *And they're dancing.*

"Excuse me, but I…" He couldn't complete the sentence. "Ahem, yes, I…" He seemed dumbstruck when a breeze gentled long red curls across her face. *Her face,* he thought. *So delicate and fair, no sonnet could do it justice.*

"Have you nothing to say for yourself?" Abbie chided.

Will pulled himself up to full height and puffed out his chest. His sparse blond facial hair that appeared to be the recent idea of a beard glistened in the morning sun. The cleft in his chin showed through when he raised it at her. Pointing with his chin rather than a finger was clearly meant to intimidate.

Her hands on her hips, Abbie said. "Just look at the unholy mess you've made of yourself."

Will glanced at his muddy shoes. "Really, now!" As if he saw himself mirrored in Abbie's eyes, he laughed, too. "Guess I must look a sorry sight."

"That you do."

"Well…" he began, then stopped. In his jumbled

thoughts, he vaguely recalled that something urgent needed attending to. He'd known what it was only a minute ago. So close to the most beautiful girl he had ever seen, he couldn't remember. Nor did he want to move for fear he was lost in a dream and the vision would vanish if he stirred.

"Well," Abbie mimicked him, then said, "Have you not got someplace to be, or do you intend to plant yourself like a scarecrow in this field the rest of your life?"

"Yes, of course." Will showed no inclination to move.

Again she laughed. "Yes, you're going, or yes, you're staying?"

He looked to be completely flustered. Finally, he collected himself enough to mumble, "Yes, of course, I have to go to work. Excuse me… I'm… I'm sorry… it's… late… They'll be wondering… Nice to have met you."

"Indeed," she said. "And will it be proper for you to show up for work with filth all over your fine suit?"

He slapped at his elbows and knees. "Oh, yes, that's right. I was going home to clean myself up before—"

She latched onto his arm. "You've got no time to cross the Common to your fine brick house, then walk all the way back to Burke's. It'll be quicker if you come home with me. I'll see what can be done to make you look presentable."

She was right in what she told me. I giggled. *How brazen of her to reach for what she wants without an invitation.*

Abigail's lips twisted. One eye closed, she said to me, "Do you see something of yourself in the way I went about it?"

"I never… I mean me and Barry… It was him who wanted to—" How was it she could so easily read my mind, then make me feel as though I were stumbling over my feet?

She snickered. "It wasn't you who put the idea in his head?"

"No. It was all him."

"Uh-huh." From the way she rolled her eyes, I might have said that's my story and I'm sticking to it. "Look there instead of at me," she said and pointed to the window.

On the Common, Will Bender's eyebrows drew together. "How do you know I work at Burke's?"

Blushing, Abbie released his arm. "Don't I see you crossing the Common each morning, stepping this way and that like you might keep the fine shine on your shoes?"

"You've watched me?"

Her blush grew deeper. "And why shouldn't I be watching whoever I please?"

"But you're pleased to be watching me."

Abbie stood mute while a broad smile lit Will's face.

Love has silenced her ability to disclaim it. I wonder who said that. Someone must have. I'll have to ask Richard— At the thought of him, my smile faded. I twisted my engagement ring. For the first time in days it moved a little. I looked at my hand. *My finger's gotten thinner from not eating.*

"Don't think of your ring. Watch now," Abigail said.

***

The window clouded. When it cleared, it appeared to be later that same morning. Will Bender was in his office. Hands clasped behind his head, he leaned back in his chair, staring down at the lumber yard through the narrow window.

Tom Burke walked through the door. "Excuse me, Mr. Bender, but I'm not paying you good money to dream on my time," he said.

Will's chair clattered heavily from two legs onto all four as he abruptly straightened up. His face flushed, he grasped at a document on his desk. "Sorry, Mr. Burke," he said, then muttered, "Damn," as the pages slipped from his hands. When he grabbed for them they floated to the floor, scattering like frightened birds.

The old man bent to gather a few pages. While handing them back, he said, "If I know anything, I'm looking at a man in love."

"Yes, sir… I-I mean… no, sir," Will said.

Burke pulled a chair over. "Which is it? Are you in love or are you not?"

Will patted his waistcoat pockets, as if the answer might be found in one of them. "Of course not… I-I don't know. Maybe. No. How can I be in love with someone I've just met? Of course I'm not in love. How could I be? And with someone as brazen and stubborn as— Could I be? I should see her again, just to find out. But that wouldn't be proper. I mean—"

Tom Burke laughed so strenuously it brought tears to his eyes. "Don't think I've ever seen anyone fight himself quite this hard." With two fingers, he lifted his spectacles and pinched the bridge of his nose. "You do understand, Mr. Bender, whichever part of your mind wins, the other part's going to lose. So why don't you stop right there and let an old man help you figure out what's going on."

From the look on Will's face, it seemed a Dutch uncle was what he needed. His eyes turned down to his shoes, and he said, "I met this girl on the Common—"

Burke sighed. "Yes, yes. Start at the beginning. I can see I'll not get any useful work from you until this is resolved one way or the other."

Will sighed. "I slipped in the mud this morning. When I looked up, as if she were a specter suddenly materializing, she stood there, laughing at me."

"Yes?" Burke encouraged.

"I meant to be angry at such rudeness. But when I looked into her eyes… Then she spoke, and her voice was like—" He shrugged. "I don't know words to describe it."

"It was like the rustling of leaves on a summer day?"

Will's eyes widened. "Yes, exactly. How did you know?"

His hands locked behind his head, the old man lounged back in his chair. "Goodness, do you think you've invented such feelings? You young people never seem to understand the rest of us were young once and fell in love."

"Oh, I-I didn't mean to imply—"

"You're forgiven," Burke said. "Now, if you're so taken with her, there's only one thing to do. Call on the young lady."

Will heaved a deeper sigh. "That's the problem. I don't dare."

"In heaven's name, why not?"

"My family. That is, my mother, mostly—"

"I don't understand."

"My mother has this idea there's an appropriate sort of girl for me to court."

Burk grinned. "The young woman you met is inappropriate? Is she one of the wenches that service men at the Angel Inn?"

"No! Heavens, no. She's fine and good and too kind to ever be— No, of course she isn't."

"So then tell me why this girl isn't appropriate?"

"Well, she's not the sort of person… Uh, that is, she doesn't come from the kind of family—" Will gulped a lungful of air, before blurting out, "She doesn't come from what my mother would call our sort of people."

I was shocked. *What's wrong with him? Doesn't he understand how hard it is to find love?*

I heard Abigail say in my mind, *Indeed. You can*

think that about someone else, can you? Aloud, she said, "That's what Mr. Burke's about to tell him."

The old man glared at Will. "She's not appropriate because she's not from the Town?" He sounded scornful.

Picking at his fingers, Will said, "It isn't me, you understand. *I* don't feel that way."

"You don't feel that way but your mother does. And like a good little lad, you'll accept such drivel? Knuckling under to such an attitude is as good as saying you agree with it."

"But I don't."

"In that case, Mr. Bender, who'll be courting this young lady, you or your mother? Because if it would be you—" Burke stopped. His head cocked, he said. "Just who is this young lady that's taking up so much of my valuable time?"

"Abigail." At the mention of her name, Will almost crooned, "She has hair as red as the sunset and dancing green eyes. When I looked into them, like I was bewitched I lost track of time… and myself."

Laughing again, the old man said, "Yes, you certainly seem to have been bewitched. Abigail with red hair? Would this be Abbie Kirby?"

"You know her?" Will sounded surprised.

Burke nodded. "Not well. But from what I hear, there aren't many lads she'd give the time of day to. I know her family, though. So do most in town. And sure as I'm sitting here, I can say without risk of contradiction, if the Kirby family isn't appropriate, none here is. They're all hard workers. They keep to their own business, and not a single scandal has ever attached to their name."

"But my mother—"

"Your mother, indeed!" Burke rose from his chair. "If it's only that barring your way, lad, let me tend to her. Meantime, since you've a mind to see this young lady again, do it. And if I were you, I'd do it quickly before she decides your foolishness isn't worth the waste of her time."

When Tom Burke left, Will tried to focus on work. It appeared to be a Herculean labor. After several minutes he gave up the effort. "Mr. Burke's right. I should call on Abigail," he said to his office walls. "Abbie, he called her. Abbie." He seemed to take pleasure in rolling her name on his tongue. "Yes, I'll take his advice. I'll see Abbie again." His face fell. "But how do I explain to my mother I'm courting the daughter of a fisherman from the Dock?"

His feelings floated across the years and through the Abigail's window. As if he spoke directly to me, I heard him think that regardless of the difficulty, he had to make Abbie Kirby his own. If he didn't, his heart would forever be restless.

Abigail's voice again spoke in my mind. *Do those sound like the words of someone you know?*

A swarm of butterflies flitted in my stomach. I forced a blank expression onto my face. "What if it does? They're just words. I've heard it all a thousand times."

"*Hmmm.*" Abigail looked disgusted.

"I'm not going to discuss this!"

"*Hmmm,*" she said again.

I tore my eyes from hers and turned to the window.

Will laid his head on his desk. "Maybe I can see her and not say anything," he said aloud. "Father will believe my being out at night's just another Railroad run. Mother will think I'm off fishing with Charlie. It could work."

Even as he contemplated the possibility, his heart told him to stop. "No," he said. "Abbie's far too good for such sneaking around."

Shoving aside the complicated issue of his mother's disapproval, he pondered what seemed to be the greater problem: what excuse could he find to meet Abbie again?

"Why doesn't he just pick himself up and go to her house? Uh… your house," I said to Abigail.

"Queen Victoria's time was very different than the

one you know," she explained. "When I lived, men—both single and married—were free to find release with ladies of the night. But courting a lass with a view to taking her to a marriage bed was a different matter. My Will had no experience at courting. Look at him, poor lad, trying hard to think of a way to see me again."

While Abigail spoke, Will stood and began to pace. With each step, he muttered, "No, that won't work. Ah, that won't do, either. Damn, damn, damn!"

Half an hour of plotting brought him no closer to a solution. Each scenario he constructed seemed to leave him at risk of embarrassment, or worse, of rejection if Abbie had been merely flirting. After the first rush of certainty, doubt—the Devil's greatest invention—settled over him. At last he concluded the only safe plan was to wait until the church social at the end of the month. Abbie might be there. She might agree to dance with him.

He imagined her smile when he invited her to waltz. He closed his eyes. His arm around the waist of an invisible partner, he moved in a slow circle thinking of how he'd hold her while they danced, of how he would lift and carry her off when the music ended. He knew Abbie would be as light in his arms as in his heart.

What followed was an entirely different sensation. His face red, he quickly sat and covered his crotch with the hem of his jacket.

Next to me on the window seat, Abigail tittered like a schoolgirl. "Thinking of undressing me, of running his hands over my breasts and thighs wasn't gentlemanly—not *seemly*, Mother Bender would've said. Just look at the poor lad, will you, suffering so for thinking of doing it. Ah, isn't he adorable?"

Isn't he just, I thought, picturing Richard in place of Will.

Abigail's face lit with the love she clearly had for her young man. The warmth of it radiated outward until it filled the air around her. She put her fingers on one of the windowpanes, as if reaching for him, as if wanting again to be in his arms while his hands strayed across her—

I felt what she felt. I fought against it.

Preoccupied by her love, for once she didn't crawl into my thoughts. Blushing now, she took her hand from the glass, and laughed. "Poor lad, he knew he'd better put such thoughts of me aside or he'd never be able to rise from his chair. The only way he could do it was to tell himself God would grant good fortune in his desire if he stayed restrained and patient."

She leaned back, the twinkle gone from her eyes. "Och, but it's impossible to know the mind of God, just as it is to see the working of fate. And fate, you see, already had me and Will waltzing to a tune of its own. Though we didn't know it, our next meeting had already been arranged."

Chapter Twenty
Tryon's Folly

Abigail said, "After he decided to be patient, Will finally settled down." She rested her cheek against a windowpane. "It's late afternoon now, and there he is working hard on the contract he began before thoughts of me made him—" Her face turned as red as her hair.

I couldn't help but laugh. "Go on, say it. He got all hard when he fantasized about having sex with you."

She slapped my arm.

This was too good to let go of. I put on the clinical expression my shrink always wore. With a German accent, I said, "So tell me, Mrs. Bender, what was it like when you two finally did it?"

Her eyes crinkled. "Did what?"

"You know, the—"

"Camel with two humps?" she said with a salacious grin.

"You slattern," I said. "That's exactly what I mean —did the dirty deed. Had sweaty, hot, pig sex."

She poked me. "You mean like you and Richard have?"

"Okay, okay—" Unable to push more words through my laughter, I waved my hand.

"Should we keep playing like harlots, Kaitlyn," she said, "or would you rather know how we came to it?"

I fell back against the wall of the window nook, holding my stomach. "Oh, I definitely want to see how *that* happened. This is getting better than an x-rated movie."

Her expression darkened. The lightness gone from her voice, she said, "It didn't happen the way you're thinking. It wasn't like in one of the movies you and your friends have been watching, where people fall into each other's arms while music plays."

The sorrowful cast of her eyes drained my mirth. "What… happened?"

She pointed. Through her window I saw Will's office and the paper spread haphazardly across his desk. His jacket hung on the back of his chair. His sleeves rolled up, he quickly struck lines from a page and scribbled new ones in their place.

Charlie Bolton's head poked through the door. "Train needs to run tonight," he said.

Will glanced up and rubbed his eyes. "Tonight? Look at this mess. I've got to get all this finished before leaving here." He brushed a hand through mussed blond hair. "Can we put it off until tomorrow? If not, maybe you and Brian can make the run without me."

"Not this time." Will's office was so small everything in it could be seen in a single glance from the doorway. Still, Charlie gazed furtively around before moving close to hand over a scrap of paper. "Reverend Tryon left this with Minister Cox when he come across from Lewiston this afternoon."

Unfolding the note, Will read the sprawling script aloud: "The three parcels you asked after have arrived at this Station, and are now in the lowest storeroom ready for delivery. However, the merchant is disgruntled at them having been sent on without approval. His clerks stopped here this morning seeking to recover the packages. This merchandise must be forwarded no later than eleven o'clock tonight or it might be mislaid."

He refolded the note. "You'll see to disposing of this properly?"

"Always do." Charlie said.

"Almost didn't recognize the reverend's hand—must have written it in haste. And his warning about clerks wanting to retrieve their packages—" Will looked past Charlie. "Guess it *will* take three of us to make sure they're transported without damage. Could be trouble on this trip." His shoulders tense, his fingers rapidly twisted a pencil.

"Bound to be if hornets are buzzing 'bout the nest at Tryon's Folly," Charlie said.

"I suppose it can't be helped." Will took a deep breath. "It's delicate merchandise. Can't risk it getting lost or broken."

As if he were entirely indifferent, Charlie sprawled on a chair across from the desk, his chin on his chest. "I suppose."

After a minute, Will said, "Better take precautions, then."

Charlie's head popped up. "Taking that kind of precaution, sooner or later you might make use of it."

"Haven't needed to yet." Will leaned to look out the door. "Seems to me, keeping it close by my side's the best way to make sure I won't have to."

"But, would you… if things came to it?"

Will's gaze wavered. He laid the pencil on his desk and carefully arranged it on top of the pages. "Don't know, and I pray I'll never find out."

"Best way to be sure you won't, is not take it."

His eyes cast down to the pages on his desk, Will said, "I need to have this contract finished and in Mr. Burk's hands if I'm going meet you on the beach. Meanwhile, you'd best get your ketch ready for the parcels waiting at Tryon's Folly."

I tapped Abigail's arm. "Tryon's Folly?"

She nodded. "It was called that by those who knew of it."

"They keep mentioning the place. Was it important?"

Her voice heavy, she said, "It was to the runaway slaves who hid there in the darkness, waiting. The Folly was four cellars going down to the river below the First

Presbyterian Church in Lewiston. Josiah Tryon was the pastor there. It took him years to dig those cellars, so runaways could be snuck out unseen."

"Why did they have to hide? After all, Lewiston was in the North."

Abigail rolled her eyes. "Have you not listened to all I've told you? The *safe* North, indeed. Have you never heard of your Fugitive Slave Act? Did they teach you nothing in school?"

"I told you—"

"I heard what you said. History doesn't touch you so you pay it no mind. But it touched *us* every day. Your American law gave slave-hunters the right to come into houses to take back their property. And those who came didn't give much care to what they broke or who they slaughtered while they were about it."

"But the law—"

She cut me off with a sharp laugh. "This was border land, the frontier. The only law was money folks could make by working with the slavers. For a few dollars, even the soldiers helped them. Those soldiers were the most dangerous, since the law you care so much about did nothing to them when they killed—or stood by while slavers lynched a Railroad Conductor. In those days no one, South or North or either side of the river, could be trusted. So the three runaways the boys went for had trembled over every mile of the Railroad till they got to the basement of Buffalo's Michigan Street Baptist Church."

With a rueful look reflecting every running slave's fear, Abigail explained that Buffalo had been a center of the abolitionist cause, its docks a major port of departure for Canada. For this reason, movement there was heavily scrutinized by roving bands of Southern slave-hunters—also by local rowdies and hooligans who wanted a share of the reward for slaves they found. Crates were broken into, workers on the docks beaten if someone thought they were hiding slaves or even knew of someone who might be. So the runaways were sent on to Josiah Tryon's church.

Abigail held up a hand. "Now enough of your questions. There the lads are, sailing the Niagara on their way to the Folly." She turned back to her window. "You won't understand what this night meant to me and Will if you don't see for yourself what happened."

As we watched, Charlie Bolton's cat-ketch rode the center of the channel to a point where a church spire poked up above the trees. There, Brian furled the lugsail and the boys quietly paddled toward the eastern shore. The dip of the oars in the water and the soft call of birds were the only sounds along the river.

When they neared the bank, they slipped into the water. Dressed in black, their faces smudged with soot, Brian and Charlie pushed at the sides of the boat. His back to the riverbank, his head wrapped in a dark bandana to hide his blond hair, Will shoved at the stern. They slid the boat ashore so carefully the scrape of the hull on the pebbles could barely be heard.

"Hope they don't keep us waiting long," Brian said while he pulled sailcloth from the boat.

"*Shhh*," Charlie cautioned.

Will leaned forward, peering into the dark woods. A twig snapped. He cocked his head.

"Gotta be the church caretaker," Brian whispered. He turned toward the sound. "C'mon, c'mon, don't have all night."

"*Shhh*," Charlie said again.

The birds stopped chirping.

Will fidgeted. With his rifle at his side and a pistol in his hand, he mouthed, "I'm going inland a bit." Bent low, he quickly disappeared into the forest.

Charlie and Brian crouched against the cat-ketch. Minutes later, the underbrush rustled. Brian reached into the boat for a small lantern. Holding it close to the ground, he waved it twice. In a moment, a stooped, gray-haired man poked his round red face from the thicket. He glanced around then signaled behind him.

Three blacks, two males and a female, dressed in what appeared to be new clothes, moved cautiously, hand-in-hand, out of the ebony forest. The old man pointed to the boat. "Down there. Those boys will show you the way."

The runaways edged into the moonlight's glare. As they broke from the thicket, the last turned to the old man. "Thank yuh, suh, for these fine clothes… for ever'thin'."

"*Shhh*," Charlie said.

"C'mon, c'mon!" Brian whispered.

The first black hesitantly lifted one foot into the boat. Charlie held up a large piece of sailcloth to wrap him in.

A shot rang from the trees. "Halt there!" a husky voice ordered.

Two men stepped forward, both dressed for the road. From the smudges on their grizzled, unshaven faces, it looked as though they had hidden in the brambles for days. The first had stringy long hair. He held a pistol in one hand, swung a rope loosely in the other. A musket was slung across his back. His nearly bald companion held a smoking rifle across his chest.

"Thought we'd catch up with ya if'n we waited long enough," the man with the rope said. "You boys step back now. We got papers say we got a right to take this here property."

The female runaway began to tremble. "No, Lord, no," she moaned. One of the males squeezed her hand, and the three stood frozen like startled deer.

A rustle in the underbrush off to the left marked where Will slid behind a tree at the edge of the woods, fifty yards away.

Brian and Charlie glanced at each other. The slump of their shoulders indicated they understood they'd be taken into custody. Charlie thought, *if Will's smart, stays quiet, he'll escape with word of our capture. If we survive it.* His body tensed.

Alerted by a slight movement, the bald man stepped forward. He leveled his rifle with one hand, and used his other to pull a pistol from the pocket of his deerskin jacket.

The other slave-hunter called, "You, old man, git over here by them niggers and nigger lovers. Authorities gonna want a few words with all of ya." He held out the rope. "You other two, take this here, tie them niggers and the old man together."

Nobody moved.

"Luke, whyn't we just shoot them nigger lovers and be done with it," the bald slaver said. "Legal to do such back home when a body's stealin' yer property. Don't see why we cain't do it here. 'Sides, it'll save us a heap of time and trouble if'n we don't have to haul 'em all up to Fort Niagara."

One of the black males lifted his head. He thought, *Better to drown in this river than go back.* With a quick movement, he turned and bent to dive for the water.

The click of a rifle being cocked sounded like a slap. A slave-hunter glanced at his companion and laughed. "Don't shoot nothin' important. That nigger ain't worth much if'n he cain't stud—and he ain't worth nothin' dead."

The black man straightened and turned defiantly. Hatred glowing in his dark eyes, he yanked open his shirt, pushed out his chest and took a step toward the gun. "Better a bullet," he said.

Brian moved quickly to block the black man's path. A pistol and a rifle swiveled toward him.

Charlie slowly lifted an arm. "Hold on. No one needs to die tonight."

From the way Charlie stood up with a hand behind his back, his long, pockmarked face calm and his eyes hard, he looked like he would try to brazen their way out of trouble the way Will had once done. When he spoke, he sounded confident, though his knuckles were white where he grasped the boat.

"Just two of you to stop six of us from moving on? Can't shoot unarmed men and get away with it, and none of this here's legal if there ain't no one from up at the fort along to make it so."

The long-haired slave-hunter scowled. "Don't need no blue bellies to make anythin' right."

His companion chuckled. "'Sides, this way ain't no need to share the reward with no Yankees."

"If you're gonna shoot, better make the first one good," Charlie said. "Six of us, some will still be standing to get you."

"Please!" the female slave cried. With a blur of motion, a slave-hunter's arm shot out and back-handed her in the face. She crumpled to the ground.

Brian inched forward. One of the black males followed.

Fear filled Will's mind. Could he raise his gun, fire it at the men?

"Hold fast there!" The long-haired slave-hunter pointed his pistol at Brian's stomach. "Could be an idea to drop this trouble right here, John, I'm thinking. Put an end to this leg of the Railroad right fast, maybe."

The bald man's laugh was the snicker of someone so indifferent to death he could easily impart it. He cocked his pistol, applied gentle pressure to the trigger.

"No!" Will cried out.

Crack. Crack. Two shots rang in rapid succession from the trees. *Crack.* Fire flashed from the barrel of Luke's pistol. Just a fraction wide, the bullet missed Brian's chest but tore a gash on his side. He twisted to the ground, grabbing at the wound.

At the first shot from the woods, long-haired Luke's rifle slipped from his hands. He clutched his chest, as if he might stop the blood seeping through his fingers. The second shot felled the bald slave-hunter. He dropped with the leering grin still on his face. A dark spot on his forehead marked where the ball had struck. The back of his skull was shattered.

Will sprinted from beneath the nearby trees. "Get moving!" he said, his face ashen. Wisps of smoke wafted up from the rifle and the pistol he carried.

"Ya killed me," Luke groaned.

"Didn't yet." The red-faced old caretaker took two steps to where the slave-hunter lay staring up at the moon. He hefted a sharp rock, weighed it in his hand, then smashed it into the dying man's skull. "You're dead now, slaver," he said, and heaved the blood-covered stone into the underbrush.

Brian still lay on the ground. His face showed both shock and relief. "Now what'll we do?"

Kneeling, Will lifted Brian's shirt. "Not too bad. Not good, but it could've been worse." He glanced at the dead slave-hunters. "Much worse."

Charlie's head spun back and forth. His thoughts were frantic. Were those footsteps down the shore? Other slavers, soldiers, townsfolk who hated Negroes worse than the Southerners did? They couldn't stay to find out.

One of the black males crouched beside the woman. All three runaways wept.

His back turned on the dead slaver-hunters, Will looked into the woods, into the dark river, then up to the sky. He looked everywhere but at the slave-hunters, at what he'd done to them. "Toss them in the water," he said at last.

"Yeah, let the whirlpool suck 'em under," Brian muttered. "Take 'em right to hell where they belong."

Charlie shook his head. "Current's running the other way, toward the lake. The bodies will float past the fort."

"Can't risk someone might spot them," the old caretaker said. "Setting slaves free, Reverend Tryon says it's our duty to do that. But killing people—" He dropped his head. "Up at the fort, they'll call it murder."

"Is there a shovel in the reverend's cellars?" Charlie asked.

The caretaker nodded. "Leave me to see about getting this filth buried somewhere they won't be found." He turned toward the thicket. "You boys get them Negroes across afore someone comes by to see what the shooting's about."

Charlie glanced at the dead slave-hunters, then his eyes shifted to where their weapons were scattered on the ground. Pointing, he said, "Can't leave those here. Someone finds 'em, gonna know somethin' happened."

Clutching his wound, through a groan, Brian said, "Forget 'em. I gotta get home." When he lifted his hand from his side it was red with blood. "Gotta get this cared for."

Charlie knelt and picked up the slave-hunter's pistol. "Looks like one of them Colt's revolvers," he said. Kinda new, too. Might be worth somethin'."

"Never gonna be able to explain how you come by it," Brian said. Again he groaned. "Dammit, get me outa here!"

"No, see this?" Charlie said. "I know a man who'll pay good money for it."

His tone flat, Will said, "Forget that pistol. Forget all those guns. Dump them in the river so we can be done with this place."

"But—"

"No *buts*, Charlie!" Will grabbed the revolver and hurled it into the water.

"Stop fightin' over them guns!" Brian said. "Get me home!"

The old caretaker returned to the shore where he stooped and picked up one of the rifles. "You boys get going. Take those runaways 'cross the river afore someone comes looking. I'll take care of burying these 'long with the bodies."

Will turned Charlie around and pushed him toward the runaway slaves. "Grab that sailcloth and help me get them wrapped!"

No joyous banter over a successful mission, the boat trip back to the beach at Niagara-on-the-Lake was as silent as the night. Waves lapped against the small boat's hull. Soft sobs rose from the three blacks wrapped in sailcloth. Now that they were clear of Lewiston, what had happened filled Brian's and Charlie's minds. In their silence, they might have been struggling over the sight of blood and death at their feet and fighting the fear of how near they came to filling unmarked graves on the river bank. What work was needed to bring them home, Charlie did at the tiller and Brian did at the sail. His face pale, he appeared to be in shock.

Will sat in the prow. His back to the others, he stared out to the dark horizon. He recalled how he had learned to hit the center of targets set up by Nathan Kinsley. Time and again Nathan had made him fire his rifle until he never missed. This was the first time he'd fired at humans. The first time he ended a life.

***

While the boys sailed the dark river, Abigail whispered to me, "Later, when Will could think again, he spent days berating himself because he didn't find something—anything—he might have done to keep from killing those men."

Able to overhear Will Bender's thoughts, I knew he didn't consider the metaphor of killing men named Luke and John. Still, his taut face said his conscience throbbed with such an ache he might have dispatched that biblical duo. The only words he spoke on the trip home were, "There's no glory in killing—"

Abigail turned to me. "Will didn't finish what he was saying that night." She almost couldn't get the words out. "He would in a few years."

The pain in her voice caused a chill to run up my spine. Silently, I prayed her plans worked out better than mine had. Needing to know, I asked if it came out all right in the end.

She gazed through her window and brushed her fingers along a pane. "I got what I asked for."

Hearing only the reassurance I sought, I relaxed until she added what might have been, "for a while." She said it so softly I couldn't be sure.

Chapter Twenty-One
Homecoming

By now I understood it was pointless to push Abigail, so I leaned back in the window nook, watching through the window while the boys sailed into view. They showed little energy when they reached the shore. It seemed to take their combined strength to lift their passengers from the cat-ketch and free them from the sailcloth shrouds.

Hidden among the trees in a hooded cowl, Abbie watched their lethargic dance. From the way she leaned forward, pulling at the hem of her cloak, something in the end of this trip must have looked very different from those before. She moved quickly to the shore.

"What is it, Brinny?" she said when she reached the boat.

At the sound of the light brogue, Will's head turned. He stepped toward the hooded figure and stared into her eyes. "You?"

"And what did you expect? she answered. "Did you think while the three of you took your sweet time securing the boat, your cargo found their way to the Calvinist Baptist Church themselves?"

Will showed no delight at finding the woman he had recently rhapsodized over was one of his coconspirators. He turned silently away. I heard him think, *.After the evil I've done this night—*

Charlie also turned away. Brian sagged against the boat.

Abbie looked at her brother. "Brinny?"

"Get these people to the Colored Section. Move!" Charlie ordered.

"Brinny?" she said.

"Later," her brother said through gritted teeth.

"Yeah, talk of it later if you'll do it at all," Charlie said. "Get these packages delivered so we can be finished here."

***

Snowflakes flying past the window obscured the scene. When it cleared again, I watched Abbie enter the cottage on Ricardo Street. She tiptoed into her brother's room.

Brian sat on his bed in the dark, his back against the pine slats of wall. He had his right arm tightly wrapped around his chest, as if his heart would fall out if he let go. He chewed at the index finger of his left hand.

Abbie tossed her hooded cloak aside. Sitting at the foot of his bed, she said, "Tell me."

He shook his head.

"I'll have the truth from you, Brinny Kirby."

He stared past her, biting his lip. "Two men died tonight," he said to the oilskin coat hung from a hook on his door."

She gasped. "How…? Who…?"

He didn't answer.

She placed a hand on his side. He grimaced.

"Are you hurt bad, Brinny?"

"No." He winced and shook her away.

"Charlie… and Will. What of them?"

"Can we talk of this tomorrow?" Brian moaned.

"No, we cannot! I need to know. Tell me *now* what happened."

The firmness in her green eyes seemed to pull the words from him. He told her all of it, finishing with, "and Will shot them both."

Her eyes went wide. "He did that?"

"He had to, don't you see?" Brian said. "Those men were slave-hunters who caught us."

"They'd have turned you in for a trial. We'd have done something about that without the need for killing." She sounded outraged.

Brian grabbed her arm. "You're not listening, girl. Did you not hear me? They was gonna kill us all! Raised their guns to do it when Will shot first." He touched his side. Blood came away on his hand. "Abbie, we was dead men, me and Charlie. Will Bender saved us." With a pained groan, he fell back heavily against the wall.

"Let me see your wound." She pulled open his shirt, dabbed at his torn skin with her skirt. "I'll go for Dr. Bernard."

"No!" Brian said.

"Your wound must be properly cleaned before it gets gangrene."

Brian shook his head. "Can't be explaining what happened. Abbie, you'll have to see to it yourself."

She jumped from the bed and quickly returned with a basin of water, clean cloths and a roll of gauze. Tears formed as she washed the blood from her brother's side.

"No need for crying, girl. The ball barely hit me," Brian told her.

"But just a bit to the right… you would've been—" She stopped, her hand in the air. At last she understood how close death had come to claiming her brother as a prize.

Brian took the blood-stained cloth from her. "But it wasn't, and I'm not."

She wiped her eyes. "Will saved you."

She thought back to that very morning when she and Will Bender stared at each other on the Common. She'd felt something strong pass between them then. Now she knew what it was.

***

Through another windowpane I watched Will toss and

groan in his bed. He had shot two men. While their lifeless eyes stared, he stepped over them as if they were nothing more than branches fallen from the trees. Now he knew what death looked like. In his sheltered room, it surprised him how easy it was to cause. He punched his pillow, then sat up.

"Brian didn't do it. Not Charlie, either. It was me!" He stumbled to his window and peered down the street. "Charlie, you were right," he whispered. "Taking guns along, sooner or later I'd use one for more than show."

His logic answered, *It would have been the end of your friends if you didn't shoot.* His conscience argued back, *It was you who hid in the dark, you who aimed, you who pulled the triggers.* The sound of the shots still rang in his ears.

In bed again, he buried his face in a pillow. It didn't blind him to the way those men looked, broken on the ground. The sulfur smell of burnt gunpowder filled his nostrils, the acrid tang was bitter on his tongue. *Never again will I see a horror to match it,* he thought.

"I needed to do it," he said again and again, until it almost became a mantra. "If I hadn't, Brian and Charlie would have died instead." He had to make himself believe it. *I do believe it, dammit!* "There was no other way. If I hadn't shot first, Brian and Charlie— and Abbie— She was on the beach, a witness to my crime."

Tell her about it later, Charlie had told Brian. Will knew he *would* tell her. Every sordid detail. Brian couldn't hold any part of it back. By now his Abbie knew what he had done, and knowing, her heart would become like granite. *Someone as fine and gentle as she could never care for a... a... killer!* The word slammed against his skull. *Will Bender is a killer! I won't be accused and brought to trial for my deadly sin, but a killer is what I am. And a girl like my Abbie—*

What if she didn't find him odious for what he'd

done? After all, he'd saved her brother. She should be grateful. She *would* be grateful. He caught his breath.

Killer! Again the word invaded his thoughts, eroding what hope still lingered. No! He would not allow his Abbie to link her fate to a creature such as him. Tears running unchecked down his cheeks, he moaned, "Never again will I have a right to think of her as mine."

***

When I blinked, the windowpanes went blank. The next thing I saw was Will slouching across the Common. I knew it had to be the next morning, because he looked haggard after a sleepless night. When he reached the street, he stopped to look toward to the Kirby's cottage, then turned and hurried off.

"Will," Abbie called out. Clearly, she had been waiting beside her house for a sight of him.

He glanced quickly over his shoulder before, head low, he continued toward Burke's Coal and Lumber.

She chased after him. "Will!" She caught up and grabbed his arm. "Will Bender, why are you avoiding me?"

"I…" he said. "I'm sorry… I… I must go."

She turned him around. "Must you now?" Her hands on his cheeks, she gently twisted his head until he had no choice but to look at her. "Will you not let me thank you for Brinny's life?"

With the morning sunlight and half of the Dock to witness her brazenness, she gave him a long first kiss.

On the window seat, Abigail sighed as if she were again in Will's embrace. "Before I knew it was happening," she said, "I was wrapped in his arms so tight I couldn't tell where my body ended and his began. Then, like that kiss was to be our final parting, a tear ran down his cheek. When he let me go, I leaned close, wiped his eyes, and whispered, 'I love you, Will Bender. With all of my heart I do, and I mean to have you.'"

Chapter Twenty-Two
Times that Change Everything

Snow swirled outside Abigail's window. The image of her staring into Will Bender's eyes faded into the whiteness. In response to the ghost's sigh, I said, "He was very special. A real keeper, my friends would say." My words sounded flat. I didn't know such a man, yet I was pleased that the woman beside me on the window seat had—the more we spoke, the more she showed me of her past, the more I liked Abigail Bender.

She favored me with a brief smile, then her eyes drifted back to the window. "He was the only one I ever... But loving someone so much, wrapping him in all your hopes... Och, it's a terrible, hurtful thing.

I caught my breath. I had once used those very words to describe love.

She glanced at me sideways. "You know the truth of it, don't you?"

I sobbed. "I..."

Abigail reached for my hand. "You don't need to say it."

"Why does it have to be this way?" I moaned.

"You've asked a thing I've no answer to, though I've often pondered it." She patted my hand. "But listen to me going on like a leprechaun when you need to rest. Look at you, eyes all red and drooping."

No sooner were those words spoken, than my eyes began to burn. I rubbed them and yawned. "I wish I'd known you when you were..."

"Alive?" Abigail finished my sentence. "No need to feel strange about saying it. I know I'm dead. I must say, though, I'm sorry not to have known you before then. I'm thinking we might've been great friends. We can talk of such friendship later."

She took my arm, urged me to the bed, then sat next to me.

I shifted onto my side and looked up at her. "I think we *are* friends. We must be. Why else would I be so glad to see how Will made you... *makes* you feel?"

Abigail gave me a smile as warm as the fire in the hearth. Brushing a tendril of hair from my face, she said, "Friends we are, then. Hush now."

Through another yawn, I said, "You and Will had a happy ending, didn't you? Please tell me you did."

"We knew happiness. We did know it... for a while." Her voice broke over each word.

Fearing what would come next, my heart ached for her. "But people grow old, die. It's the way of life. Those we love..." I couldn't go on.

"Sure, and so it is. And so it should've been for Will and me. If..." She took a breath, and held tight to my hand. "If I hadn't done what I did to get him, I might've had years of memories instead of the fire in this room to warm me. Our first kiss should've led us to a long road filled with laughter, sorrow, friendship, hope—all that's a loving life. And children." She gently wiped away my tears. "Ah, if a body could know what's coming. Thinking back now—and all these years I've had naught but thinking to do—with that kiss, fate bent our lives."

"I don't understand."

"Don't you? Have you not known a time when everything changed?" Not waiting for yet another denial from me, Abigail placed her hand across my eyes.

Instantly, an image took form.

I was in the small kitchen of the garden apartment where Barry and I once lived, one of many in a large complex near the Long Island Expressway. My life-plan was working out: I'd become a lawyer, married him—not a wedding at the Plaza as I'd dreamed, yet I was a Mrs. and now I was pregnant. I held a cookbook open on a shelf with one hand while I reached across to the refrigerator with the other. When I opened the door a dozen eggs floated out. They didn't splatter on the floor. The cardboard carton lifted, turned, opened. Eggs flew across the room. They splattered against the cabinets. One broke on my forehead.

Laughter drifted down from the ceiling—the sound I'd first heard the day I wrote my life-plan. The day my father walked out on us.

I dropped the mixing bowl. My legs gave. I crumbled to the floor. "Barry!" I cried.

"Dinner ready?" he called from the living room.

"Get in here!"

"Just a minute—the inning's almost over."

"Now!"

My husband was of medium build and his face—Well, Shakespeare might have described him as having a lean and hungry look. Grumbling, he padded around the wall to the kitchen. He nearly doubled-over at the sight. "Kaitlyn, I know you're just learning how to cook," he said. "But if you read the instructions, the eggs go in a bowl not on you and the walls."

I needed to be held, protected. Barry only snickered. We ate at a restaurant that night, a tarnished pleasure since my husband wanted everyone to know about the flying eggs.

"A ghost in our kitchen? More likely a ghost in my wife's little head," he chuckled to the waitress when she brought our meal.

He still laughed about it while we drove home after dinner. When we pulled up to our apartment block, he said, "Hey, I know. Maybe it's the ghost of your cousin Fred who died in the Trade Towers. Didn't you tell me he always threw snowballs at you when you were kids?

Snowballs, eggs—" He made a weighing motion with his hands. "Yeah, could be. Good old Fred was always a joker. Figures he'd come back as a poltergeist."

I leaned against the passenger-side door and held tight to the handle, biting my lip. Could Barry be any more insensitive? What happened to the man I married, the one who vowed to cherish and protect me? The one who couldn't wait for the reception to be over so he could get into my pants? Two years past our wedding I hardly recognized him.

I looked up at our apartment. A shadow moved past the window. I trembled. Evil lurked in there, I was sure of it. I didn't want to climb the stairs, didn't want to unlock our door, didn't want find out what or who the shadow might be. But I had nowhere else to go.

Hahaaa. Laughter came from the back seat.

I grabbed Barry's arm. "Didn't you hear that?"

"Hear what?"

"That… voice. Here… in the car!"

He laughed at me. "Old Cousin Fred's still rattling around in your brain, huh?"

My husband wasn't quite so smug the next night when Ronnie and Ken Hoffmann came over for dinner, though he started out that way.

I had just finished washing the dishes when I heard laughter in the living room. I leaned around the kitchen wall. "What's going on?"

"I'm telling them about your kitchen helper," Barry said with a snide grin. "You know, Kaitlyn, your ghost."

As if someone snuck up behind me, the hairs stood up on the nape of my neck. Afraid to turn around, I threw the dishtowel into the sink and ran to the living room. Ronnie and Ken lounged on the sofa. My husband sat in an armchair next to them with his legs stretched out on the coffee table.

Embarrassed by both my husband and my fear, I

whined, "It isn't funny. Come on, guys, don't laugh at me. I was scared silly."

Barry chuckled. "Certainly silly. I'm not so sure your breaking a dozen eggs is scary, though. Unless," he mocked horror, "you're throwing them at me with that look in your eyes."

I perched on the arm of the sofa.

Ronnie put her hand on my shoulder. "You shouldn't pick on her." She patted my cheek. "Men—they're all alike. Everything's a joke to them."

"Thank you." I said. "At least *you* understand."

Her long, black hair shook when she laughed. "Still, you have to admit it's funny—the idea of a poltergeist heaving eggs across your kitchen. Do you think you could keep it as a pet? I wonder what poltergeists eat."

"You too?" I pushed her away.

"Hey, ease up," Ronnie said. "There isn't a ghost in your house—there aren't such things. And I've got news for you, there's no tooth fairy either."

"Also, there's no Santa," Barry said.

"Really?" Ronnie faked a gasp.

The others laughed. While I pouted, a light in the unfinished nursery down the hall turned on. The light flickered twice.

I reached for my husband. "Barry…"

He leaned away. "Come on, Kaitlyn, it's just a lose bulb or something."

The light flickered again.

"It isn't!" I started to shake.

"You're being ridiculous," he said.

The light flickered a last time, then died.

"Barry, stop it!" Ronnie said. "Ghost or no ghost, can't you see she's terrified?"

He rolled his eyes. "There's nothing to be frightened of. Look, I'll show you." He pulled his legs from the coffee table and rose.

"Don't! Barry, please don't go in there," I said.

"Why? You're just being a girl about this." It sounded as though he thought being female might be the worst thing in the world. He gave Ken's shoulder a good-natured punch. "C'mon, let's show her."

"You don't understand—it isn't the bulb."

"Of course it is," he insisted.

"It's not!"

The guys looked at each other, and Barry said, "Okay, electrician, how do you know?"

"That bulb burned out last night. I removed it, but I didn't replace it because I forgot to buy spares."

He shook his head. "You're always forgetting something," he said. Then, what I told him finally penetrated his skull. "Hey, wait a minute. No bulb? Impossible."

He and Ken went to investigate.

"What's wrong?" Ronnie asked when they returned.

Ken pulled at his beard. "Katy's right. There's no bulb in the lamp."

"Must have been a car's headlights bouncing off the walls or something." Barry's snide complacency was gone. "Yeah, that has to be it. Nothing to worry about."

I wasn't reassured, and within weeks things got a lot worse. I felt vulnerable in my home. The poltergeist was there, in the kitchen, in what would be my baby's room. Its laughter echoed on those nights Barry worked late and I was alone. He had moved up in his firm and often worked late.

The hoarse laughter crawled along the walls, seeped under the doors. I heard it in the hiss of the radiators. There was a curse was on my home, on Barry, on me—the more the poltergeist laughed, the more certain of that I became.

"I can't live here anymore," I said one night during dinner. "We've got to find another apartment."

Barry screwed up his face. "Why do you always start on me just when I'm putting the first forkful of food into my mouth?"

"Because we never talk any other time."

"Uh-huh." He stared at his plate.

"I can't, Barry, I… I don't want to stay here."

"You were afraid of the neighborhood we left, insisted we had to move when you got pregnant. Now you're afraid of *this* apartment? We can't keep moving every time your imagination goes haywire."

"It's not my imagination. There's really something… evil here."

He slammed down his fork. "Come on, Katy. You're pregnant. Everyone knows pregnant women's hormones make them nuts. Call your doctor. Ask for some pills or something."

His words were a knife slashing the seams of our marriage. Those seams finally tore apart when my pregnancy reached the middle of its ninth month.

Though I was a thin girl, I carried quite large. My back constantly ached. My ankles swelled, then my wrists. I felt tired all the time, some days not able to get out of bed. At last month's prenatal examination, the doctor told me I had to start my maternity leave immediately. This put pressure on our finances.

"Gotta work late," Barry announced one morning. He me gave a perfunctory kiss and pulled on his camelhair coat.

"Not again," I groaned. What did he do all those nights he didn't come? Drink with friends? Another woman? Suspicion crawled like a spider up my spine.

Hahaaa, the disembodied voice wheezed.

"Gotta do it, Kaitlyn."

"Can you at least stop for some groceries on your way home? Here's the list." I tried to hand the page to him.

He brushed my arm away. "Sorry, don't know how late I'll be. Get to the store yourself."

I glared at him, tears in my eyes.

Hahaaaaaaa. The laughter grew louder, longer.

"Dammit, do something for yourself instead of lying around all day!"

My eyes overflowed. "I can't." I spread my arms to show the mess pregnancy had made of my body. "Look at me!"

As if detesting what he saw, his eyes flicked to the apartment door. "Don't know what to tell you. If you won't go out, you'd better find out if the market delivers."

Desperate to make him stay, I tried to shove the door closed. He jammed it open with his foot.

"This isn't fair! I'm stuck in here while you're out—"

As he slammed the door behind him, he said, "Someone's gotta bring in the bucks to keep this family going!"

Now the laughter rang in the hall outside. How could he not hear it?

That afternoon I noticed blood in my panties and telephoned the obstetrician. He instructed me to get to the hospital. He would meet me there in a half hour.

I telephoned Barry. His secretary answered.

"Beverly, is my husband there?" I said.

"He's in a meeting, Kaitlyn," she said coolly.

"I need him, Beverly. Get him!" A sharp needle shot from my chest to my abdomen. "Now!"

Hahahaaaaaa.

Barry came on the line. Obviously, he'd been in his office all along. "What is it now?" He sounded impatient.

"I'm staining."

I heard him breathing.

"Barry?"

"Call the doctor and call me back."

"I already spoke to him. Do you think I'm an absolute idiot?"

"Not absolute." His laughter mixed with the ghostly

wheeze, became one with it, swelled until it filled every inch of the apartment. The walls closed in. I felt as though hands were at my throat. I struggled for air.

"The doctor said I have to get to the hospital right away." I groaned when another pang doubled me over.

Hahaaaaaa. The laughter was at my feet. Now it crawled up my leg.

"I'm in an important meeting here," Barry said. "I'll get home when I can. Hang in there. I'm sure nothing's really so wrong another couple of minutes will matter."

Though his office was but a few miles away, he didn't make it home until two hours later. By then I was lying in a small pool of blood. Ronnie Hoffman was beside me, trying to lift me into a sitting position.

"Nice of you to get here, sport," she hissed at Barry.

His face blank, the image of innocence, he said. "What happened?"

"While you were deciding whether to bother coming home, Katy called me. Good thing I got here. She passed out while I was phoning for an ambulance."

Emergency Services arrived just then. Fifteen minutes later two EMT's and a nurse rushed my gurney through the emergency room.

Now I lay on a cold metal table beneath glaring lights, a tiny lifeless body on my stomach. People in masks and green gowns tried to gentle the small body from my arms.

"Take it from her, nurse," one of them ordered.

"No!" I shouted—

***

"No!" Trembling, I cried out in the quiet of Abigail's Room. I had sworn to forget Barry, my baby, forget that horrible time. If the only way to forget was to never again feel anything, so be it. But the sorrow of the past lay in bed beside me now as it had for years.

"Stop it!" I shoved Abigail's hand away.

"There's no hiding from this," she said. "You know as well as I do what's risked by daring to hope."

I moaned. "It's a good thing I didn't know what would happen. Otherwise I never would have done something like… like— Dammit, something bound to bring such heartache."

Her lips pursed, she said, "Give yourself over to love, you mean? For a husband, for a babe even before it's born? If you hadn't, you'd never have known the days of joy before. I'm thinking it's better to know. Leastwise, you could still cherish each glorious moment—even if you can only hope the end will be changed."

"And if it can't?" I sniffed. "Would you have accepted Will's love if you'd known you'd lose it?"

Tears ran down Abigail's cheeks. "I don't know. But if *I'd* known… If I'd known…"

I forced my past back down to the steel vault in which I kept it locked. I told myself my sorrow was behind me. Abigail had to relive hers every day in images seen through her window. It felt so unfair.

She patted my hand. "When I first knew I loved him, I also should've known, no matter how right Will was to shoot those men, fate would demand payment for what he'd done."

"But even then you would have loved him," I told her. "Seeing the two of you together, I know it's true—" I caught my breath. Ronnie had said the same about me and Richard.

Abigail wiped her nose on her sleeve. "I would've loved him even more. But maybe I'd have thought of another way at the beginning—something to show him he had no guilt in what he'd done without making him strong enough to face the killing again. Maybe then I wouldn't have had the sorrow of his leaving."

I pushed myself up on my elbows. "He deserted

you? How could he?"

In Abigail's words I found justification for breaking up with Richard. He would eventually grow tired of me and leave. Men always did.

"He did leave," she said, "but not in the way you're thinking. And not before we had a grand two years together. But, och, such a foolish, stubborn, lovesick child I was, I didn't stop to see fate shaping things so the end began at the start. You see, at the beginning I didn't trust fate to give me Will."

Abigail settled against the bed's headboard, staring into the fire. After a very long moment, she spoke the next part of her tale. I closed my eyes. By now I knew Abbie and Will and the town where they lived so well, I didn't need the ghost's window to see this part unfold.

Chapter Twenty-Three
The Dock and the Town

"On the street, I told Will I loved him and meant to have him," Abigail said. "But after our first kiss, he dropped his head and walked away. I called after him, 'I mean to have you, Will Bender, no matter what.'"

She waited outside the huge gate of Burke's Coal and Lumber that evening. "I'll have a word, Will Bender," she said when he came through.

She took his arm and tried to steer him toward the shore.

"I must get home. My parents are waiting dinner," he said.

She refused to release him. "You'll talk to me first."

He pulled his hand away, leaving her again to stare at his stooped shoulders as he plodded off.

A similar scene occurred each morning and evening during the following week. Will changed his customary route, went to and from work by a different path, yet guided by some instinct, she always found him.

"I'll have a word with you," she would say when he tried to brush past her.

Though he shook his head and refused to speak, she persisted until one evening he didn't turn from her. Hopeful, she held tight to his hand. Her long skirts swirling around her ankles, she led him down to the beach where Charlie Bolton's cat-ketch rested on the grainy sand. Certain his memory of Tryon's Folly held him from her and that memory sat in Charlie's boat, she decided it was there she'd begin to free him from its grip.

On the deserted beach, while gulls crooned to the

waning day, she leaned against the boat's pine hull, clasping his hand in both of hers.

Shoulders hunched, Will gazed at the lake.

She took his other hand. "Don't I understand what you're feeling?" she said. "But, Will, you've done no wrong—you must see that. You were meant to be there. Fate meant you to save Brinny."

He shook his head. "I killed two men."

Abigail smiled inside when Will at last admitted his perceived guilt. Now that its name had been spoken, the demon gnawing at his soul could be exorcized.

"If there was anything else you could've done," she said, "would God not have shown it to you?"

Sails billowed in the distance on Lake Ontario. A stiff breeze pushed a schooner northward. The wind ruffled Will's blond hair. "Could've just let them see my guns like I did that other time. The men might have backed down."

She took his face in her hands. "There's no might about it, Will Bender. The way things were, those two would've killed you along with the others. Evil walked among you that night. You've a duty to defend yourself from it. Defend your friends, too."

"Duty's fine, but… and Brian… If I'd just—"

"There's no maybe, don't you see?"

"Still, there must… What else could I have done?" He broke into sobs.

She wrapped him in her arms.

When his crying eased, she placed his hand on her breast. "Can you feel my heart, Will? It's the love I have for you, gives it strength to beat. Would it beat so if you'd done wrong?"

She stood on her toes, and kissed his forehead and eyes. She wound her arms around his neck and covered his lips with hers.

His body responded. She felt his hardness when he pulled her close. A groan rose from his throat. He buried his face in her red hair, then laid her gently on the sand. In the shadow of Charlie's cat-ketch, he fumbled with her blouse. She barely felt the pebbles scrape her back when he rolled onto her and began to explore each part of her body.

She arched her spine. "Let go of it, Will. Let me take the aching from you."

While his tongue traced the length of her thin neck, she guided him into her. Hips raised and gently swaying, she drew him deeper inside. A tingling grew in her vagina, rushed down her thighs to her knees, to her feet. The evening exploded. Pin-lights like a million stars filled the sky. Never had she felt such joy.

***

For a minute, Abigail sat quietly. She hadn't blushed while she spoke of making love to Will, though her face appeared warm from the memory.

Finally she went on to tell me how she spoke with Will night after night on the beach while he struggled against his inner devil, and she made love to him each time. Armed with what could only be an instinctive knowledge of the heart, she led him from the cave of his private hell.

Brian and Charlie couldn't help, she told me. When shock at seeing the slave-hunters' violent end wore off, they were filled with gratitude to Will for their deliverance. They wanted to celebrate their friend as a hero, wanted Will to go to the Angel Inn with them while they did. They couldn't understand why he refused to toast the glory of that night on the Niagara's bank.

Nor, Abigail said, could Will's parents provide the needed comfort. He refused to tell them what he'd done. Cut off from everyone else, it seemed as though he could only find peace of mind in Abigail's embrace.

Though she wasn't present when Will told his parents of her, she knew of it because she'd often watched the scene through her window. Having witnessed what her window could show, I didn't question the veracity of her recollection.

"Mother Bender called me an urchin of the Dock." Abigail laughed. "Early on, Mother Bender didn't try to come between Will and me. One day she even told Father Bender she was grateful for our friendship—what she actually said was, 'The only time our son smiles is when he's with that unkempt urchin.' When a few months later Will told her he intended to marry me, Mother Bender stopped being so kind."

As I listened to Abigail's words, the careful way she described everything, I had no trouble forming a mental picture of what occurred.

***

The Benders sat in what was now the carefully manicured garden behind their brick house. Red roses grew along a latticework trellis. Lilacs lined the cobbled path. A pitcher and glasses of lemonade were on a wicker table between George and Elizabeth. Will sat slightly apart from them.

In that peaceful haven, Elizabeth Bender bristled. "Spending time with an urchin as a friend is one thing—she's a nice enough child, I suppose. But she's from the *Dock*. To think she might be part of our family— Well! Mr. Bender, tell the boy."

"Now, Mrs. Bender, our son loves her," George said. "I don't see what's wrong."

"You don't? I'm surprised at you. How can you not see our son and that… that urchin could never be happy?"

Will sprang from his seat. His hands clasped behind his back, he paced along the cobblestones. When Elizabeth at last stopped complaining, he turned to her, eyes cold. "It's a different place we live in, Mother. This isn't Erie. Those silly notions you hold dear don't apply here."

She gasped. "How dare you speak to your mother like… like a guttersnipe? You see, George? You see what comes from hanging about with… with…" She raised her painted Japanese fan and waved it rapidly.

"Mother, your act is quite old," Will said. "You can faint or not. It won't change my mind about marrying Abbie."

Elizabeth clutched the fan to her chest. "How can you let the boy speak to me in such a fashion? Talk to him, George. Tell him!"

George Bender had retreated to a corner of the garden when his wife began to rant. In the shade of an elm, he smiled. "The boy is at last behaving like a man," he said. He returned to the table and moved a wicker chair next to his wife. "I can't scold him, Mrs. Bender. The lad is quite right in this."

Her lips in a tight thin line, Elizabeth glared at her husband, at her son. When they didn't melt from the heat of her stare, she heaved a melodramatic sigh. With a swish of skirts, she stormed into the house, muttering, "Taking up with a girl so far beneath his station, it's the end of civilization, *that's* what it is."

Elizabeth Bender now punished her wrong-headed men with silence. She turned her back when they spoke to her during the next two days and primly sought solitude in another room. Later, when they spoke of that time, Will told Abbie that his mother's resistance was comparatively light. In Erie, she would have resolutely put down her tiny foot without a thought to whose neck it crushed. Will would have been made to understand what such an ill-conceived match would do to the family's social position. But in living three years in Niagara-on-the-Lake, without friends of her class to support and encourage her elitist attitude, she had begun to mellow. Then, after having tea with Tom Burke—the acknowledged leader of local society—she ceased any attempt to curtail the relationship. In fact, by the time Mr. Burke departed, she gave the marriage her blessing.

Again, Abigail described the scene in detail:

After less than an hour in her sitting room with Tom Burke, Elizabeth sighed. "I suppose if it must be, I shan't try to prevent it."

The old man adjusted his spectacles and patted her hand. "I believe you're being wise, Elizabeth. Why, looked at the right way around, a wedding between Will and Abbie will do more for your social standing here than anything. It'll open a whole avenue of new friendships." He fluffed his white beard. "I suspect the result of those friendships will be the glorious success of George's haberdashery—I don't have to tell you how a woman's gentle approval can influence her husband's sense of fashion. You might even find women coming to you for advice on social matters."

Her eyes fluttering, Elizabeth nearly cooed. "Do you really think so, Mr. Burke?" Carefully she replaced her dainty tea cup in its saucer and rested it on the table at her side.

He took her hands. In the heavy tone of an oracle, he pronounced, "I see that happening, yes, I do. And if we're to be great friends, Elizabeth, if I'm to help you in this, you must call me Tom."

She blushed. "Why, of course… Tom. Let me pour you another cup of tea. Perhaps we might discuss arrangements for the children's wedding. You take sugar with your tea, as I recall."

Though he'd been drinking his tea unsweetened, he said, "How kind of you to remember, Elizabeth. Yes, a spoon of sugar will be fine."

She lifted the delicate white china teapot with red roses painted around it. While she poured, she said, "You know, Tom, when I think about it, Abbie Kirby seems remarkably well mannered for a child who hasn't had the benefit of proper training."

He turned his face. From the growing redness on his cheeks, he might have strained to hold a leash on his laughter. When he looked again at Elizabeth his smile betrayed no hint of his thoughts. "I'm sure you'll be able to train Abbie properly."

"Yes, yes," she agreed. "The girl might be the perfect clay for me to mold."

***

Abigail left Elizabeth Bender and Tom Burke at the tea table, and in words, she painted another scene.

She said, "I wonder what Mother Bender would've said if she'd known word of me and Will planning to wed was not welcome to my mother, either, and it was *Will's* character Ma questioned. You see, Kaitlyn, it was impossible Brinny could keep his wound secret for long—not once Da saw how he winced and favored his side the day after the shootings at Tryon's Folly."

Her father pressed Brian about his injury, and soon the entire episode came out. Then her father told Abbie's mother. Her explosion came that night when they gathered around the kitchen table in the candlelight.

With the hem of her apron, Mary rubbed an imaginary spot on the table. "I knew from the beginning the Bender boy would lead our Brian into danger," she grumbled. "I told you that, didn't I, Sean? Didn't I say that?"

A summer evening, no fire burned in the hearth, yet Mary's face flushed as if she stood in front of a flame. Abbie hooded her eyes. Brian twisted in his chair.

"No, wife, I don't recall as you did say that." Smiling indulgently, Sean Kirby lifted a candle and lit his pipe.

"Then I should've warned you, because I knew right off. When Brian came home talking about this new friend like he was the beginning and the end—well, I knew it would bring him nothing but trouble."

Sean moved closer to his wife and wrapped a

calming arm around her. "I think you're wrong there, Mary. Our Brian and Charlie Bolton would've been making them runs even if the Bender lad had never joined them. And think on it, woman. If the lad hadn't been there to save them—"

Mary Kirby snorted, as if to say anything her husband argued would be fit only for the rubbish heap outside of town.

She did the same thing a few weeks later when Abbie stated she intended to be courted by Will Bender. As soon as those words were spoken, Mary turned on her daughter.

"Not if I've a word in it!" she said. "A boy who could do something like that—"

Dinner had been cleared. With no fire in the hearth or stove, the Kirby's living space was lit only by fading daylight that leaked through the two windows at the front of their cottage.

Her hands on her hips, Abbie stared her mother. "Like what, Ma? Brinny's life was lost. Will gave it back. That's what *that* boy did."

"The girl's got a point there, wife," Sean Kirby said from the seat he's taken at the far end of the table.

"Sure, go defending her, would you. I know what I know, and I won't permit it!" Standing above her husband's chair, Mary waved a wooden spoon to emphasize each phrase.

"How do you expect you'll keep me from seeing him? I'm a grown enough woman to do as I please," Abbie said.

Mary raised a hand as if to strike her daughter. "Don't you be talking to me in such a way, Abbie Kirby. Me who gave you life—"

"Will gave my brother *back* his life, or do you choose to forget that?"

Brian rose from his chair. His hands on the table, he

leaned toward his mother. "The girl's right, Ma, Will Bender did that for sure. Without him there to do it, I'd not be in this kitchen listening to you disparage his name."

Mary looked to her husband. "Tell them, Sean. Tell them I'm right in this."

"I can't, wife—not when I know you're being foolish for no reason." He sat back and sucked on his pipe.

Her wooden spoon pointed ominously in the direction of each in turn, Mary said, "All right, then, the lot of you. Have it your way if you will. But *you'll* see I'm right."

The spoon clattered as she threw it on the table and stormed to her bedroom. Before she slammed the door, she turned and said, "One day you will. Oh, yes, when fate demands payment for what the boy's done, you'll see!"

Days later, when Abbie informed her parents she'd agreed to marry Will Bender, Mary's temper again raged.

Standing near the dead hearth, her eyes burning like the glow of molten coals, Mary shouted, "I'll not have it!"

"He asked me, and I said I would," Abbie said.

Mary untied her apron and threw it to the floor. "You'll not!"

Brian glanced at his father. In the presence of two angry women, both were wise enough to remain still.

Nose-to-nose with her mother, her eyes aflame with equal heat, Abbie said, "I'll marry Will Bender and no one else! And if I haven't your blessing in this, I will anyway and you'll never see your grandchildren."

"Abbie Kirby! You're not—" Mary gasped. From the way she shuddered, death's fingers might have been running along her spine.

"No, Ma, not yet I'm not," Abbie said. "But Will and me'll be married, and I *will* be with his babe one day. So if you've any hope of seeing a grandchild grow in my belly, you'll be there to witness me wed."

Mary turned away from her willful child. Through

moans and sighs, she mumbled a soliloquy to the stucco wall: "What can be done if no one but me sees danger lurk? Fate won't be kind to the lass if she gives her life to that boy. It won't! Still, could it be fate's decree that she must wed him first, then find it so?"

She turned back to her family with sad acceptance on her face. No enthusiasm in her voice, she said, "If it's to be, I'll be there to see you wed, daughter."

Abbie hugged her. "Thank you, Ma."

Sean Kirby clapped his hands. "It isn't every day a man hears his daughter will be a wife. This calls for a toast. Brian, bring the bottle."

Drinks poured, the Kirby family raised their glasses. Three among them joyously saluted life. Not Mary, though. Her face was so pinched that in the wine, she might have tasted a blood sacrifice to a demon god.

Chapter Twenty-Four
Wedding Plans

Now Abigail described another scene.

Her wedding to Will was planned for September. Over the preceding two months, influenced by the love the young couple clearly had for each other, Tom Burke sought ways to bring the two families together. At his urging, Elizabeth Bender sent a note across the Common to invite Mary Kirby for tea.

Elizabeth opened her arms in a sisterly greeting when her future in-law was shown into the sitting room of the brick house. "I did so want to meet you, Mrs. Kirby," she said. "If our children are to be married, it seems best you and I be friends."

Unable to hide her curiosity, Mary examined the room which accounted for a third of the Bender home's second story. China vases and statuettes crowded the floor. Wandering Jew crawled along the walls, and ivy draped its tendrils over heavy loveseats, armchairs and tables.

Perching on a corner of a loveseat, Mary brushed at her sleeves and skirt. "I came because Tom Burke said I must. But I thank you for asking me."

Elizabeth settled daintily in an armchair across from her guest. With a polite, if distant smile, she replied, "And I asked you because Tom insisted I should. But I am indeed glad you could come."

The hoop of Elizabeth's skirt knocked against a leg of the low table separating the two women. She rose slightly and pushed back her chair. Now she had to stretch uncomfortably forward to pour their tea. The delicate cups filled, she sat back. With her cup and saucer balanced on a knee, she patted her lace cap. "We really should make a habit of this," she said. "Maybe next time I'll visit you."

"Ah, and that would be pleasant. Stop by any time you find yourself in the Dock." Mary glanced around, as if to calculate how different would be a visit in her modest kitchen with its bare walls and open hearth.

"Yes, of course. I'll be certain to," Elizabeth said. "Today I thought we might talk about the wedding. I think we could hold it outdoors on the Common."

Mary laughed. "Have you not seen the Common, then? I don't think many would find the footing suited to celebrating on. It'd be better to have it at the church."

"Fine, fine. I'll talk to Father Francis." As if to show magnanimity, Elizabeth Bender suggested the nuptials take place where the Kirbys worshipped.

Mary sighed. "Abbie says they've asked Minister Cox to marry them." The shrug of her shoulders asked what could be done with young people who are determined to have things their own way.

In the nature of their relationships with their children, Mrs. Bender and Mrs. Kirby at last found common ground. "I do understand," Elizabeth said. "It's not easy, knowing what to do when they grow up."

Mary nodded. "You're certainly right in that. Especially when my Sean refuses to appreciate why I worry so."

"There *is* so much worrying a mother does, isn't there?" Elizabeth said. "My husband's no help to me, either. Why, when Will was young and fell from the roof of our porch while trying to catch a bird, George scolded me for fretting. 'He's just being a boy, Mrs. Bender, stop fussing over him,' he said."

"That's nothing. Once when my Abbie was young—couldn't have been more than eight—I caught her trying to swim out to Sean's boat one morning. And Sean, he says to me, 'If the lass wants to come along for the fishing, Mary, let her. I've taught her how to swim.'"

Laughing through these small remembrances, the women soon had tears in their eyes.

"May the good Lord watch over them both, I canna see how a mother can," Mary said a while later. She took the last sip of her tea and glanced at her hostess. "Shall I pour us another cup, Beth? I find I'm enjoying this talk with you."

By the time Mary Kirby left, the difference in the women's backgrounds, the way they dressed, the surroundings in which they dwelt, seemed less important. It seemed the recognition of a mother's love stretched across the Common in the same way Will and Abbie's passion for each other did.

***

While the women shared their tea, Sean persuaded George Bender to close his shop early and join him at the Angel Inn. There, he introduced his future in-law to the Dock and Irishtown when he called, "Drinks for all!"

Abigail described the Angel Inn as a modest colonial building on the corner of Market Street. Yellow clapboard walls broken by windows with white shutters rose two floors to a wood-shingled roof. A bar just inside the front door divided the ground floor into two rooms. As they entered, Sean Kirby draped an arm across George's shoulder and steered him toward the larger room.

"Drinks for all," he called a second time.

"And what'd be making you so free with your money this day, Sean Kirby?" someone said from a table in the corner.

"I'm here with my new friend George, Jack Boyle, to thank him for having a fine son like his Will."

"Why would that be?" Harold Clement appeared ready to show gratitude if it meant a free drink.

"Haven't you heard? The lad's gonna marry my

Abbie," Sean said with a great grin.

More than a dozen men gathered around to pat George and Sean on their backs.

"That's fine!" someone called out.

Another raised his glass. "It's far better news than a shipwreck on the lake."

"It's surely that," Sean agreed.

"Are you celebrating something without inviting me?" Tom Burke asked when he walked through the door an hour later.

"We are indeed. We're here to celeb… cel… raise a few glasses," George slurred. His face was as red as Sean's. "T'day marks the joining of the Benders and Kirbys." He reached out a hand. "'N 'cause I s'pect, Tom Burke, your talk with my wife had something to do with it, c'mere and raise a glass with us."

Burke slapped both men's backs. "I'm glad if it did. And because it might have, all the drinks this fine afternoon are on me."

As a new round was passed, Tom Burke led Sean and George to a table by the window. There they sat while one well-wisher after another came by to salute them with whisky or beer. As he introduced each to George, old Tom said, "This is the man I told you about. George Bender. He's the one opened that fine shop on Victoria Street."

And each in turn replied, "Is he now? It's a good time to stop there, then. I'll be needing something fine and new for the wedding."

The party broke up at supper time, and George stumbled home with an open collar and florid face.

"You appear to be a bit drunk, Mr. Bender," Elizabeth remarked prissily when her husband slid into his place at the table's head.

Will snickered. Abigail, who had been asked to dine with them, sat up straight in her smocked dress, straining to keep a smile from her face.

"Drunk? I am indeed, Mrs. Bender," George said. "And I must say I had a fine time getting this way."

***

In July and August, Abbie was a frequent visitor at the brick house on Victoria Street. Elizabeth seemed to enjoy telling her about the fine pioneer stock she was about to marry into. She also spoke about life in Erie, and Will as a child who always found his way into mischief.

"I swear to you, Abbie, the ceilings weren't high enough to contain my son." Elizabeth adjusted the ribbons on her lace cap. "And curious? Each time I turned around, he'd pulled everything out of the cupboards and spread it across the floor. If there was a crate in the back of Mr. Bender's shop, young Will soon thought of how to get into it. And there was his fishing." She raised her arms in mock despair. "Why, I felt as though every day I'd be visited by Will's schoolmaster, who complained my son convinced his friends to play hooky and go out on Lake Erie."

Abbie looked forward to those times, because Elizabeth Bender dropped her veil of proper constraint and laughed easily. "You do truly love him as much as I do," Elizabeth would remark when Abbie's face lit at the mere mention of Will's name. She sounded less surprised each time she said it.

Then there was the time Elizabeth learned Abbie had an inquisitive mind of her own. She discovered this on a day she walked into the sitting room to find her future daughter-in-law quietly reading a volume George had left on a table.

Elizabeth once told Abigail her mother taught her the precepts of a proper wife: to play the piano, sew, speak a little French, and manage a quiet, efficient household for her husband. She'd also been taught to be virtuous, dutiful, and devoid of intellectual opinion. When she read, it was from some light romance. George wouldn't waste his time on such trivialities, and Elizabeth longed for a friend with whom to discuss those stories. So when she saw Abbie engrossed in the book, she watched from the doorway.

"What is it you have there?" she asked after a few minutes.

"I-I'm sorry to have taken this without asking first," Abbie said.

Elizabeth patted the girl's arm. "Not at all, child. It's fine you did. Which book is it?"

"*The Critique of Pure Reason*." Abbie closed the leather-bound volume and showed its spine.

"Immanuel Kant?" Elizabeth's eyes widened. "Do you understand what he says?"

"I'm trying to. I think he's saying there's only so much anyone can know about this world."

The older woman laughed. "My dear, I don't think my son fully realizes what he's gotten himself into this time." When Abbie handed back the book, Elizabeth insisted, "No, no, child, keep it. I'm sure Mr. Bender will enjoy discussing it with you."

Over time, it became quite apparent that Elizabeth relished the idea of a daughter to spoil. Frequently, when Abigail left, she carried with her a gift of clothing or a trinket of some kind. One day as the wedding drew near, Elizabeth gave her the published parts of what would become Isabella Beeton's *Book of Household Management*. At the time it was a pleasant, if useless gift, because, as Abigail told it, she and Will hadn't yet considered where they'd live. Elizabeth presumed the children would reside with her and George at first. But, as if he intended to separate old ideas from new, Tom Burke had in mind a gift which dispelled this fantasy.

At the wedding feast, Mr. Burke toasted the bride and groom. As he stood between them, their hands joined by his, he announced, "I've tried to think of the perfect thing to mark the union of this young couple. I wanted it to symbolize the same link between the Dock and Town this marriage does." Thumbs in his waistcoat pockets and rocking back and forth on his heels, he took a dramatic pause. "At last I have it. Will, I recently acquired a house on the corner of Prideaux and Victoria Streets—a place the sections meet. It was a bakeshop at one time, and I could swear I smell bread baking when I walk in there. That's a fine aroma for a good house to have. The house is yours, my boy, for as long as you care to live there."

Burke blushed through his gray beard when Abigail threw her arms around his neck and kissed his cheek. Holding her new husband's hand, a glow of joy in her green eyes, she said, "If we're to live in such a fine house for long as I'll love Will Bender, then the world will end long before we move out."

Chapter Twenty-Five
Senatus Populusque Romanus

An expression of pleasure filled Abigail's face. As if drawn to it, she moved from my bed to the window seat and pressed her face against the panes. I thought she must be watching her wedding out there.

I searched for a similar joy in my life. My eyes closed, I let my mind wander back to Barry, my first flame, high school sweetheart, my husband for a while. Had I ever loved him the way Abigail loved Will? Had I ever loved him at all? Ronnie was right when she said I hadn't. In the dark and the quiet of my Niagara Inn room, I had to admit that marrying Barry had been just an item to be checked off my list of things required for a successful life. My husband left me because he wanted more, deserved more than I had in me to give. I considered what Abigail had found with Will. For the briefest moment, I wondered if something was wrong with me that I wasn't able to be the wife Barry wanted. But then I thought, *what nonsense*. Before we got married, we'd been together long enough for him to realize I couldn't. Wouldn't. After all, a woman losing herself in her husband was so… retro. So nineteen-fifties. I never wanted that, didn't need it. Submerging my life in a husband wasn't on my list. I was a career woman, self-sufficient. I worked hard to get to the point at which a partnership at Cowan and Fine was in the offing—

It struck me then that thoughts of Barry might have gotten mixed into what frightened me about Richard. *It's the same thing*, I argued to my memory. *Richard's known me long enough to understand what I find important.*

When I had followed my line of thought to its end, I

said, "I think love like you and Will had belongs to another time, Abigail. Women today have evolved past such passion. I'm right, aren't I? You've seen how relationships have changed in the last century."

She didn't respond.

I opened my eyes. I was again alone.

She must be seeing to something, I thought, and vaguely wondered what might busy a ghost. Whatever took her from the room, I was satisfied she'd soon return to finish her story. Though her romance with Will might be an antique of a time I had no desire to live in, the idea of a strong woman's love for a daring man who showed the same passion for her captivated me. I'd never known such a man. But, would I have noticed if I did?

All at once I felt very alone. "Abigail," I called out. The word seemed to resound in my room. "Abbie, don't leave me!"

I heard her disembodied voice say, "Would I be deserting a friend? I'll be there soon. Meantime, you were thinking of someone."

"Barry?"

After a moment of silence, she said, "Not him, the other."

I wrinkled my nose. "Richard? What's he got to do with anything?"

"You tell me," her voice answered. "It's him you're fretting over."

"It isn't!"

I heard her sigh. "Will you *never* stop arguing? I said you are, and you know it's true. Don't deny it."

I was about to, vehemently, when she asked, "What did he do to scare you so that you're running for your life?"

Her question rankled. "How many times do I have to tell you? I'm not—"

"You can say it for as long as I've been condemned to this room. It still won't make the lie true." Again she sighed. "Humor me. I've shown you so much of me, tell me this of you. Why did you run from him?"

I leaned on an elbow. "Truth or dare, huh?"

"Truth or…?"

I smiled. "Yeah, it's a game where—" I rolled my eyes. "Forget it. Doesn't matter. And there's nothing to tell. Richard doesn't scare me."

"Tell me anyway. Something made you run—I can feel it in you."

Abigail was right, of course, as she had been about so much. Still, I refused to give in. "It wasn't Richard, it was—" Shuddering, I remembered a night last week. "I was happy being with him until—"

"Tell me," she said again, no playfulness in her voice.

I didn't want to tell her. Moments of happiness never lasted, and remembering my small portions of it—After they were stolen from me, I found thoughts of them unbearable. My lips tight, I muttered, "Why are you doing this to me?"

"Remember!" Abigail demanded.

I attempted to hide the memory beneath others. But the ghost had again taken control of my will. Even when she wasn't present, she seemed able to strip it away. At her command, I grew too weary to fend off the image of a taxi pulling to the curb in front of SPQR.

Abigail's voice sang like a Siren in my mind. *Don't fight the memory. Tell me.*

The Devil lives in the details. The ghost's insistence forced me to recall every one of them.

As if in a dream, I saw Richard shove aside the tails of his overcoat and fumble with his wallet. Though we'd ridden only a few miles, he handed the driver twenty dollars.

***

"That's a bit much for tip, don't you think?" I whispered as he reached back to help me from the cab.

"A tip? Oh, that's right… need to tip the driver." He pulled another bill from his wallet.

I covered it with my hand. "Richard, you've already given him far too much."

When he looked at me, his eyes seemed to be unfocused. "Uh, yes, that's… true. Still, you know what Aristotle would have said—"

I tugged at his arm. "It's cold out here. Tell me inside."

Stammering about this wasn't at all like Richard. I wondered if he was getting ready to break up with me.

The maitre d' rushed over when we came through the door. "Ah, Dr. Slattery, Ms. Novacs, you've made it. I've held the table you asked for."

Richard had asked for a table? He hadn't said he wanted go out to dinner until half an hour ago.

We were led to same table we sat at after the Cowen and Fine Christmas party. It was in a corner, beneath the mural of the Roman Forum. Richard dug into his pocket and slipped something into the maitre d's hand.

"Another tip?" I said. "What's with you?"

The dining room was crowded for a Sunday night. Waiters in starched white shirts and black trousers hurried between tables, taking orders, sliding meals in front of customers. The clink of knives and forks on sturdy china added to the din of forty conversations. In the midst of this chaos, Richard mumbled, "Wrong with me? Nothing… Uh, I'll tell you later." He tried to smile, but his lips didn't quite make it.

The waiter brought us glasses of wine. Richard swallowed half of his in a single gulp, then stared into his glass. "I-I've been thinking—"

I shuddered. His thoughts had a habit of putting me

in uncomfortable places.

"—and I've concluded it's a very logical thing for us to do. Kaitlyn, we're not children anymore. As Epicurus wrote… Uh, or was it Demosthenes—"

I started to ask where he was going with this, but he stopped me with a raised hand. "No, no, wait. Let me explain." He hurried off on a tangent.

While I sipped my wine, I inspected the mural behind him. The men scattered through it wore togas. I considered how Richard might look in one—he certainly had the legs for it. My eyes crinkled and my lips turned up. I raised my glass to toast his legs.

When I focused again, I heard him say, "—and Samuel Richardson wrote that marriage is the highest state of—'

My fork clattered on my plate. "Richard, stop!" I sat back.

He leaned forward. "I'm only trying to explain—"

My stomach felt as though it were tied in one big knot. I leaned across the table. "Richard—"

He sat back. "—the contract between a man and a woman—"

"Slow down, cowboy," I said. "Marriage isn't a contract."

His eyes took on a far-off look. "Well, in a sense it *is* a contract. Remember that as late as the nineteenth century—"

The knot in my stomach tightened. The last thing I wanted from him was a history lesson. No, the last thing was to have him propose. And, to have a proposal mixed into a history lesson… I had a life-plan. Another wedding? Definitely not on my list. I had to stop him before he ruined everything.

Thinking quickly, I threw a quote at him. "In the *Remarkable Andrew*, William Holden said 'A good businessman never makes a contract unless he's sure he can carry it out, but every fool on earth will sign a marriage contract without considering whether he can live up to it.'"

"No, no, I can… we can. That is, I thought—"

I wiggled my fingers to suggest Groucho Marx's cigar. "And what about the contract's sanity clause?"

He grabbed my hand. "Can you please be serious?" He sounded annoyed.

Annoyed is what I wanted him to be. Anger would be a distraction.

I pulled my hand away. When he reached for it again, I dropped it on my lap and twisted the tiny beads on my evening bag.

"Kaitlyn, I'm trying to ask you to—"

"Don't," I whispered.

He stopped.

All at once the horrible hoarse laughter filled the restaurant. It mocked me. I slid as far back in my chair as I could. A strand on my bag broke. Small beads scattered on the floor.

Richard opened his mouth—

As I recalled the restaurant, the laughter, the tiny glass beads bouncing on the carpeted floor, I began to shake in my Niagara Inn bed. I felt as though I were locked in a dream in which I fell into Richard's open mouth. "No, no, no! Don't! Please, please don't ask me," I cried.

Abigail's voice pulled me back. "Do you love him?"

I clutched the bedcovers. "Do I…?"

"It's a simple enough question," she said.

It wasn't. "I love him. Of course I do… in my way."

I heard her laugh. "What does that mean?"

I'd been so busy skipping though life, skirting serious relationships, I hadn't thought about what *my way* meant. Now I tried to make Abigail—or perhaps myself—understand. "I felt comfortable with him. We were together when I wanted to be, apart when I needed my own space."

"What did he want?" she asked.

"He was fine with it… Well, if he wasn't, he never said anything. But he changed after we had dinner at the Hoffmanns' apartment. When I was too busy or tired to see him for a few days, he wanted to know why. Wasn't I happy with him? Then at the restaurant, he wanted to ask for more—a lifetime of more. After Barry… I couldn't—*wouldn't*—promise that to anyone."

"Why?"

I didn't answer.

"When he started to propose, you thought about the sanatorium and what brought you to it," Abigail said. "What happened when he gave you the ring you keep trying to twist off?"

My mind returned to SPQR. I smelled the richness of the food, the earthy spices. I heard dishes clatter, heard an undercurrent of voices around me. I saw Richard's lips moving. With the laughter echoing in my ears, I couldn't hear what he said. I reached for my wineglass. When I lifted it, drops of red spilled over the rim. I wondered if the ground were shaking, then realized it was my hand.

I rose from my chair. "Excuse me a minute. Too much wine. Need to use the ladies'—"

Richard stopped me with a look so intense it weakened my knees. "I know what you've been through," he said. "I won't let that happen to you again. I'll never let anything bad happen to you. I'll write that down, have it notarized. Kaitlyn, I adore you. Please, marry me."

The dreaded words had escaped, couldn't be retrieved. I knew what I had to do—it would only require a few boxes and one trip to remove my things from his apartment. I glanced at him. He looked so hopeful while he waited for my answer. He would be shattered when I said no. I wouldn't do that to him in front of all those people.

I scanned the room. Still half-risen, I pointed. "Oh, look. Over there—third table from the door—isn't that the mayor?"

Again I failed to distract him. In a stage whisper, he recited a Browning verse: "*I love you as freely as men strive for right; I love you purely, as they turn from praise; I love you with the passion put to use in my old griefs.*"

I fell back into my chair.

"Marry me," he said again.

The kitchen doors swung open, waiters scurried in and out. New customers were seated, others rose to leave. Outside, the temperature was below freezing. In the restaurant, heat shot to my head. "Gotta get out of here." I grabbed for my purse.

Our waiter dashed over. Instead of handing Richard the bill, he put a dish of chocolate mousse in front of me. A thin ladyfinger rested next to the pudding. An engagement ring circled the lady finger. People at other tables stood and applauded. The maitre d' scampered over with a bottle of champagne. "On the house," he said.

Cold sweat broke out across my forehead. I fanned my face with a napkin. The air felt as thick as mud. I could hardly breathe. I stammered, "Richard, I-I..."

He took my hand and slid the ring onto my finger. "I don't ever want to be without you."

I heard the laughter again, this time behind me, low, wheezing. The sound of it reminded me I wasn't to be allowed this happiness. Panicked, blinking rapidly, I dropped my hands under the table, struggling to remove the ring. I had to get it off, give it back. My finger had swollen around it. The damn ring wouldn't budge.

Now the laughter surrounded me, a sound so loud and clear. How come no one else heard it?

***

When I finished telling Abigail about the night I got engaged, I was panting.

"It's then you lost your appetite," she said.

How could she know?

"You're not as complicated as you think," she said. "It's love you're afraid of. Fate led you to this house to escape that fear's grip."

I yanked the quilt up to my neck. "Fate didn't bring me here! I told you, Ronnie kidnapped me. I planned to go somewhere much further away. Los Angeles is a place where love comes easy and walking away from it is easier still. When this weekend is over, I'm moving to Los Angeles.

"Do you think what you fear won't find you there?"

"If it does, I'll go somewhere else—to Tahiti, if I have to."

"Uh-huh," Abigail said.

"I would! That's what I tried to tell Ronnie Hoffmann the day after Richard gave me this ring."

Another memory flashed through my mind.

***

Ronnie and I were having lunch at an East Side deli. When the waiter brought my corned beef sandwich, Ronnie said, "You don't look right. You're just nibbling at your meal. And why are your gloves still on?"

"I have a rash."

My voice must have been very loud, because she said, "Hey, don't snap at me, girlfriend. Whatever's eating you, I'm on your side."

"Nothing's wrong." To prove it, I took a bite of my sandwich. My mouth dry, I couldn't swallow. I spit the chewed food into a paper napkin and started to cry.

"Nothing wrong, huh?" Ronnie said. "Okay, start talking."

I wiped my eyes with a napkin Ronnie took from another table. "Richard spoiled everything."

"What? How? Did he break up with you?" The way she held her knife and fork, she looked as though she'd cut him into little pieces if he had.

I pulled the gloves off my hands and showed her my finger. "He wants to get married."

She gasped. "He certainly does. Look at the size of that stone."

I blew my nose. "Don't get comfortable with the idea you're about to be a matron of honor. I won't marry him."

"What? Why not?" It sounded as though she couldn't believe I could be such an idiot. "You practically live together already. How would being married make a difference?"

"Don't know. Just will."

"Oh, come on. Think! There's something you're not telling me."

I didn't want to tell her, but found it impossible to hold in. "It's… the damn ghost!"

Ronnie sat up so straight I thought she might jump from her seat. "The what?" She leaned across the table. "There *is* no ghost. It's just in your mind. Dr. Carver explained to you why you made it up."

"It's real! I heard it again last night when Richard gave me this. Something horrible will happen if I marry him. Maybe another— " I shook my head. "That's what the damn ghost wants." I tried to twist the ring. "It made my finger swell or something. See, I can't get it off. I've tried soaking my hand in soap… Nothing works. My house wasn't haunted, Ronnie. It's me!"

She dug in her bag for her cell phone. "I'm calling Dr. Carver. He'll—"

I grabbed the phone. "No! Can't let them lock me up again. I won't live through it this time. Ronnie, I've got to get out of here!"

She took my hands. Gently, as if soothing a wild woman, she said, "Good idea. Go home. I'll go with you. You'll feel better after you rest awhile."

I shoved back my chair. "I'm going, but not home."

She stared at me as if she had no idea what to do next. “Where, then?”

“California. Los Angeles,” I said. “I thought about it all night. My firm opened a new office there.”

“The hell you are!” She grabbed my shoulders. “You’re running away again, like Dr. Carver said you did when you lost the baby.”

Right then Ronnie decided to kidnap me. She and Andrea had already booked rooms at the Niagara Inn—

The vision faded.

“She made me come with them.” I told Abigail. “Stayed with me in my apartment the rest of the week to make sure I couldn’t get away.” I waited for her to say something. When she didn’t, I said, “So you’re wrong about why I’m here.”

Still no answer.

“California,” I whispered, and thought, *or maybe further. Maybe... all the way into...*

The silence was total, the darkness in the room complete. Fine with me. Truth be told, it’s what I wanted. No need to run anymore… Or fight… Fright… So tired… Just float… away…

I heard a cruel laugh. When it stopped, Abigail said, “If that’s what you truly want.”

Chapter Twenty-Six
Filling the Gaps

I felt as though I was drifting far from where I lay in bed. Against a background of an infant's cries, I heard snippets of conversation. People sounded concerned.

"Getting worse—"

"My God, she's hardly—"

"Call the doctor!"

I heard running in the hall and up the stairs.

Someone shouted, "He'll be here soon!"

"Let him look at her," came next.

I felt something cold pressed against my chest.

"—isn't good—"

"Get her there!"

From everyone's tone, I thought I ought to be worried. I didn't care enough to get up and find out what the fuss was about.

I learned what went on later when I overheard Ronnie and Andrea talking.

***

Concerned by my shallow breathing, Ronnie tried to shake me awake. When I failed to respond, she leaned over my bed then quickly pulled back. Apparently, I looked like the picture of an unwrapped mummy she once saw in *National Geographic*: my face had no color, my eyes were sunken and my skin seemed to be pulled taut on my skull. I looked like her mother had just before the doctor turned off the respirator the day she died of cancer. When my friend saw me in this condition she howled, afraid I'd left her too. She realized I wasn't dead yet when my lips moved as if I were speaking.

"Andi, get in here!" she shouted.

Andrea ran down the hall. She nearly fainted when she poked her head into my room. "Ohmigod, ohmigod!" she cried.

Ronnie grabbed her. "Tell Mrs. Hughes to call that doctor. Now!"

Leah Campbell hovered in the hall, craning her neck around the doorframe. "Christ protect me from Satan's evil," she muttered. "This is just like what people say happened to that other one."

For a minute Ronnie believed the grizzled old housekeeper had put some kind of curse on me and that I was dying because of it. "Damn you! Get out of here, you witch," she hollered. "Get that idiot out of here before she does any more harm!"

Andrea latched onto the housekeeper's bony arm, yanked her from the room and dragged her down the stairs. When Andrea returned, Mrs. Hughes came with her.

"Dr. Early's on his way," the innkeeper said.

Ronnie sat on the bed beside me. Though I didn't feel her do it, now and then she rubbed my hands. Once she shook me and cried, "Come on, open your eyes. You're gonna be okay. Come on, dammit! I'm stronger than you are. I didn't let you get away the last time, and I'm not gonna let you go now."

At last the doctor arrived.

"I see, yes, I see," he said when he walked into the room.

He felt my forehead, then checked my pulse. He pulled a stethoscope from his bag and held it to my chest. "This isn't good—much worse than I had any reason to expect. She should be in the hospital."

Ronnie spewed anger at him. "What's wrong with you? Get her there!"

He unwound his wire-rim glasses from his ears and

stared out the window. "Wish I could. Everything's shut down in this blizzard. Can't drive two blocks without skidding off the road." He turned to the innkeeper. "Fact is, Naomi, I can't even get home. I'll have to stay here until the weather breaks."

"What about Katy?" Ronnie demanded.

He patted her arm. "Yes, yes. I'll do what I can to make the poor girl comfortable until…"

Ronnie understood what the doctor left out. She leaned over his shoulder while he continued his examination.

Dr. Early told Mrs. Hughes to take Ronnie downstairs and give her something to drink—something very strong.

"You've gotta let the doctor work," Andrea said.

Ronnie refused to budge. "I've got to be with her. Can't any of you understand? I won't let her die with only strangers around."

Mrs. Hughes wrapped my friend in her arms. "Dear, please, you *must* let the doctor look after her." She led Ronnie to the door and told Andrea, "Dr. Early's right. There's a bottle of brandy in the parlor. Both of you take some of it."

When Ronnie resisted, Andrea said, "Come with me. You've gotta call Richard."

"I forgot about him," Ronnie said. "He'll never forgive me for letting this happen. What'll I tell him?"

"Tell him to get up here so he can be with her when… at the end," Andrea said. "He'll hate you if you don't give him that chance."

Ronnie yanked her hair. "And Ken—he'll hate me, too. He told me to let Katy and Richard work things out. Don't interfere, he said, they love each other, they'll figure it out. I screwed things up by trying to fix them—" She grabbed Andrea's sweater. "She's always been there for me, my twin, everyone used to say when we were in high school. What'll I do without her?"

Mrs. Hughes said, "Make your calls."

"We have to tell Richard," Andrea said again.

"Yeah, I-I have to—" Ronnie patted the pockets of her jeans, took two steps in one direction then two more in another. "Where the hell's my cellphone?"

"Use the phone in my office if you need it." Mrs. Hughes pushed them toward the door. "Make as many calls as you have to."

In the small office off the kitchen, Ronnie made the call. Holding the phone in both hands, she sobbed all the time it rang. When she heard a voice on the other end, she gulped back her tears, and said, "Richard… Oh, Richard… Katy…"

"Give me the damn phone," Andrea said. She held it to her ear. "Richard, this is Andi O'Rourke."

"What's going on there, Andrea?" Richard demanded.

"Excuse me a second, Richard," she said. She put down the phone, sniffed back tears, blew her nose, then picked up the phone. "Richard, you have to get up here. Katy's very, very sick. The doctor…" She fought a sob. "I… don't think she's gonna make it."

***

Richard later filled in this part of the story.

That Saturday morning, Ken Hoffmann had just come into Richard's apartment. With Ronnie and me out of town, he and Richard planned to play racquetball, have dinner and maybe take in a movie afterwards.

"Hello, hello? Ronnie, is that you?" Richard said into his cellphone.

Ken said. "Tell my wife I miss her."

"Ronnie? Are you still there?" Richard said. "I can't understand you."

"What's going on?" Ken asked.

"Damned if I know. Sounds like she's crying."

Now Richard heard Andrea's voice on the line. He stiffened and demanded, "What's going on there? No!" he shouted and dropped the phone.

Ken picked it up. "Andrea— Andi, slow down, I can't understand you," he said. "Where's Ron, maybe she can explain— Oh."

Richard leaned over him, ear close to the phone.

Ken shrugged him aside. "Okay, I understand. Yes, yes, we'll get there as fast as we can." He turned to Richard. "You'd better sit down."

"What?"

"Katy's gotten very ill—"

"They told me that!" Richard took Ken by the shoulders. "What is it? Tell me!"

"There's a doctor with her," Ken said. "They don't know if she'll last the night."

Richard's jaw dropped. "No! They're wrong. They must be."

"Doesn't seem to be anything they can do."

"Isn't there somebody up there who can— What kind of place is that? Give me the damn phone!" Richard grabbed the cellphone and frantically jabbed at the numbered buttons. His hands shaking, he hit two or three buttons at a time.

"Who're you trying to call?"

"Nine-one-one!" Richard pounded on the phone. "Got to send a Medivac to get her back down here where somebody knows something."

Ken gentled the phone from him. "There's no way—" He got no further.

"I was losing her because I insisted we get married when I knew she didn't want to," Richard groaned. "How stupid can I be? Ken, if she's that sick, I could really lose her. What am I going to do?" He turned to the window. As if his words could carry across the five hundred miles between us, he shouted, "Dammit, Kaitlyn, you can have it any way you want. Just don't die!" He snapped a quick about-face and started for the apartment door without taking a coat.

"Where do you think you're going?" Ken asked.

"Got to get to her."

"Not in the condition you're in. No way I'm letting you drive alone."

His hand on the doorknob, Richard said. "If you're coming, then come on. Only dammit, stop talking!"

Ken threw a coat to him. "You've got no idea where to go."

"We'll figure that out on the way," Richard said as he raced past the elevator to the fire stairs. The guys didn't stop for the next nine hours, except for the couple of times they needed gas. Snow along the Thruway slowed them in places, sometimes to almost a crawl. Impatient, squirming in his seat, Richard said, "What the hell's the good of my owning a Jaguar if we can't let it race the way it's supposed to?"

Behind the wheel, Ken said, "Calm down. We'll get there."

The snow tapered off a little when they reached Syracuse. Beyond the plow in front of them, few cars were on the road. Ken stomped on the accelerator. The Jaguar fishtailed, then sped off faster than was safe. As they neared Buffalo at the end of the Thruway, Richard called the Niagara Inn on his cellphone. On the back of a gas receipt, he scribbled the directions Naomi Hughes gave him.

***

While Richard and Ken raced to the Niagara Inn, Dr. Early watched the seconds pass on his wristwatch while he counted the beats of my pulse. A minute later, he placed my arm on top of the comforter, and shook his head. All of his experience said I was dying, he whispered to Mrs.

Hughes, but nothing explained why. I had no fever, no chest congestion. The day before, he'd been concerned enough to draw a vial of my blood, then risked the raging storm to find a medical lab that would test it while he waited. Nothing obvious showed up. The medical technician said he would keep testing and call if he found anything.

Andrea and Ronnie wept at the foot of my bed.

The doctor told them. "She's comatose. Wish there were something I could do. Only chance is for me to get her to hospital for a battery of tests. But even then— "

Chapter Twenty-Seven
Disembodiment

I woke to what sounded like the scrape of a snowplow on concrete. When I turned my head on my pillow, I saw Abigail perched on the window seat with a blanketed bundle cradled in her arms. For several minutes I watched her gaze into the blanket with a tender smile, then bow her head to nuzzle whatever lay within. Curious, I swung my legs over the side of the bed.

Abigail grinned at me. "You're awake, and risen at last."

"Had to happen sooner or later," I said.

My head tilted, I thought for a moment. It had been a while since I had either the desire or strength to climb out of bed. The last time I tried, I couldn't get up without Abigail's help. Standing now unaided, I felt wonderful and strange at the same time. I had a sensation of weightlessness. It was as if… well, as if the law of gravity no longer applied to me.

"I feel absolutely buoyant," I said with a giggle. My arms outstretched, I turned a perfect pirouette. The long flannel nightgown swirled around my ankles.

Abigail nodded. "Sure it's like that, feeling as if you've never ailed a day in your life."

My brow furrowed, I tried to make sense of what had happened during the past few days. "I *was* sick, wasn't I?"

"You've been that for a while, one way and another. Still are, I expect."

"Don't be ridiculous. Look at me, I'm fine." Again the nightgown billowed out when I spun.

"Are you now?" Her head cocked, Abigail glanced past me.

The look in her eyes told me something dreadful lurked back there. I thought I ought to peek, if only to avoid whatever it was, but didn't want to stop swimming in the sea of tranquility where I floated.

Abigail cast her eyes sideways. "Might as well know now as later."

This time her glance brooked no resistance. It pulled my head around until I saw what she looked at. What I saw shattered my euphoria as if it were a crystal goblet dropped from her second floor window. It couldn't be! I squinted. My eyes… had to be lying. I saw—

I gasped. "No, no, no!"

I felt as though there was more frost on my brain than on the windowpanes. *I'm hallucinating, that's what it is. Fever. Yeah, that's it. I'm still sick, have a high fever.*

"Your mind's not playing tricks. You're seeing reality." Though Abigail didn't add, *for the first time*, I knew that's what she meant.

"It can't be!"

"It's where you've threatened to go for a long time."

I glanced over my shoulder. The floral paper hung on the wall, the matching carpet covered the floor. No fire burned in the hearth, no kindling sat in the tin holder nearby. I saw the dresser with my things scattered on top of it, my overnight case on the floor. I saw the antique bed. I saw—

My heart flip-flopped.

I saw—

Abigail nodded. "The truth is before you. Will you believe it now?"

I saw *me* in the large bed with the comforter pulled up to my chin. The me in bed seemed so calm. But my face— I looked as if I was—

I grabbed the bodice of Abigail's dress. "Am I… am

I…?"

A mournful look in her eyes, she slowly shook her head.

I touched my arm, half expecting my fingers to pass through as if it was mist. They didn't. I touched my legs. Same thing. Relieved, I began to say, "I'm not—" But then, unsettled again, in a quivering voice, I asked, "Am I?"

"The choice of living or dying isn't so easily made," she said. "And now you've seen what *real* is, it's you that'll have to decide which you want."

"I'm not deciding to… I haven't wanted… How can you think that?"

She rolled her eyes as if to ask how I could be so dense.

When she focused again on me, I felt forced to respond with a little truth. "Well, once, maybe. Not anymore."

"You still do," she insisted.

"I don't!"

"Och, have it your way then. You're still too stubborn to admit what's plain to everyone else."

Sulking, I searched for an argument to obscure the truth of Abigail's words.

She laughed at me. "This isn't a place to hide from yourself. I thought you'd have seen that by now."

As if facing an inquisitor, I stood, arms at my sides, fingers picking nervously at the flannel cloth of my nightgown. "Am I being punished for something—is that why this is happening? Abigail, I don't understand."

"No more do I," she said. "Except that for some it seems easier this way."

"Easier than what?"

She glanced through the window, as if the answer might be found in the falling snow. "Facing the truth," she said at last.

Unable to deny it, still I refused to make what

lawyers call an admission against my interest. I struggled to find a way out. There had to be a loophole—there always was. I turned and looked at myself on the bed. *Maybe if I climb under the covers, I'll be able to slip back inside me.* Even as I had the idea, it sounded rather confused, but I couldn't think of another way to explain the evidence of my own eyes. This wasn't something the people who wrote *Black's Law Dictionary* or the *Law Journal* considered, so I had no way to name my situation. My mind paged through things I'd experienced, things I'd been told, read about, searching for a precedent. I thought, *Divorce, hmmm. Maybe that's it—I've divorced myself from... uh, me?*

Blocked by what felt like a brick wall, my mind wandered down a different avenue. Though Abigail hadn't confirmed it, I *was* being punished. I knew why. I had tried to kill myself when I lost my baby, and when I failed, I became emotionally withdrawn and refused to share my life with anyone, even Richard. In all the time I'd spent with him, had sex with him, no matter how hard he tried, never once had I let him get near me in a way that counted. Now, like Abigail Bender, I seemed to be condemned to be apart from everything I knew. From everyone I… loved. There it was: when I lost my baby, I'd sworn never to feel love again, never to leave myself vulnerable to it. Yet somehow love had slithered beneath my defenses. Would the realization be enough to get me back into my body, or was I stuck in some purgatory for as long as it took to be cleansed of my sin? Though it wasn't listed among the deadly seven, in this moment of complete honesty, what I had done seemed just as wrong. Now, like Abigail Bender, I would forever thereafter be a Niagara Inn ghost, a memory some future Leah Campbell would warn others of.

All the while as my mind churned, Abigail sat quietly on the window seat with her bundle. When I at last looked over at her, she said, "You would have argued if I told you of this. You had to come to it yourself."

In a very small voice, I asked, "What can I do?"

She bowed her head. "I suppose all there is for it is for you to hear the rest of my story. Don't know the why of it, but I'm feeling like I won't rest till I've told you. And I'm thinking maybe there's something in it to answer both our needs…" She glanced over to the bed. "If it's not too late."

Because she said her story offered some small hope I might get out of this fix, I now thought the most important thing in the world—the only thing—was to know what happened between Abigail and Will Bender.

As she had so many times before, she read my mind. "Yes, the story has to be finished," she said. "It's easier for some that way."

I nodded, as if I understood.

She patted a place on the window seat. "Come sit by me. I've something to show you."

"It's a baby," I said when I looked into the bundle. With one finger I stroked the newborn's cheek. "She's adorable."

"*His* name is Jeremiah," Abigail corrected.

I cringed back in a corner of the nook, recognizing something about the name. "Is… he yours?" I asked.

She sighed. "Will's and mine? I wish it could've been so. Maybe if he had been— Ah, but all the world's maybes won't change a moment of what was."

"Whose is he, then?"

"That's part of what I'm needing to tell you." Before I could inquire further, she asked, "Would you like to hold him?" Ignoring my hesitation, she placed the bundle in my arms.

My body went rigid. I desperately didn't want to hold the infant, but with no avenue of escape—in my disembodied state, where could I go?—I had no choice. My eyes darted. Then the baby cooed and I relaxed.

"You have a way with Jeremiah," Abigail said.

I gazed at the small face while I cradled him. The fresh smell of him seemed as intoxicating as a warm spring morning. All at once, feelings I had long ago locked away broke free. I ached for the rhapsodic joy of possessively holding my own child. I longed to sit with my baby in my arms for hours, nothing more important in life than his happiness.

I should have had that!

The thought left a sour taste. For me, a baby's smell would forever be mixed with the reek of hospital disinfectant. My dreams for him would end in the dark soil of a small grave. I fought back tears.

"You should have had the joy." Abigail looked at me, into me. "Ah, I see now. Even if you won't say it, giving your babe life would've taken yours."

Tears I'd held in for years burst from my eyes. "No!" I said. "They were wrong. He was my *baby*. They should have saved *him*. Even if it cost me—" I caught my breath, locked my lips.

Abigail reached out her hand and brushed my cheek.

"They should have," I groaned.

She let Jeremiah take her finger in his tiny hand. "Maybe we'll talk of this later. But the time for you to hear the rest of Will and me is as brief as this darling child."

She patted my hand and leaned back.

"Mine and Will's wedding was a glory," she said. "The church was lined in daffodils and a chain of daisies led us down the aisle. Everyone from the Dock and Town, the Colored Section and Irishtown too, came to witness my joy. My friend, Annie Stark, came arm-in-arm with the Morgan lad she'd had her eye on since she was twelve. Though he still flirted with every lass down at the beach, he now found comfort in Annie's company when evening came. Tilda Riley had wed in the spring and was already with child. Seeing her belly six months full made me dream of a time mine would be also. Charlie Bolton and Brinny were there, looking uncomfortable as if their suits were a wee bit small on them.

"I wore the most beautiful lace gown, the dress Mother Bender wore when she wed Will's father. Ma spent weeks with a sewing needle to make it fit.

"The day of the wedding, Mother Bender arranged my hair. She fixed it up in a bun—not the tight kind so many women wore, but looser, like. She called it a knot. It was how French noblewomen wore their hair, she said. Then Ma tied a crown of daisies around the bun. When they were done, Mother Bender called to the photographer and I had to stand stiff as a statue in front of the church door, waiting for him to adjust his camera.

"My heart leapt when the church door opened. Will stood between Father Bender and Brinny. He cut such a grand figure in his gray morning suit, bent-down starched wing collar and all. I could hardly believe fate had given me to so fine a lad. All aglow, I memorized the moment and how wonderful I felt. Then Da took my arm. As we walked past all my friends, the sun shone so bright through the church windows, I felt sure God sent it as a gift to light our way.

"I hardly remember all the words, but after me and Will swore our vows, Minister Cox raised his hands and smiled at us. I looked up at my husband—*my husband*, the word sent a shiver of joy through me—and I thought it surely would always be so.

"Father Bender had hired a band he saw advertised in the *Buffalo News*—that's the paper he'd taken to reading once he moved here. Me and Will danced till my feet hurt. Mother Bender kept telling people how lovely I looked, and how she'd always been glad at the thought I'd be Will's wife. Mr. Burke laughed when he heard her say that, and he took her hand to dance.

"On our wedding night, we came to our new marriage bed in this fine house old Mr. Burke gave us, to this very room. I stood over there by the hearth while Will took my dress off me, then kissed my neck and breasts with a passion he hadn't lost since the first time we made love between the boats at the shore. My Will lifted me to the fine feather bed Ma and Da gave us and loved me till the moon was high. Then I snuggled in his arms, waiting for sleep to bring me sweet dreams of tomorrow…"

Abigail's voice seemed to drift into the past. When she spoke again, she said with a sigh, "It was September of eighteen-sixty. As I lay in Will's arms late in the night, I would have sworn I heard a rasping laugh. Though I couldn't know it then, that was fate laughing because it saw that two months later you Americans would elect Mr. Lincoln to be President, and seven months after *that*, the Confederates would capture a group of Union soldiers in the New Mexico Territory. Everything changed after that."

Chapter Twenty-Eight
Nathan Kinsley

Abigail handed me a wrinkled newspaper clipping she pulled from under the cushion of the window seat. The dateline read 'Mesilla, New Mexico Territory, July 25, 1861.' On the clipping I saw an artist's rendering of tumbleweed blown across a field. Gray-clad soldiers surrounded a rag-tag group in dark uniforms. In the center, a white charger reared over the bowed head of an officer who held out his sword. The article told how the Seventh United States Infantry, tired and hungry, had been chased through the badlands until they finally had to surrender.

When I handed back the clipping, Abigail said, "For a long time, I believed the end for me and Will began in that desert."

I stared at her, bewildered. "For heaven's sake, what could Union troops surrendering after a minor skirmish in the Civil War have to do with you and Will?"

"You couldn't be knowing that from the words of the article, could you?" Abigail showed it to me again. "Look down the list of officers who were captured that day."

I scanned the row of names. "I still don't see—"

She pointed to one. "Nathan Kinsley!" She spat the name as if it were a curse. "You heard Will thinking of him when the boys sailed to Tryon's Folly?"

I nodded.

"I knew you had," Abigail said. "What happened in Mesilla brought him back into Will's life. After the surrender, Nathan got sent to the fort in Youngstown across the Niagara from us."

I looked a question at her.

"Och, do you know nothing of history? Even your own?"

"History was never my strongest subject in school. These days I only have time to read casebooks and the *Law Journal*…" I glanced at me in bed and moaned, "I only *had* time…"

With what might have been a touch of haughtiness, Abigail said, "I read everything. Leastwise, everything in books left behind by people who come to stay in this room." She moved her skirt to reveal *Anna Karenina* beside her on the window seat. The folded letter still marked her place. "I've no need to worry like you did about things going on in life, and there's not much else for me to do but read… and think." She stared out the window.

I touched her hand. "It must be hard, sitting here with only memories all these years and no friends to talk about them with."

She dabbed at her tears. "Ah, but I have a friend now, don't I? I'm grateful to you, Kaitlyn, for listening and sharing my memories with me."

My eyes also filled with tears. "It's what friends do. That's how Ronnie and I have always been. In fact, I sometimes think she knows me better than I know myself. Oh, Abigail, I wish you could know her."

"I see how she cares for you. I like her for that. She's dying inside, you know, seeing you fade from her."

I again turned my eyes to the bed. "I wish it could be different."

"I also wish I could change things." Abigail's fingers wiped away frost that had formed on the inside of a windowpane. "I've often wondered if it's possible to go through life without hurting anyone."

"Sounds like you caused people pain."

She nodded. "That was a worse sin than what I did to myself."

I locked my eyes on hers.

She adjusted her dress. "That's also part of my story. But my time with you is fleeting and I must finish what you need to hear." She fingered the newspaper clipping she had dropped on her lap. "You asked what this had to do with what happened to me and Will. I once read when your American War started, both sides still thought to fight like gentlemen—in word at least, if not in deed. So when Nathan and his people surrendered, they gave their parole to not fight again till they were formally exchanged for Southern prisoners. But I'm thinking the Confederates only agreed because they didn't have enough food for themselves, much less for all those soldiers they captured." She shrugged. "Whether for honor or food, the Union believed it was bound by the oath Nathan and his men swore. To keep the oath, the generals sent a small lot of them here to Fort Niagara, where they'd not be able to rejoin the fight. From the moment he came, Nathan began to pull Will away from me."

"So that's why Mesilla was the beginning of your end?"

She sighed again. "I once thought it so and blamed Nathan."

"You don't anymore?"

"Nothing's ever so complicated or simple as that." Abigail peered through her window to where Fort Niagara still stood on the promontory across the river. She explained that in death she at last shed the remnants of self-pity and her vision cleared. In a wider perspective she saw fate's full design. Because of what Will believed and the things he had done, sooner or later he would have joined the fight. Still, Nathan Kinsley did come to Fort Niagara in early 1862 and became the catalyst.

"For months before he came," she said, "Will read every story the *Buffalo News* wrote of your American War. Sometimes I'd hear him and Father Bender talk about it late into the night. When he read that Fort Sumter had been attacked, he said, 'It's sure to start now, Father. Surely now President Lincoln will declare a war to free the Negroes.'

"I don't need to look out my window to remember Father Bender's voice sounding so heavy it might have been soaked with the tears of every man who ever lost a son. 'Declare war? Yes, I fear so,' he had said.

"And Will had said, 'Why fear, Father? That will be the day Charlie and Brian and I—even Abbie—have prayed for. It's to that end we've worked to bring the Negroes across here to Canada.'

"Father Bender reminded him, 'Before that, too. Yes, Will, I knew about you and Nathan Kinsley carrying runaways to Olean. Don't think that didn't fill me with dread.'

"I wonder what Father Bender would have said if he'd known what happened at Tryon's Folly. Not knowing, he said, 'Now this war has begun, it will be a long and bloody time before it ends. Be glad you'll not know the pain which comes from taking another's life.'

"Father Bender was right about what the war would be. Soon the newspaper told the blood-stained details of more fights than I can count on both my hands. There were pages of pictures showing dead men and horses spread like so much straw across the fields, and trees and farms burned to ashes. Someone told me those were woodcuts of photographs a man named Matthew Brady took days after the fights ended. The pictures looked so real I felt like I stood among the dead." Abigail shuddered at the thought. "I used to wonder how anyone could choose to save such sights and how a man could live having seen them."

She continued to finger her clipping all the while she spoke. "Each story was more terrible than the last, and with each I saw a stirring grow in Will's eyes. But this one—" She held out the crumpled piece of newsprint. "Looking back, this first article was worst of all."

So I would understand how Nathan Kinsley gained the ability to tug at Will's conscience, Abigail explained that Will met Nathan at Allegheny College and the two became fast friends. They roomed together while Will remained at school. They fished together, growing closer in the joined silence of early mornings beside rivers and streams. Together, they frequently called on two sisters who lived near their rooming house, and eventually Nathan introduced Will to the one thing they hadn't yet shared—working a section of the Underground Railroad. Dressed in black, speaking little, they drove horses ahead of a rickety wagon heavy with human parcels. With slave-hunters wandering the fields, it could be dangerous work. Nathan never let them go unarmed.

As if to stress her next words, Abigail looked hard at me. "The shot that killed either Luke or John at Tryon's Folly came from the rifle Nathan gave Will when he started to work the Railroad. Then, when Nathan got sent to the Niagara Frontier, he found a way to send someone to do the fighting he couldn't." She looked at me. "Can you hear fate laughing now?"

The silence when she stopped was so poignant, for a moment I thought I also heard fate's voice. Strange, though, almost a shock—what I heard was the low wheezing laugh I sought for so long to escape.

"Do you understand now how all that was and will be is tied by a single cord?" Abigail asked.

At last I saw it all: fate had used a strand of thread to carefully weave a tapestry for Will and Abigail. Whatever happened after would be dictated by what came before. Fate had also woven me a tapestry. My father leaving pushed me down a path that eventually led to a Niagara Inn bed.

Chapter Twenty-Nine
A Call to Arms

In telling me of the war's start and Nathan Kinsley, Abigail had painted a broad landscape of places outside her small world in Niagara-on-the-Lake. Now her focus narrowed to a crisp Sunday morning in March of 1862, a day on which Elizabeth Bender crossed the Common to visit Will and Abbie at the house on Prideaux Street. Through the window, I saw Mrs. Bender enter the kitchen, a wide room lit by morning sunshine that flooded through large windows. A fire blazed in a brick hearth.

Elizabeth pulled a chair from the claw-foot table in the room's center and watched Abbie knead dough for breakfast biscuits.

"You do that well, child," she said. "From the way my son's stomach grows larger each day, it seems you've learned to cook everything quite well."

"I try hard to please him." Abbie didn't look up from her work.

With a sideways glance, Elizabeth asked, "How are you feeling this morning?"

Abbie brushed at a tendril of red hair. The motion streaked her cheek with flour. "I'm well, Mother Bender. I'm always well." She knew what was really asked. It had been eighteen months since the wedding and still she had no morning sickness.

Elizabeth took a handkerchief from her cloth purse and wiped the flour from her daughter-in-law's face. "It's bound to happen in God's good time."

Smacking the ball of dough, Abbie said, "It'll be a wonder if God will ever grant me the blessing."

Moments later Will strolled in. As he adjusted his shirt collar, he chirped, "Good morning, Mother. How are you on this fine day?" He pecked a quick kiss at her cheek.

She looked up at him. "Your father's been asking after you. The shop's so busy he thought perhaps you might return to work there."

Will laughed. "I'm pleased to hear father's business is growing and I'm quite certain he'll find the help he requires. For myself, I'm content where I am at Burke's."

A smile played on Abigail's lips.

"Your father works terribly hard," Elizabeth said. "I really do worry about him. He's not getting younger."

Will took his mother's hand and kissed it. "Father cherishes hard work—in that he'll never change." He looked slyly at her. "And neither will you. You just want me to leave Burke's so Abbie and I would be forced to move in with you and Father."

With no alteration in Elizabeth's smile, she said, "It would be so pleasant to share our large house, Abbie, wouldn't it?"

Will stepped behind his wife and placed his hands on her shoulders. "I believe we're both happy as things are. Aren't we, my love?"

Abbie turned up her face to accept a long kiss.

"I wish you wouldn't do that." Elizabeth averted her eyes. "It isn't at all seemly to show affection in public."

"Not seemly to kiss my wife, Mother? Adoring her is too much a pleasure to be sinful." Will winked, then, in what could only have been a small act of rebelliousness, he dropped his head and kissed her again.

Elizabeth gasped. "William Jeremiah Bender, how can you do such a thing? If your father saw this… this display he'd disown you. I assure you, Abbie, your husband never learned such behavior in my house."

"No, not in your house, Mother," Will agreed. "However, when I roomed with Nathan Kinsley I did learn a thing or two from his frontier manners. And I must say that some of what he taught me is rather worth knowing."

"Really!" Elizabeth gave a small cough.

"It is worth knowing, isn't it, Abbie?" Will said. "From all the activity on it, I think we'll soon need a new bed."

Again he kissed her and the two of them giggled.

"You're a heathen, that's what you are. Not fit for polite society," Elizabeth said. "Why, if Minister Cox heard of this—"

"He'd remind you, Mother, that I'm only following God's dictate to be fruitful and—"

"Really!" Elizabeth dabbed her handkerchief at her cheek. After another sputter, she pulled a crumpled envelope from her purse. "Oh, I nearly forgot. This came for you last week."

Will turned the envelope over. As if to test whether it had been broken, he felt along the seal. "Mother seems to have learned a bit about privacy since we moved to Canada," he whispered to Abbie.

"Well!" Elizabeth said.

He waved the letter at her. "Why didn't you bring this sooner?"

She smoothed her cloth cap. "If you lived with us, you would have had your letter as soon as it arrived."

Abigail asked, "Who is it from?"

"Nathan Kinsley," Will said. "I've told you about him, Abbie." He shook his head. "I've not heard from him since he wrote to tell me the army sent him to some dusty outpost in the west."

He read the front of the single sheet then quickly flipped it to read the other side. When he finished, his face lit with pleasure. "See what it says, Abbie?" He handed her the letter. "Nathan's here, just across the river from us."

Will quickly wrote out a reply.

What wonderful news that you are so close. How did you come to be here? So much has happened since we last corresponded, my dear friend, I hardly know where to begin. The most important news first: I am married! I know having seen me at my worst and so clumsy around girls, you will find that difficult to credit. But I am these last eighteen months. She is a wonder, my Abbie, and such a constant source of joy even Mother has grown to love her—although she is not the bride Mother would have chosen for me. Nate, you must meet my dear wife. Leaving this to stimulate your active imagination, I will close by asking when Abbie and I might come across to visit you.

"Nathan's answer wasn't long in coming," Abigail told me. As if she had placed these items there so she could illustrate her points, she pulled his reply from under the cushion of the window seat.

Come whenever you can, the sooner the better. My life here is so quiet and boring it would be a blessing from heaven to spend an afternoon with someone only slightly less quiet and boring. And please, bring your dear wife. In her company, I might find something to brighten my spirits.

While I read the letters from and to Nathan Kinsley, a scene appeared on the panes of Abigail's window. Pointing to the scene, Abigail told me it was now a mild day in mid-April. She and Will were ferrying across the river to Fort Niagara.

While I watched, Will chattered excitedly about his friend and of the times they shared in Allegheny. He told her how Nathan had taught him to be a conductor on the Railroad, and how Nathan's father, a bible-thumping country preacher, had lit the fire of passion for the abolitionist cause. At last able to get a word in, Abbie said with a laugh, "Ah, but tell me, are you glad to be seeing him?"

Now ashore, they climbed the rampart on a flight of stone stairs. After stating their purpose to a corporal who slouched at his post, they stepped into the mayhem of a construction site.

Laborers laid new stones on the riverfront wall. A sergeant shouted at them, "You there, those ain't straight. Gotta be straight and six deep or it'll crumble, first cannonball that comes flying—"

The sergeant's voice mixed into the complaint of an officer who called, "No, no. Not that way. Dammit! Who told you to do it that way? Where's the mason?"

Men hauling bricks and stones scurried along a network of planks laid across mud puddles left by recent spring rains.

"Gotta get this wall finished before—" someone said.

"Hut, hut," came a command from the yard. Two dozen soldiers in a ragged file marched toward the gate. "Halt! You call this close order? No wonder Johnny Reb had such easy work taking you lot."

An officer with long black hair and a full mustache waved to Will and Abbie. He broke from a crew that appeared to be sponging a cannon barrel. "Will! William Bender," he called. "As I live and breathe, you've made it after all."

"Seems we might have arrived at a bad time," Will said.

Nathan Kinsley glanced at the chaos around them. "Nonsense. Every day is like this. We've a hodgepodge of masons and laborers hired from Youngstown and Lewiston. It's a hard task getting this rabble to do things the way the army wants." He pulled off his cap and ran fingers through his hair. "I must apologize for the condition of this place. The fort was left to rot for fifty years after the last war with Britain. Now some genius has decided they might attack again from Canada, so we've been commanded to rebuild the fort into a proper military camp—and do it in a month."

"That would be quite a feat." Will winced when a shard of stone bounced close to him.

"Indeed," Kinsley said. "But enough of my problems. Let me look at you." He took Will by the shoulders. "How many years has it been? Four, five? You've grown older, but I'd say not a day wiser for it."

Will patted Nathan's stomach. "You've also grown a bit, though it looks like a lazy life, not age, has done it."

Kinsley's grin broadened. "Ah, Will, you never change. I may one day be a general, and you'll still treat me with the familiarity of—"

Will threw an arm around the other man's shoulders. "A very dear friend."

Again Kinsley laughed, deeper this time. "Indeed. Now introduce me to this beauty you've brought to brighten my day."

"This is Abbie, my wife." Will's arm circled her slim waist.

Her eyes lowered, she flared her skirt and bent as if about to curtsy, then she shook her head, and said, "I can see I'm cursed to a day of schoolchildren's banter."

Kinsley clapped. "Not just beautiful, but clever too. Ah, my friend, I can see you've done at least one right thing in your wasted life." He took each by an arm to steer them along the rampart. "The noise and flying stones here won't make for a civilized visit. We'll retire to someplace quiet—the officers' ready-room, I think." He pointed to the insignia on his shoulder. "See, I'm a lieutenant. I'm allowed in there. Oh, I do fancy a comfortable talk with an old friend, and, I hope, a lovely new one. In the officers' room we might do it over some glasses of a reasonably good sherry." He looked around once more, then called to a nearby sergeant, "Schmidt, take over here. I'll be in the barracks if the colonel needs me."

"Oh, how I've missed our times together, Will," Kinsley said when they were seated near a fireplace in the damp hall. Around them, new timbers rose up the walls and across the low ceiling. Small windows allowed little of the sun's warmth to penetrate. He sipped at his sherry while talk of times past brought a wistful smile to his lips. Elbows on his knees, he leaned toward Abbie. "Your husband was quiet and serious when we first roomed together. But under my tutelage he soon learned to have as a good a time as anyone."

"I don't dare imagine," she said.

"Oh, yes. With me to teach him, he became quite the rake," Kinsley said. "All the women in Allegheny had their caps set for him. Will, do you recall those sisters who lived near our rooming house? Irene and Clara Stephenson, they were. Yes, yes, those were their names." He twisted the ends of his dark mustache, then drew long fingers through his hair. Tilting back in his wooden armchair, he grinned suggestively. "Abbie, you should have seen the fuss those sisters made whenever your husband came to call."

Will glanced at his wife from the corner of his eye. "Now, Nathan, you know that's not true. It was you with whom the Stephenson sisters were anxious to sit on their front porch swing."

"No, no, Abbie," Kinsley said. "Upon my oath as an officer and a gentleman, I'm being entirely truthful in this. As a matter of fact, the few times I dared call upon them alone, the ladies pined so for your absent husband they pouted all evening."

"Is that so?" Abbie feigned jealousy. "I think Will and me have a bit to talk over when we get home."

"Don't believe this cad." Will smiled and shook his head. "An officer and a gentleman? Nonsense. The man's a born liar."

Kinsley poked at Will's ribs. "Liar, am I? Now let me see if I remember. It was Clara with the long red curls you were sweet on." To Abbie, he said, "I can see in his attraction to red hair, he hasn't changed."

Turning her eyes down and sideways at her husband, Abbie said, "Was he sweet on this Clara Stephenson, now? That's fine to know, when before I agreed to marry this wastrel he swore an oath I was his first and only love."

Will laughed. "Oh, the two of you will be cursed for all eternity for telling such falsehoods."

"Probably." Kinsley reached for the glass of sherry resting on a rough-hewn table at his side. "At least I will. I doubt that'll happen to this angel you married, though. Will, you must have locked her in a cell and threatened harm to her family to induce her to spend even one minute in your sorry company."

"He did that and more." Laughing, Abbie slapped Will's hand away when he reached for hers.

"With the two of you enjoying yourselves so grandly at my expense," Will said, "perhaps it would be best if I leave."

"Perhaps it would." Again Kinsley twirled his mustache. "Then I'll be able to learn how you managed to win this angel and perhaps win her from you. No, no, Will, don't go off in a huff just yet. Ah, I surely have missed jesting with you. And more, too. Do you recall those late night trips we used to make? The Railroad lost a fine conductor when you left Allegheny."

Abbie glanced around before quietly assuring Kinsley, "Will wasn't lost to the cause when his family moved to Niagara-on-the-Lake. He, my brother and their friend Charlie made many night trips on the Niagara to ferry runaways across."

"I'm not surprised." His expression now serious, Kinsley turned to Will. "But what are you doing for the cause now it's come to war?"

"I'm married." Will said.

Abigail grabbed her husband's hand. "He is! And Will's a Canadian now. The fight isn't his."

Abbie had sat quietly sewing on those nights Will and his father read the newspaper and talked about the war. She recalled the faraway look she saw grow in her husband's eyes. Now, recognizing the direction in which Nathan Kinsley had taken this conversation, she felt a chill.

Kinsley poured himself and Will another glass of sherry. "Isn't the fight his? Isn't it the God-given duty of every right-thinking man to take up arms in this cause? Isn't that what my father taught us? Will, have you grown so complacent these past years you no longer recall all we swore we'd do?"

Abbie rushed to respond before her husband could. "If it is, why are you sitting here so comfortable, drinking wine in front of a fire while you dare others to do the work?"

"Can you think I'm here by choice, Abbie?" Kinsley rose. Hands clasped behind his back, he began to pace. "Do you not think I'm frustrated, barricaded in this wreck of a fortress, doing nothing but watch the river flow by? If I were able, I'd lead men into the fight. Especially now I've had word about my friend, James Wells—you remember him, Will? He was a year behind us at Allegheny. He and I roomed together after you left. His mother wrote to say Jamie was slain at Shiloh. I should be in the fight so I might find the gray-belly bastard—excuse me, Abbie—the rebel who killed my friend."

"Then why not put in for a transfer?" Will asked.

Kinsley sat heavily back in his chair. "I can't.

Technically I'm still a prisoner of that rebel Colonel Baylor and his Texas Mounted Rifles."

Will's eyes narrowed. "A prisoner? Here?"

"Yes. Last July when the Rebs galloped into Mesilla screaming like madmen, we were ordered to abandon Fort Fillmore." Kinsley shook his head as if he still failed believe it. "After two days of living on nothing but sagebrush while we ran like cowards from a fight, we were ordered to surrender to the Rebs at that cursed San Augustin Springs—may the Devil choke on its name. Surrender, by God! How could they command us to do such a thing?" He snatched his glass and gulped the sherry. "When we were paroled, my detachment was sent to this godforsaken purgatory of a place so our commanders could stand by their oath to hold us out of the fight."

"I'm sorry," Will said.

Kinsley again rose and stood by Will's chair. "As am I. So *I'm* bound to be here, but you're not. It strikes me if you went, I'd have been replaced by a good man."

When she glanced in her husband's direction, Abbie saw a fire burn briefly in his eyes. She looked away, thinking, *You'll not be going off to be slain in that bloody fight, William Jeremiah Bender. Not if I've anything to say about it, you won't.*

Chapter Thirty
Loves Lost

Will didn't respond to his friend's challenge that April day. Abbie believed he was prevented from pursuing it by how upset she became. She hoped her reaction would put an end to the matter. As I watched the scenes shift on the window-panes, I saw Will grow quiet at home over the following weeks. Acutely aware of his every expression, Abbie knew an internal battle between love and duty churned in his mind. Afraid duty might win, she did her best to distract him.

"Looks like it'll be a fine year for us, Will," she trilled to fill the silence. "Mr. Burke told my father you're so valuable to him, he's thinking of making you a partner."

His voice flat, Will said, "That would be fine." The unspoken *if* hung like a rain cloud between them.

Abbie tried again. "One day there'll be a child for us to care for. Won't that be wonderful, Will, having a babe to bounce on your knee?"

He closed his eyes.

Will Bender made a few more trips across the Niagara to talk with Kinsley. He went alone on those occasions. On his return, he seemed even more lost in thought. After his last trip, as if his moral scale had carefully weighed and balanced duty and his love for his wife, with a heavy sigh, he told her, "I think I must go."

"I'll not let you!" she cried.

He shook his head. "Abbie, I must."

"But why? It's not your fight, Will!"

He knelt and took her hands in his. "It is, my love. In this Nate is correct. This is the fight of every right-thinking man. If I don't engage in it, I won't respect myself."

"But—"

He rushed on. "I believe I know now why God led me to Tryon's Folly. It was to make me strong enough to face what's to come."

"It was to save Brinny's life you were there. Nothing more!" She shoved him away.

"No. It was so I'd be able to do the job set before me now." He rose to his full height. "I have you to thank for helping me see I can do it. Yes, Abbie, you did, when you taught me there's no guilt in what I did that night." He looked at her. "If you hadn't loved me enough to bring me through my confusion about slaying those slave-hunters, I might never have found the strength to do this."

Abigail told me her heart tore on Will's words. What he said about her being the cause of her current plight rang like the bell in the church steeple. But how could she have known it then? When day after day she sat beside him on the beach, held him, found words she didn't know she possessed to strip off the guilt he wore like a mourning coat, how could she have foreseen it would lead to this? The realization of what love would cost her felt like a slap. She recoiled when he again reached for her and said he knew must go.

Instead of her husband's voice, she heard an echo of her mother: *You'll see I'm right when fate demands payment for what the boy's done.*

Fate had indeed laid a clever trap for her.

Two weeks before he left, Will told his parents of his plan. An argument immediately ensued. Elizabeth lost control.

"You tore me from Erie, away from everything and everyone I cared for, because you swore this was the one way to keep my Will safe from the killing!" she shouted at George. "As a good Christian wife, I did as you demanded.

After I've suffered through everything up here, now what? My son is going off to be slaughtered anyway!"

"Father, is this true?" Will asked. "Is this the reason we moved here?"

"It is, son," George admitted. "And if I thought I could keep you safe from what's happening, I'd pick up and move us all again."

"I'm grown now, Father. I've made my own decision."

"I know you have, son." As if hoping he might still reason away the madness, George said, "But think of the life you've made for yourself. You have a wife—"

Will turned to where Abbie stood crying near the parlor door. "I'm aware of that." He set his jaw. "And everything will still be here when I return."

"What do *you* say of this, Abbie?" George asked.

"I…" Her voice gurgled with tears.

"Abbie will learn to understand," Will said.

"She will never understand!" Elizabeth shouted, and the argument raged again.

It continued even as Abbie waited at the station for the train that would carry Will back to Erie. There, among his childhood friends, he planned to enlist in the Union Army.

"Why must you go, Will?" she demanded for what might have been the hundredth time. She had dreaded this day for a month. "Why? Give me an answer I can understand. Give me something I can hold onto during the long, cold nights ahead."

For the hundredth time, Will responded, "Because you couldn't respect me if I were to behave like less than a man, and if I don't go, I'll not respect myself."

Choking on tears, she reached to straighten his jacket collar. "While you're out there, have caution, Will Bender. I'll die with you should anything happen."

He held her close. "I *will* take care, Abbie. My love

for you will see me home when this is over."

The engine's whistle shrilled. Will kissed her and boarded without a backward glance.

As the train pulled from the station, Abbie ran along the wood platform.

Will leaned from the window and touched her hand.

The last words she called to him were, "Hear what I say, Will. I'll not stay here as your widow. By all the love I have for you, I swear I'll not."

***

I watched tears run unchecked down Abigail's cheeks. Her voice cracked on each word as she described how she ran alongside the Pullman coach that carried her husband away. Her pain shattered my heart. I reached out to the woman who sat next to me on the window seat.

"Oh, Abbie, I can't begin to imagine how devastated you were. I hate that you had to go through it."

She lifted the hem of her skirt to wipe her eyes. "It's a kindness for you to say so—especially kind because I know you also lost one you dearly loved."

"Barry?" My face crinkled. "I don't think he ever loved me. I'm not sure I loved him, either. We'd been friends so long I was just… used to him."

"Still, you wed him."

I giggled. "Yeah, I did. I used to have this fantasy about a perfect husband who'd give me the perfect life my mother never had. I married Barry because I feared that perfect love would never find me. I figured if I tried hard enough, I could make him fit into my plan. As for what *he* wanted—" I shrugged. "Guess it was easier for him to climb into my bed than go looking for— Hey, don't laugh. I know this sounds ridiculous, but we were young. Impatient children." I let out a breath. "I've never admitted this before, even to myself. Now that I have, I guess losing him to a woman who really loved him… Well, there's no comparison to Will leaving you for a war."

Abigail took my hand. "There is. Your husband stole your childhood when he left. Still, it wasn't him I was thinking of."

"Richard? I've seen too much of modern men and their relationships with women to have any illusions about him. He wants me the way I wanted Barry—a comfortable sofa in the dream house he's built."

"It isn't him I mean, either," Abigail said. "Though I expect the thought of him not being there hurts more than you let on. No, I'm thinking of someone smaller—someone whose existence was terribly brief."

I gasped.

"Ah, you know very well who I mean. And knowing, you understand why I'm grateful for your kindness in sharing my pain. But you see, Kaitlyn, though I hurt to see him go, I didn't lose Will that day at the station." She leaned back, and her eyes seemed to cloud with memory. When they cleared again, she said, "I'm thinking he might have lost himself long before he was finally gone from me. Here, I've something to show you."

Chapter Thirty-One
Letters from the Front

Abigail pulled a packet of letters from a hidden panel in the mantel of the fireplace. They were tied together with a red ribbon.

"Will wrote these while he was away," she said. "They tell of things he saw and did, of comrades he lost. His pain is there, too. None have read these letters but me and Father Bender. Now I'm thinking I'd like you to read them."

For a long moment she stroked the letters the way she might have caressed her husband while begging him not to go. I sensed in her distant gaze that she watched him walk through those memorized pages. The only love she'd known, clearly he lived on in the words he'd written.

With a sigh, Abigail returned to the window seat, took the bundled infant Jeremiah and handed me all she had left of Will Bender. Touched by the gesture, I hugged the packet to my breast.

"When you read these," she said, "you'll see they're as revealing as Mr. Brady's pictures."

I turned the letters over in my hands. The paper looked and felt remarkably well preserved—though a hundred and fifty years old, they might have been written yesterday. How could that be? And now that I thought about it, why wasn't the article that told of the Union surrender at San Augustin Springs yellowed and brittle? I glanced at Abigail.

Again reading my thoughts, she just smiled, and said, "When you read these you'll know how my Will was lost to me."

I untied the ribbon and took the first letter from its envelope. Erie, Pennsylvania, July 10, 1862, was written in neat script on top.

"Read it to me?" Abigail asked.

I unfolded the letter.

Dear Father,

I arrived in Erie six days ago. It feels strange to be back here after so many years away. How different everything is, while at the same time being so much the same. Main Street is as crowded as ever. The shops are as noisy, though the talk in them is about the war instead of trade. The great houses along Millionaires' Row look even grander than when we left, yet there is a feeling of sadness about them. Perhaps this is just a trick of memory.

I'm staying with the Ewings next door to where we used to live. It is evening now, and after a long day I'm writing this letter on the steps of their front porch. John Ewing has just come out. He asks to be remembered to you.

I saw Mr. Ewing the moment I arrived. He was at the station to pick up a shipment of tobacco for his shop and saw me step down from the train. After greeting me as if I were a long-lost son, he asked why I returned. When I told him I'd come as a volunteer for the fight against the Secessionists, he nodded appreciatively. He said his Johnny has also volunteered. I was a bit startled—in my mind Johnny Ewing is still the twelve year-old in overalls whose nose was always running. It is difficult to think of him as he is now, a seventeen-year-old corporal in a new blue uniform.

Many young men in Erie are readying themselves for this fight. I saw the number of their ranks when I visited the camp outside town where the new unit they formed is training.

I must admit I had not thought so far ahead when I left Niagara-on-the-Lake, however Mr. Ewing told me that with my education, and because of the important people here who fondly remember you and mother, I should apply for a commission as an officer. When I reminded him I have no military background, he said few officers in this regiment have. Leadership ability, he insisted, and good contacts are the keys to making a good officer. Taking his advice to heart, I visited your old friend Artley Hess—he is now one of the city leaders who have taken responsibility for forming this regiment. Mr. Hess's son is Major Thomas Hess of these 11th Pennsylvania Volunteers. I did not know Thomas well when we lived here—you'll recall he is several years older than I. But I remember the few times he encouraged me to play hooky and go fishing with him on the lake.

When I stopped by his office, Mr. Hess welcomed me home as heartily as Mr. Ewing had. He said it was fortunate I arrived when I did. After training for almost six months, the regiment has recently been turned over to the Federal government. It will leave in a few days to join a corps of the Army of the Potomac at a place called

> Harrison's Landing. I told Mr. Hess what I've been doing since he saw me last. When I finished, he said, 'My boy, it sounds to me as if you're officer material.' After securing from me the $250 dollars he said was the fee being charged for a junior officer's commission, he directed me to another office where I was sworn in as a lieutenant. I then went to what used to be your haberdashery and there I purchased my uniforms.
>
> I must say it concerns me, Father, to learn these young Pennsylvania men will shortly be led into battle by officers whose primary qualification is having the funds with which to purchase their commissions. However, I suspect this will matter little once the shooting has begun. It is generals with years of military training who will direct our troops.
>
> So, with but a few days to know the thirty-five men I have been assigned to lead, tomorrow we are off to war. Please send my love to Mother. I've written to Abbie how much I already miss her. In my letter to her I bragged of how I was appointed a lieutenant because the officers quickly saw my leadership qualities. I did not tell her how cheaply commissions are bought, for fear she would find such news troubling. Please, Father, don't tell her or Mother—

When I reached for the next letter, Abigail picked up *Anna Karenina* and removed the folded page marking her place in the book.

"This letter—" She showed it to me. "I keep it near

me, because in it I hear Will the way he sounded the day he left. It's the last time…" Her voice broke.

I had been overcome by sorrow when I first touched that piece of paper. Did Abigail's sadness emanate from the page? Did Will's?

I took the page from her and was surprised to see the words were no longer faded, and the paper was no longer brittle. Dated the same as the letter I had just read, it began, *My Darling Abbie—*.

> Please, dearest, forgive my not writing more than a few lines to you before this. Even in my silence, I long with all my being to feel your gentle touch. I have been so busy since I arrived—I was appointed a lieutenant almost before I disembarked from the train, and given a unit of men to command. They tell me I have a natural ability to lead. I think this must be true after so many years on the Railroad. I was flattered at first, but then I thought of what leaving you behind has cost and my heart ached. Sleep is difficult, my love, without you curled up beside me in bed. To ease the pain of our separation, I stay busy drilling my men and getting to know them. That helps for only a short while. Too soon evening comes and I go off by myself to think of you. I pray this fight will be quickly won so I might return to our home and again be warm in your embrace. Until that happy day, I am, as always, your faithful Will.

The next letter I read, Will wrote to George Bender twenty days later. It was dated Harrison's Landing, July 30.

After being bivouacked in this horrid camp since we arrived two weeks ago, it is rumored the 2nd Corps to which we are attached will soon be sent to battle. Together with the other junior officers, I stopped for a drink of brandy at Major Hess's tent last night. He told us he does not know where we will be sent.

Leaving Harrison's Landing will be a blessing, Father. Morale has eroded quickly here. There has been little to do, save listen to men gripe, and suffer through arduous retellings of battles fought by others. Still, sitting night after night with so many crowded in here among the wagons, artillery and crates of supplies, it is impossible to keep from listening.

I will refrain from feeding your fears by repeating stories I have been told. Most of those sound too horrid to credit. I am certain much of it is the invention of soldiers seeking to raise their glory in the eyes of us newcomers. Yet, from wounds I have seen being tended to in the medical tent, I suspect at least some parts are true. I choose not to consider that for the moment.

Except for the cleared ground we occupy near this landing, there is nothing for miles but dense pine forest. It has been raining for days, and there is no place for the ground water to run off. As a result, we live in what feels like Nickerson's Marsh. You know the place, Father—it is just inland from the Niagara River. Abbie and I went exploring there once. What a wonderful day we had—shoes hung like scarves around our necks, holding tight to each other we waded through the mud and reeds. We were so lost in our dreams the swamp seemed to be a garden. Far from my beloved wife, I cling to such memories.

This Harrison's Landing is not the Eden my memory has made of Nickerson's Marsh. It is a bog we are camped on—a mire of filth, I heard somebody call it. The earth is so wet our tent poles will not hold. Last night, a strong wind blew heavy rain like bullets against the faces of unhappy sentries. Those soldiers soon cared little if they would be shot for deserting their posts as long they could find some shelter. This morning I awoke to find most of the tents had collapsed. To make matters worse, the constant rain has made it near to impossible to strike a fire the men might seek comfort around.

Also, there is much sickness in the camp. The water is bad and is dangerous to drink. I have tried to ease my men's thirst by securing beer for them at my own expense. Because it is hard to come by, too often it is this evil water they must drink. Almost all have fallen ill with dysentery, and each must now take daily doses of quinine. Recently a large supply of onions was sent from Washington. That was necessary since the food has gone bad and there is also much scurvy in camp.

I have not been ill. At the moment my only worry is the foul odor surrounding us. The garbage pits and latrines reek to the point at which I am often forced to walk a distance into the pine forest to escape the fetid waste for a short precious while. Also, I leave camp to escape the bite of swarming black flies and mosquitoes. These insects do us more damage than an enemy we have not yet met.

From what I have written, you will understand why I am pleased to learn we will soon leave this place. The fighting ahead cannot be worse than what I have experienced here. It would be interesting to learn whether these conditions were planned by the generals in order that the men would find fighting less odious by comparison.

Please kiss Mother for me, and please, please, see after my beloved wife. Keep her spirits up. She can be no more lonely for me than I am for her. I ache with guilt at the thought a single tear for me might fall from those green eyes to stain her gentle cheeks. In thoughts of her I find comfort even in this terrible place—

I refolded the letter and placed it on Abigail's lap.

"Just the thought of you brought him comfort," I said. "How lucky you are to have known such love."

I must have sounded surprised by the idea of it, because she asked, "Is being loved so hard for you to grasp?"

I glanced through the window.

"The answer's not out there." Abigail touched my chest. "It's in here."

"It isn't," I told her. "I'm not sure I even understand what it is—not to make love, but… to feel adored. My parents exhausted themselves fighting with each other.

They had nothing left for my brother and me. They didn't know love either, so I never learned from them. Then there was Barry—"

Abigail lifted the letter and kissed it. "Yes, you were badly hurt, and I'm thinking you've locked love from your heart. But, Kaitlyn, the heart isn't an iron vault. It's a living thing that'll have its way even when the one it pines for begins to change. I loved Will no less when *he* did."

I didn't answer.

"Is it because you've had no experience with real love that you've nothing to say?" she pressed. "Or is it you're afraid to know the joys and tears love brings?"

When I still said nothing, she gave me a knowing nod and put the next letter in my hand.

Port Corcoran, August 26, 1862
Dearest Abbie,

This war is beginning to remind me of our Saturday socials in the church. Like dancers moving around a large floor, we and the enemy do nothing more than circle each other, then back away until another waltz begins. Since leaving Harrison's Landing, we have been engaged in a long march through dense forests and overgrown fields. We have walked down roads so dusty we now look more like millers covered with flour than Union soldiers in blue. It does not seem as though anyone knows what to do with us or where we should be.

After departing the camp we occupied at Harrison's Landing, we crossed a river at night on a pontoon bridge that creaked and swayed under our weight. It looked and felt as though it had been made from scraps of wood broken from crates of supplies strewn about when we left. Many of the men cannot swim and feared stepping onto the bridge, because they were certain it would be unable to hold them. I am now hoarse from shouting to coax them across. A sergeant from another troop, who walked beside me for a while, said we had come across the Chickahominy River. Although it is called a river, it has nothing of the majesty of our broad Niagara.

On the other side, we camped for two days at Newport News, then embarked by ship for someplace called Aquina Creek. No sooner had we settled in than we were ordered to march into the country before being ordered to return and re-embark for Alexandria, Virginia. From there we marched another eleven miles to where we are now camped on Arlington Heights opposite Georgetown.

With all the aimless marching we have done, Abbie, I begin to believe that in this war I shall have more need for new shoes than ammunition. Take care of your dear self and have no fear for me,

Always, Will

The letter he wrote to George Bender the same day, told a very different story. In it he said:

—While this constant trudging from place to place has been wearisome, Father, it would almost be bearable were it not for the Rebel snipers. They swarm along our path like wasps with stings of death. I wrote to you about Billy Jackson, a private in my company. He was a large blond farm boy from just east of Erie. I say 'was' because three days ago we marched down a rutted road beside a sparse stand of oak trees. I was next to Billy, yelling at him to not loiter when he stopped to admire crops he insisted were grown taller than any he had ever seen. Suddenly shots rang out, from where I could not determine. Before I realized what had happened, Billy Jackson lay sprawled in the road, left eye gone and cheekbone shot away.

If that were not horrid enough, cannonades send shells screaming overhead. Last week one landed among a group of men who rested on a knoll near a barn a hundred yards in front of us. When the shell burst, so much dirt flew from the ground it was hard to breathe, much less see. I heard loud cries from within the cloud. When the dirt at last settled, I saw tattered men with their arms and legs torn off. The ground on which they lay ran with a river of red. All of this, Father, from an enemy we have not yet seen—

Chapter Thirty-Two
Will Bender's War

A bit stunned from what Will Bender had written, I picked up the next letter. Will wrote it at Harpers Ferry on September 25, 1862. In it he told his father:

> —After leaving Arlington Heights we were ordered to Centerville, about thirty miles distant. We marched through the night and arrived to the roar of artillery. A heavy battle was in progress. We cheered because we would at last have a chance to inflict damage of our own upon the Secessionists.
>
> We were to fight beside troops under General McDowell's command, but it was impossible to find our positions. Confusion reigned up and down the line. 'Where's McClellan?' the men called while they waited for instructions our senior officers seemed reluctant to give. Finally, Little Mac rode onto the field. What a sight he was, Father, in his plumed officer's hat, boots so polished they reflected the sun, and a uniform blouse bedecked with medals. He trotted from one end of the line to the other on his white gelding, shouting words of encouragement. It is easy to see why our men love and trust Little Mac.
>
> Soon his spirit restored the confidence of our troops. Formed into ranks, we advanced two miles over open ground

through constant skirmishes. Men on either side of me fell like grass cut by the swipe of a sickle, crying from the pain of balls that tore their flesh. Still, we inflicted more harm to the Rebels than they did on us. Now I have tasted battle. Though for all the confusion I cannot be certain, I fear I may have slain a Rebel soldier. I say fear, because my conscience aches over the thought I might have. How much more will it do so as the number I kill mounts?

My regiment was held in reserve when the city of Frederick was taken two weeks ago, so we missed the fight for it. Frederic is a charming place, with a long main street lined by shops of every description. Allowed to rest there for two days, letters from home at last caught up with us. Thank you, Father, for the money you sent. With it I purchased new socks and boots. I had a good laugh while speaking to the merchant in the general store where I bought these things. He was a thin, horse-faced man named Edward Mitchell. He told me we had received a grander reception in Frederick—even from someone like him who is a most ardent Secessionist—than had the Rebel forces we drove from the city. He complained that the South's paper money is suspect, and none in Frederick would take it. So the Rebels appropriated what the businesses refused to sell them.

There is a lesson to be learned from this: causes are wonderful to shout about, but the passion for them chills quickly among merchants and farmers when the goods needed are not paid for with hard currency. Having witnessed this, Father, I cannot believe this war will be a long one.

After we left Frederick, there was a desperate fight at a place called South Mountain, although we were not part of that, either. I am told our lines stretched fourteen miles from what is called the Hagerstown Road to Harper's Ferry. Determined to hold the pass through the mountains, the enemy were well placed along the ridge. It was a steep half-mile climb to them. Line after line of our troops swarmed up, only to be driven back by the fire of Rebel musketry and canisters that left dead and dying shredded like raw meat on the rocky slope. Finally the entire line was ordered to attack up the hill at once and well after dark a company from Wisconsin took the crest. It cost them dearly with half of their company killed. From the crest, the Wisconsin boys poured fire down on the running Rebels, whose bodies fell in heaps. The next morning I saw the remains of the battle and thought it must have been the bloodiest affair the world would ever see. I was wrong in that.

On the morning of the 17th, after a night in which our camp was shelled until past nine o'clock, we awoke to an enemy lined up in force along Antietam Creek. When I looked out on that sunny morning over the beautiful landscape dotted with cottages, neatly plowed fields and orchards heavy with fruit, I found it hard to believe the fields before me would soon and forever be stained red.

Artillery shells screaming like banshees overhead shattered the morning calm. They burst among our ranks, blowing souls heavcnward. After suffering the shelling for a time beyond endurance, I felt relief to run in a mad dash toward the creek. I was in a line that moved to within two hundred yards of the Rebels. Having achieved that point, those of us still standing massed in the safety of an orchard on a slight rise. Below us, the enemy was caught unsheltered in a cornfield. We blasted them with round after round of such raking fire that after an hour their front line had been decimated. The few who could, retreated over a hill with us stepping on fallen bodies as we chased them. On the other side of the hill we came up just short of a lane where the ground had been so washed away by rain it formed a natural breastwork. The Rebels crowded in there where we could not reach them. Reinforced, the shots they threw tore at us with such deadly precision that in moments our ranks were as broken as theirs.

Still, one after another our men stood and fired back, then one after another fell—including Johnny Ewing whom I'd promised to protect. I had no time then to consider what I would tell his father. I still don't know how I will find the strength to do it.

We were saved from annihilation when our cavalry charged from the woods to drive the Rebels back. The brief respite gave us time to reform our lines. Though our ranks were thin and our sixty rounds of ammunition almost gone, we joined the final charge that broke their center.

The next morning I walked on a portion of the battlefield, perhaps only a mile of it. Father, nothing I have ever seen prepared me for the sight. I can make no estimate of the number of good men killed and wounded on both sides—more than a few of them slain by your son. Wherever I turned, the dead and dying were piled on each other and lay among slaughtered animals and shattered caissons. Soft moans haunted the morning. Those of us who survived now searched among the dead for fallen comrades. We held cloths over our mouths and noses, because the air was so heavy with the acrid stench of death it burned our lungs. I cannot believe this place will ever again be clean. I cannot believe I will ever again be clean.

I will write no more for now because I need time to let dry the tears I cry for my fallen friends—and for myself that I have been a part of this slaughter.

Your faithful son, Will

The next letter Will wrote to Abigail. Sent from Harpers Ferry on the same day, in it he mentioned none of the horror he had witnessed and done. The few lines he wrote said:

—I miss you this morning more than I ever thought possible. I long for your touch on my arm so I might know I am alive. In thoughts of you I find sanctuary from this world of madness.

I have been through a battle. Have no

> fear, my love, your husband is uninjured. Rather than bore you with details of that minor skirmish, let me talk to you of what I have seen in this place—of beautiful fields, high with corn and wheat, and orchards of fruit so bountiful the Garden of Eden would weep with shame—

When I refolded the letter, Abigail said, "Drivel he wrote of. Beautiful fields of corn, indeed! He sent me bad poetry when I longed to be beside him to share the worst."

"He wanted to keep the terrible things he'd seen from you," I said. "What's wrong in that?"

Tossing her head, she glared at me. "Och, love cannot be sheltered. It doesn't live only in a garden. If you lock it behind a fence in a meadow where flowers bloom and larks sing, it soon finds that meadow has become a desert. Thought to protect my eyes from death, did he? Never would he have done that if I were near enough to scold him. Wasn't it me who held him after that night at Tryon's Folly? Wasn't it me who loved him enough that he could stand to face the next day?"

I laughed. "You're still angry about it."

"I am."

"And still you loved him no less?"

Abigail's eyes snapped up from the folded letter. "What has one to do with the other? Love doesn't so easily turn on itself. I felt angry and disappointed, yes, but I loved him no less." Again, she looked at the letter. "Keep the worst from me, indeed! Father Bender knew better, though. He gave me each letter Will wrote to him and I soon put a stop to such foolishness from my husband. But not until he'd tried to keep the horror from me one more time. Here, read this letter."

I picked up the letter she pointed to. Stafford Heights, December 21, 1862 was written on top. After a brief description of the camp he dwelt in, Will Bender wrote to his father:

> —Many of our engineers perished in a burning hell of shot and shell while bravely trying to build pontoon bridges that would carry our brigades across the Rappahannock River. Though a dear price to pay, their heroic deaths allowed a force of our men to cross. Soon Fredericksburg was ours. But only after what the bloated bodies of our fallen troops confirmed was brutal street fighting to dislodge the damn Rebs from the houses and yards they hid in to fire upon us.
>
> It should not have been necessary to suffer such losses. It seems one Union commander after another is determined to delay until there is no longer surprise in our presence. We had arrived at the Rappahannock without the enemy being aware. Surely if we had forded the river immediately the Rebels would have been caught unprepared. Father, we could have driven them all the way to Richmond! But, having achieved surprise, General Burnside would not give the order to attack. Still, several of our junior officers—and I count myself among them—spoke of doing it without orders. Major Hess soon put a stop to such talk. So we sat in our tents while the Rebs had a month's time to gather forces to throw against us.
>
> December 12th was cold and foggy as our troops swarmed across the river. Instead of continuing the attack that brought

us this far, General Burnside again halted us. In the delay, we lost control of our men and they ravaged the city. Looters roamed the streets. Doors of houses were broken down. Cavalry rode inside. When I passed along what once was a lovely lane of neat Federalist houses, I saw strewn there somebody's fine furniture, piano, china and bedding.

The greatest folly is what occurred the next day. By then the enemy forces had regrouped in strong positions along the surrounding high ground. We marched out of Fredericksburg under a withering hail of artillery shells thrown down from the heights. Those of us who survived the bombardment were ordered to run up the hill in waves. We were like cattle in a slaughterhouse. Late in the afternoon, General Humphreys led us in a final assault on that corner of hell called Marye's Heights.

The damn Rebels were well entrenched along the portion of Telegraph Road we were told to take. Being the main thoroughfare to Richmond, years of wagon traffic had worn away the road surface until it was now sunken behind a stone wall. The Johnnies crouched there, protected from our guns. Between fusillades from mounted cannon that rained havoc upon us, they fired endless volleys of musket balls at our boys as they raced across the open ground, then fell as shattered corpses.

My unit worked its way up the hill through the human debris of failed attacks. Blood from bodies shorn of arms and legs, some without heads, had turned the ground to mud. Halfway up I slipped and fell to my knees. When I glanced around to get my bearings, I stared into my sergeant's lifeless eyes. His mouth was open wide, as if the last thing heard from him was a scream of horror. Withering fire poured from every side. Major Hess's legs were taken from under him by a combination of three shots. The last I saw of the Major he was tumbling like a log rolled downhill. Captain Daniel Barnett—a school teacher from Erie with ashen skin and eyes sunken so far into his skull he seemed a corpse in life—was just in front of me when his head exploded from a ball tearing through it, and he fell at my feet. Now my mouth opened with a scream of horror that mercifully could not be heard above the cannons, and I dove for the ground. With fire raking every inch of the hill, I could not stay there long. I rose and fired on those Rebs—killed one, then grabbed my dead sergeant's rifle and shot another. To save my men? To save myself? I may never know. Soon, so few of us survived, I was the only officer left. I tried to rally my boys, but with the rest of the brigade flying like hunted geese down the hill, we could only give covering fire, then, because of God's grace, retreat alive down to where we'd begun.

I too have been wounded, Father, but it is not at all life-threatening—merely a fragment from a shell-burst yards away that tore some flesh from my shoulder. I will soon be healed and able to rejoin my troops. I will be their new captain. Then, God willing, I shall use my men to inflict as much pain on those damn Rebels as they have on the friends I have lost.

Please, Father, do not tell Abigail about my wound or that I received it in retreat. Let her believe, as I have written to her, that I am well and bringing glory to the Bender name—

Two weeks later, Will Bender again wrote from Stafford Heights, this time to Abigail.

January 4, 1863

Darling Abbie,

I received your letter, and now know Father has been giving you my missives to him. Though I thought to spare your gentle green eyes the sight, reading them you know what hell must look like. There is no need for you to be cross with me, Abbie, since Father has already scolded me for attempting to withhold this from a wife who loves me more than life and would gladly be in the fight beside me if she could. I have taken your and Father's words to heart and now see that holding the truth from you is the same as a lie. I apologize, my dearest one. That is not the foundation on which our love is built. Still, I am glad you are not here to witness what I have. So much death has made the killing of two slave-hunters seem a trivial matter. After all of this, my love, how shall I ever be free to lie beside you without seeing death when I close my eyes? How shall I put aside the anger I feel and find

> peace in making love to you? I fear, Abbie, there are hard days to come when I return to our home.
>
> Yet, I continue to love you with all of my heart—

In letters that followed Will told of the sickness and death that shared his tent. Between the lines, I saw his anger grow to hatred. As I read, I wondered how Abigail had found the strength to heal his heart, now so scarred it could utter few words of love. When I read the letter he wrote on June 13, 1863, from a place called Pipe Creek, I feared she never had.

> We left Stafford Heights on April 23rd, and moved a half mile to the top of a hill. There we ordered the men to build log houses to bunk in. Soon finished, our barracks stood in neat rows with the houses of two companies side-by-side. No sooner had this work been completed and we were comfortably settled in where it was dry than the houses were abandoned when we received a new order to march. Need I tell you, Abbie, when we set out it was again raining?
>
> Once more our engineers fell to work without question, and died with cries that haunt my dreams as they erected pontoon bridges on which we would again cross the bloody Rappahannock. Again we were commanded to wait before facing the enemy on the river's other side.
>
> During that day and night artillery shells flew overhead with such deadly effect we were forced to move a mile back from

the riverbank. At noon on the 1st of May, some way below Fredericksburg, we quick-marched across the pontoon bridges and ran four miles into the woods. Our divisions that had crossed the river the previous two days had been mauled by clashes with the hated enemy and were badly in need of reinforcement. After only the briefest greeting, our combined regiment was ordered to engage in a forced march of twenty-five miles. Before the night ended we were in the line of battle, fighting off a wave of those Rebs—may the Devil eat them and choke on their bones. They came at us screaming their heathen yell, determined to break through. Many of our good men fell, their cries piercing the darkness and my heart with the sharpness of a knife. Though I cover my ears, I hear it still.

I'll not describe the scene unveiled in the chill gray dawn, since it was much the same as has been told in letters you have already read. I will say, though, the prospect I too might one day feel myself torn by bullets and shells no longer frightens me as it did when I arrived so long ago at Harrison's Landing. I have also learned, as you worked so hard to teach me, there is no evil in staining my hands red when the cause is just. Holding this thought in my heart, I know I will acquit myself well in the days to come, and, if God is willing, return to you the same man you saw off at the station.

And yet, I shall be very different. I no longer feel the horror I once did at the destruction men are capable of, because I have found how easily I am capable of it. Perhaps it is true that even the most terrifying plain of Hell loses the ability to horrify once one has camped on it. But then, perhaps I am just tired after this last fight.

The battle I am writing of came near Chancellorsville in a place they call the Wilderness. It was fought where a large brick tavern dominated the intersection of four roads. It was a good strategy to bring us there. We would have succeeded if General Hooker had continued our attack. This army is plagued by commanding generals who plan boldly, then quickly lose their desire once the fight has begun.

In the morning, part of our force had run into what a prisoner told us were General Jackson's Confederate troops. It was clear to those of us on the line that we greatly outnumbered Johnny Reb. Victory, though it would have cost us dearly against an enemy we now know to possess the Devil's own fearlessness, could have been won. Instead, Hooker ordered us to retreat into the tangled underbrush of the Wilderness forest, there to dig in for a defensive fight in a nest of brambles.

In the early morning of the next day, the heavens raged so with the thunder of cannons, I thought surely the world was ending. With the suddenness of a summer downpour, the devil Rebs rained upon us, flooding in from both sides of the road at once. Bursting shells set fire to the woods and chased us from our bramble nest. Half the men I lived with, led and loved, fell, grabbed by the twisted underbrush. Those not consumed by the hungry blaze were trampled by charging Rebs, bayoneted and shot where they lay. Blood again turned the ground to mud. Men slid in it, their blue uniforms dyed red. No quarter was given. Eyes gouged, bodies torn, veterans of other deadly campaigns whimpered like schoolgirls as the Rebs swarmed them under. Trapped by the brambles, men gladly tore their own skin on the thorns to free themselves, only to be caught from behind and slaughtered like beef. Once more we retreated across that Bloody Rappahannock, leaving our dead to be buried by the enemy.

In retreat, I turned once to look back. There stood Johnny Reb, illuminated in the glow of the burning Chancellorsville Tavern. Jubilantly, he raised his guns in victory that could so easily have been ours. I felt a sting in my shoulder while we ran and was nearly knocked from my feet. A ball from a Rebel sharpshooter had struck me. Do not cry over this, my love. I suffered no more than a scratch. Once we were safely across the river, a doctor easily removed the ball. Although he insisted I must rest for a short while, he promised I would once more be fit for duty.

So I have now returned to my regiment here at Pipe Creek Line, where we are trusted to defend Washington, Baltimore and Philadelphia if a Rebel attack comes this way. We are in a strong defensive position, yet I cannot help but wonder if we will ever be led by someone who is determined to

> seize the advantage. Given the opportunity, I will do just that. I wonder, my love, if I survive this dastardly war, how I will ever learn to live again in the quiet of Niagara-on-the-Lake. More and more I think of retaining my commission once this is over. Perhaps then Nathan Kinsley and I might ride together in the west, where I am told there are vast lands to conquer—

When I finished reading I sat in silence, rubbing my thumb on the page. At last I said, "So that's how you lost him. Having seen so much—" I shook my head. "I don't like it, but I almost understand why he needed to go somewhere else when the war ended."

Abigail turned to me. Her voice gurgled with so many tears I couldn't decipher a single word. At last she wiped her eyes and nose on her blue, buttoned sleeve and twisted her swan-like neck to her window.

Chapter Thirty-Three
Fire on Coattails

I folded the last letter and placed it with the others. Without a word, I retied the red ribbon so Abigail's memories would again be held in its satin embrace. Then I closed my eyes to let her love for a man who was dedicated, brave, conscience-bound and so many other greater and smaller parts, flow through me.

For a reason I only now understand, I hesitated to give the letters back. Still, they were hers—her love, not mine. I took baby Jeremiah into my arms while she returned the letters to their hiding place.

With her back to me, in words still filled with tears, Abigail said, "My story's nearly told." Her voice, now cracked and as hoarse as an old woman's, broke through my longing.

"Did… you ever see Will again?" I asked.

She turned and pinched the moisture from her eyes that were now faded to a very pale green.

"Did you?"

In the same way each life is required to proceed in a preordained sequence, Abigail refused to jump ahead. On the window seat, she cupped her head wearily in her hands. "It pained me to read my Will had been wounded," she said, "and he'd only escaped burning in the Chancellorsville forest by the fabric of his coattail. He swore to me his wound was slight and he'd take greater care to avoid harm. But the body being hurt is one thing. A wounded soul is slower to heal."

Again she paused, but not for long. She now seemed driven to relive the rest of her story. "Since Will left for the war," she said, "it was my habit to fix a formal Sunday dinner for Mother and Father Bender. Mother Bender told me it would be a grand surprise for my husband to find me skilled as a proper wife when he returned. She said he might not understand it now, but a wife with such knowledge of manners and dress, one who efficiently runs his household, would be a blessing when, as all men must, he looked to his place in society."

I tried to lighten her sorrow. "I know you, Abbie, and one thing I know is that you'd never buy into such foolishness. Did you tell that ridiculous woman off?"

She sighed deeply. "You mustn't call Mother Bender that. Foolish she might have been at times, and a snob, but she'd come to care for me as a daughter. In my loneliness I felt blessed to feel so much a part of her."

"Still, I find it rather hard to believe you changed enough to accept her silly ideas without question."

Abigail gave me a smile filled with sadness. "Ah, I've let you see too much of me, Kaitlyn Novacs. But you're wrong. I had changed. The world had changed. Gone mad. After reading of how danger was Will's constant tent-mate, it came into my head that preparing in such a way for his return would be an act of faith—a prayer my husband would come home and again be the man I knew. I told myself the good God would not let my efforts go unrewarded. Clinging to that thought, I looked forward to Mother Bender's arrival each week. While our dinner cooked, she taught me things from Mrs. Beeton's *Book of Household Management*. So it was we were sitting side-by-side at the kitchen table of this house, the book open before us, when Will's last letter came."

She pointed to her window.

In the scene that appeared, I saw Elizabeth Bender sitting at the kitchen table. "You see, dear child," she said, "having a formal parlor where the wives of other businessmen might stop for afternoon tea is essential. You must be certain a kettle is always nearly at a boil so you're prepared to pour for them."

At that moment George Bender entered the kitchen. "The post has arrived," he said. "See here, Abbie, it's another letter from your husband."

Abbie grabbed the letter from his hands like it was food and she hadn't eaten in days. She tore it open.

George laughed. "You're quite a sight, young lady. Did you think you'd never have word of him again?"

While she read, Abbie said, "It's been so long, I've near forgotten his voice."

George touched her shoulder. "You mustn't be cross at his silence, child. From the reports in the *Buffalo News*, he hasn't had time for writing." He spread the newspaper across the table and pointed at the front page on which was a rendering of soldiers fallen across a stone wall and others lying broken in a road.

At the sight, Abbie froze.

"You've nothing to fear, child, because… see here—" He touched Will's letter. "It's word from your husband. He's alive and well." Then he pointed to the article in the newspaper. "You've not had word of him because the Army of the Potomac marched thirty miles in one day to reach the Rappahannock River. Then they broke camp three times to remove themselves from the Southern cannonade."

"Mr. Bender, don't tell this poor child such things!" Elizabeth scolded. "You'll frighten her."

Tears filled Abbie's eyes. "It's a fright I live with each day. Does the paper say when this war might end?"

"That foolish journal never says anything pleasant," Elizabeth said. "I do believe this silly newspaper takes pains to make things sound far worse than they really are." She waved her hand as if to dismiss such foolishness. "What does Will say?"

Abbie pulled his letter from beneath the *Buffalo*

News and read it aloud. On four pages he described the battle at Chancellorsville. When she read at the end that husband had again been wounded, she dropped the pages, and moaned, "I fear for him, Mother Bender. I know I shouldn't, but sometimes the fear I'll never see him again gets into my head."

From the way she shuddered, it appeared as though Elizabeth also feared losing Will. She took Abbie's shoulders, turned her and looked in her eyes. "Do not speak such nonsense, child! I'll not permit any thought but of his safety."

Abbie tried to turn away, but Elizabeth held tight. "Did he not promise us both he'd be cautious? Knowing how you pine for him, I'm sure Will shall take care not to suffer grave harm."

George quickly folded the newspaper. "Have no fear for his safety, Abbie. By all accounts the worst is over."

"I can't believe it is. See what he's written?" She pushed the letter across the table.

George read it twice, then said, "I see," and let out a slow breath.

Elizabeth's false bravery faded at the sight of his concern. Her words became shrill. "Tell her, Mr. Bender! Tell this foolish child, her husband… our Will…" She choked on tears.

George wrapped himself around his wife like armor to ward off the lance of fear. Softly, he told her, "Our son will be well, Mrs. Bender. The strength of our belief will protect him."

"It won't, no matter we want it to!" Abbie cried. "An aching in my heart speaks to me of the worst."

"You must not even think such things!" George's voice was so harsh Abbie recoiled.

"How can I not?" she said. "I dread sleep, since each night I wake crying from a dream where I see him in his grave."

"That's foolishness." George rubbed his brow. "Such a dream is merely a woman's fancy. You must steel yourself against it."

Abbie explained that she had no choice in what thoughts entered her head, but he insisted, "The strain of being alone these past months is to blame for you speaking in this manner."

Elizabeth grabbed onto the idea. "Yes! The strain of being alone, that's what it is, George. That's why she thinks such things. She must come to live with us while Will's away. Tell her she must!"

Abbie's back stiffened. "I'll *not* leave my home! This is where Will's expecting to find me when he returns, and it's here I'll be."

"Mrs. Bender's right, girl." George took her hands. "You mustn't be alone.'

"Alone?" Abbie pulled away. Her laughter sounded manic. "How can you think I'm alone when Will fills every corner of this house?"

She told her in-laws that though they were separated by hundreds of miles and two armies, Will's love for her was so strong she felt it in the parlor chair he always sat in, in the books he read, in their marriage bed.

"You're speaking hysterically," George said. "That reinforces my belief you're in no condition to be alone."

Abbie stood stock-still, hands on her hips. "Then I'll have my mother come by each day to stay with me."

From the firmness in her eyes and the set of her jaw, George at last had to admit he could do little, short of tying her up and carrying her across the Common.

***

This is the sorrow that rushes in love's wake, I thought, and wondered whom I quoted. Clearly I had spent far too much time with Richard. Thinking in other peoples' words was *his* habit.

When Abigail at last took a breath, I clapped. "There's the woman I've come to know. I'm proud of you. Men might think they're the stronger sex, but it's us who shoulder most of the burden." As much as I sought to break the spell memory had cast over her, I wanted to brush it away from me.

Drawn abruptly from the scene that played on the other side of her window, she gazed around her room. "Yes, we're strong—sometimes stronger than God intends," she said. "I'm thinking maybe it would've been best if Father Bender *had* forcibly taken me to his house. Maybe being under Mother Bender's watchful eyes, I wouldn't have been stabbed to the heart by what happened. Think on that, Kaitlyn, if ever you're again given the chance I threw away like so much rubbish."

Abigail's words snapped like a whip. I looked toward the bed. *A loner, too strong for my own good,* I thought. *Could that be why I slipped out of my body?*

"It's something to ponder," she said in a gentler tone.

I refused to give in. "Being independent is better than relying on someone else, only to hear one day he's changed his mind."

"Or maybe you wake on that day to hear fate tell you there's a different place *you're* meant to be." Abigail's eyes misted. As if she now spoke to her past, she said, "But refusing to be bound by fate's intent, believing I could be stronger than it— I'm thinking if I'd been less strong, not so stubborn—if I'd gone with Mother and Father Bender—I wouldn't now be bound to this room."

I sat up straight. I'd found a hole in the ghost's argument. While I stroked the infant Jeremiah's cheek, I said, "You told me before that fate has a plan we can't break away from. Well then, it follows that you were fated to be here to tell me your story. Therefore, even if you'd gone to live with the Benders you'd still have wound up here."

Abigail shook her head. "Och, you're thinking like a lawyer. I'm here because I refused to live as I was destined to, though I didn't see it at the time. So instead of going to wait for Will across the Common, I asked Ma to spend her days with me. She was a wonderful woman, Ma was, but I'm thinking because she knew me so well, she wasn't watchful enough.

"You see, with Ma constantly underfoot, everyone expected my fear would loosen its grip. It might have if I'd been content to stay at her side. But instead of clinging to the comfort of her, I would wander off by myself. It's what I did soon after Ma arrived on the morning of July third."

Abigail told me that she left her mother to prepare the meals, and went upstairs. Perched on the window seat in her room, she concentrated on sewing. Since Will's departure, she had taken in piecework as a means of earning pin money. She didn't have to do it. Tom Burke refused to collect rent on the house, and between the Benders and Kirbys the rest of her needs were seen to. She took in the piecework because sewing required such focus her mind had no room for unwanted thoughts. But this day as she sat by her window, her resolve wasn't as firm as it might have been. Most of the time her needlework lay untouched on her lap, while she stared out the window—the same window through which we now watched.

***

Lake Ontario looked calm under the July morning sun. Light clouds overhead were as wispy as the smile on Abbie's lips. On such a fine morning, she thought, fate's gnarled fingers could scratch no one.

She heard Mary hum while she rolled the crust for a berry pie in the kitchen below. A few times she heard footsteps, and knew her mother had come to listen up the stairs to be sure she wasn't crying.

For Abbie the morning passed as calmly as the lake. Then as she sat at her window early in the afternoon, a cloud cast shadows across the street. She felt a chill. Her face drained of color. She cringed at a burning in her chest.

"Oh!" she cried. She tried to stand, but her legs wouldn't hold. Her needlework fell to the floor, then she followed it.

Mary heard the thud. She raced up the stairs to find her daughter sprawled next to the window seat. "What's happened? Are you ill, child?" She gathered Abbie in her arms.

Clutching at her chest, her eyes wide with terror, Abbie cried, "Will's gone, Ma, and so's my life." She rocked and moaned inconsolably until she fainted.

The sound of someone whistling rose from the street. Mary rushed to the window. It was Brian. She shouted down to him, "Fetch the doctor!"

"What is it, Ma?" he called up. "Has my foolish sister gone hysterical again?"

"Don't stand there asking stupid questions. Do as I told you. Be quick about it!"

Spurred by the urgency in Mary's voice, Brian raced across the Common, around two corners in the Town and up a flight of wooden stairs. On the landing he twisted a doorknob and yanked. When the door remained closed, he pounded on it. A woman leaning from a downstairs door, called, "The doctor's gone out."

Brian seemed to be unsure of what to do next. He started back, but before crossing the Common he gave one more glance over his shoulder and saw the doctor's carriage tied up outside the Angel Inn. He ran to the yellow building, peered inside and saw Dr. Bernard, middle-aged with thick dark hair going gray at the temples, sitting down to a late lunch.

Brian raced inside and pulled up at the doctor's

table. Out of breath, he panted, "Don't know what it is, but Ma said to bring you fast."

With a glance at his plate of stew, Dr. Bernard sighed. "Can it wait a short while?"

"Don't think so—not the way Ma sounded."

"Not to worry, Doc," the bartender said. "See to Mrs. Kirby's needs. I'll keep your food warm."

The doctor pushed the plate aside and took his hat. After swallowing the beer left on the table, Brian rushed to catch up. In moments, the carriage turned the corner onto Prideaux Street. As they jumped from the rig, Abbie's cries broke through the open second story window, accompanied by Mary's insistent voice saying, "You must calm yourself, daughter."

When the doctor entered the bedroom, Abbie was pressed in a corner, eyes wild, pulling her hair. "It was never any use!" she cried. "What was ever the use in my loving him?"

"You must not say such a thing." Mary tried to pull her into an embrace.

Abbie shoved her mother aside and fled to cower in another corner. "I loved him too much. Now he's gone because I did."

"Will's not dead!" Mary said. "It's the touch of the Devil has you thinking such a thing."

Grabbing at her chest, Abbie groaned and slid down the wall.

With Brian's help, Mary lifted her daughter onto the bed. She didn't fight the doctor's hands while he examined her.

When he was done, Dr. Bernard sat back. "I can find nothing physically wrong with the girl. She's suffering a bout of hysteria. A great many women are afflicted with it." He reached into his black bag and handed Mary a number of folded packets. "This is laudanum to calm her," he said.

As he descended the stairs, the doctor told Brian, "I've not seen a case so severe. The powder I left will help for only so long. Once her body adapts to it, the hysteria might well overtake the girl again. I'm no expert in such matters, but I wouldn't be surprised if she eventually has to be sent to the asylum in Toronto."

Abbie lay impassive while her mother forced a draft of laudanum through her lips.

As her daughter dozed off, Mary knelt next to the bed. "Is that laughter in the street?" she said. "Ah, Abbie, my heart says you're right, girl. Fate's laughing 'cause it's closed the circle and taken Will from you." She shuddered. As if speaking directly to fate, she shouted, "Are you not yet satisfied?"

Chapter Thirty-Four
Beloved

As the scene in the window faded, Abigail told me that Elizabeth Bender heard of her breakdown and rushed across the Common. As she said this, a new scene played on the window.

Abbie sat at her second story window, her face pressed against the glass. She wore a dress the dour color of mourning. Elizabeth paled when she saw her. Again she insisted that the girl had to be moved to the brick house on Victoria Street.

"I'll not go," Abbie said softly. She didn't turn from the window.

"Of course she won't." Mary Kirby said. "She'll return to our house where she belongs."

There might have been a dispute between mother and mother-in-law, had Abbie not settled matters. "I'll not be doing that, either. Will is here, and I'll be, too." The preternatural calm with which she said it silenced further argument.

Speaking in whispers, the older women decided that Mary and Sean Kirby would move in with Abbie until Will returned. Elizabeth would stop by each afternoon to sit with them. As a result, it was Sean who received the War Department's telegram.

> *It is with regret that I inform you your husband, Major William Jeremiah Bender of the 11th Pennsylvania Volunteers, was slain at Gettysburg, Pennsylvania pursuant to an engagement with the enemy*

during an assault upon the Army of the Potomac at 3 o'clock in the afternoon of July 3, 1863.

Yours, Etc.
Richard Coulter, Colonel
Commander,
11th Pennsylvania Volunteers

Sean held his breath when he brought the message to Abbie's room. Because she had been in mourning for weeks and dosed regularly with laudanum, reading the telegram didn't cause another seizure. After glancing at it briefly, she folded the page. "It seems Will's been promoted again," she said as she placed it on the small table near her bed.

She reacted with no greater emotion a month later when Nathan Kinsley and another soldier arrived. From her bedroom window, she heard a heavy knock on the door then heard two male voices. One she recognized as Kinsley's. Her mother thanked the men for coming, but said Abbie wasn't receiving visitors.

The door started to close then stopped when Mary whispered to herself, "Maybe this visit will get Abbie to come downstairs and let her heart start to heal." Opening the door wide, she said to the men, "On second thought, come in. I'll tell my daughter you're here."

Sean waited in the parlor with Kinsley and whoever was with him, while Mary climbed the stairs.

"Friends of Will's have come to call," she said when she opened the bedroom door. She frowned at the uneaten breakfast, now cold on a tray next to the bed. When Abbie didn't respond, she said, "They've come across the river from Youngstown to see you."

Abbie still didn't answer or even turn from the window to look at her mother.

"Daughter," Mary scolded, "these men have come

all this way to respect your husband's memory. You must let them do it."

Abbie sighed. "You're right, Ma. Will's memory…"

Mary led her downstairs without much further prodding, but slowed to a stop at the bottom. Muted conversation came from the parlor.

"Come, daughter." With a firm grip on her elbow, Mary ushered her in.

The Gentlemen's Parlor was dim, cooled by the damp morning breeze. The heavy damask drapes were drawn back. Thin rays of light stretched over the area rug of Persian design and across the beam spanning the ceiling. Nathan Kinsley rose from the upholstered loveseat, the tips of his carefully groomed mustache drooping as if in sorrow. With a stiff military bearing, his face long, he reached out his hand. "Abbie, please let me say how sorry I am."

"Nathan," she said, "I know Will was your friend and you loved him." Her voice sounded so fragile it seemed the effort to speak might cause her to shatter.

"He was a fine man and a brave one," Nathan said.

She sighed. "He was that."

Her eyes intent on her daughter, Mary Kirby stepped closer when tears made their way down her cheeks.

Nathan took Abbie's arm, led her to one of the deep chairs and introduced the soldier who had come with him. "This is Henry Beeber. He was with Will when…"

"It's all right, Nathan, you can say it," Abbie said barely above a whisper. "My Will's dead. Nothing'll change that."

Beeber, a very thin young man, had a prominent Adam's apple that rose and fell into the high collar of his military tunic when he spoke. His left arm was in a sling and a crutch rested against his chair. "Yes, ma'am, I was with the Major all right," he said as he pushed himself up. "He was a brave one, the best officer I knew. Well, I was his orderly, and I promised him I'd… So, when I got put on limited duty 'cause of these here wounds, I thought—"

Nathan broke in. "The corporal's trying to say that Will asked him to come by and see you."

"Yes, ma'am." Beeber nodded. Not seeming to know how to come to the point, he began to ramble. "I was assigned to him back when we was at Falmouth in Virginia, and was beside him that last month until… Well, and when we was down by Pipe Creek Line he was glad 'cause we was safe there, and he knew that'd please you, ma'am. 'Beeber,' he says to me there, 'if'n Bobby Lee's fool enough to attack us here, we'll have a better victory off his troops than ever he did off us in Fredericksburg.' And I remember when the orders come for us to march, he laughs to me, and says, 'Well, Beeber, that's the army for you. No sooner do I get my billet fixed in a nice safe nest and begin a letter to my beloved wife'—that's how he always called you, ma'am, my beloved wife. He says to me, 'Beeber, in all the world there ain't a woman born to match my beloved wife.' Anyways, he says to me, 'Soon as I start this here letter, some Johnnies are seen in a place called Gettysburg and we're off after 'em again—'"

"Thank you, Corporal." Abbie rose. "It was kind of you to come all this way." She turned and left the room with Mary holding firmly to her arm.

As she passed through the door she heard her father say, "I also thank you for this kindness to my daughter. Before you leave, can you tell me did the lad die well?"

Abbie halted at the bottom of the stairs, her hand tightly grasping the newel post.

Mary tried to pull her away. "You must listen to no more."

Resolutely holding her ground, Abbie heard the corporal tell Sean Kirby the rest of what he had witnessed.

"Yes, sir, I can tell you," Beeber said with obvious pride. "Major Bender, he died a hero—and I'm not the only one what says so. I was with him when we marched all night and gets to Gettysburg just in time to set up on that Cemetery Ridge for two days. It was a place called Cemetery Hill we was supposed to be at, but the turn we made was wrong and it was the Ridge we come to. So, with all hell breakin' loose everywhere, they told us to set up there with the Sixty-Ninth New York.

"When I found out what the place was called and the shootin' begun, I asks the major if it could be an omen, and he says to me, 'The only omen here will be what them Johnnies see chasin' 'em back 'cross that there open field if they come from the tree line afront of us.' Which they done, sir. 'Bout one in the afternoon, after two days heavy fightin' they come. Phew, the cannonade blowing at us—Thought they'd knock us off the ridge, they did. But them dumb Johnnies couldn't get their range right. So after two hours they come chargin' out of the smoke, right into the eyes of our cannons—"

At the bottom of the staircase, Abbie's eyes widened. Her face dropped. In Henry Beeber's words, she seemed to be living the hell of her husband's final moments.

Mary tried again to move her, but Abbie shook her off.

"What a sound it was," Beeber continued. "Them screamin' their heathen tongue-waggin' yell, and our big guns throwin' double canister down on them, our musket fire stringing them out. With all them balls flyin,' men on both sides was falling like leaves after the first frost. By the time them Johnnies gets to this low stone wall left side of the stand of trees we was under, what's left of 'em breaks into a mob. That's when I got shot—both this arm here and in the knee. Then the cannon next to me come off its wheels and tumbles on top of me.

"Lord have mercy, 'cause with that them Johnnies come swarming over the wall. Well, sir, I just about give myself up for a dead man—'specially when I hear the colonel shout all's lost, and our bugler sound the retreat. But Major Bender, he digs his heels down and shoves the gun off me. Could've run like some, but the major wouldn't do that. No, sir. He says, 'I ain't losin' you, too, Beeber.' Restin' me on the cannon barrel, he shouts to our boys, 'We're not runnin' from these damn Rebs anymore.' Then he turns and starts shootin', and so did the rest. Drove them Johnnies back down that hill. Our boys were wavin' and shoutin', and I look 'round for the major to thank him for what he done. Didn't see him first off. Then I looked over. There he is, layin' back against the stone wall, blood running fast from two holes them Johnnies blew in his chest—must've been just afore the shootin' stopped. 'Major,' I calls to him. He's just layin' there, holding this here locket up, lookin' at the picture—"

From the way Beeber stopped and took a deep breath, his mind might have been replaying the carnage he'd witnessed. After a minute, the corporal dug into the pocket of his tunic and handed a filigreed keepsake to Sean. The dried blood in crevices was Will's, he said, and sighed so deeply it was almost a moan. "I called for help. Afore they got there, the major says to me, he says, 'Promise me you'll tell my wife I died with her in my heart and the sight of her face afore me.' Then he closes his eyes, and— Well, sir, the major saved my life and I'm right glad to be here to tell you. And I thought with everythin', Mrs. Bender'd want this here locket back."

Still holding tight to the newel post, Abbie's body sagged.

Mary wrapped one arm around her daughter's shoulders. The other holding her by the waist, she helped Abbie back to the bedroom, where she sat, unmoving, by her window.

***

Abigail now leaned against the window as she had then.

When I followed her gaze, I saw Will's end through the glass panes, witnessed him standing defiantly amid the smoking guns, watched the crimson flow when the last shots fired pierced his chest.

"My life ended when he fell," Abigail whispered.

Chapter Thirty-Five
After the Storm

Though I didn't know it at the time, while through Abigail's window I watched Will draw his final breath, Richard and Ken had almost reached the Niagara Inn.

Driving Richard's Jaguar, Ken shifted from gear to gear so quickly the car nearly slid sideways on the slick road. He got it righted just before they came abreast of the clock tower—the Niagara-on-the-Lake landmark Mrs. Hughes had instructed them to watch for.

Richard looked down at the directions he'd scrawled on a gas pump receipt.

Gears grinding, the Jaguar charged past Victoria Street. Richard craned his neck to look over his shoulder. "Dammit to hell, Ken! Weren't you watching?" he shouted. "You've missed the turn!"

"Screw you, Dick," Ken said. "*You're* supposed to be looking for the street signs."

"Okay, okay, we missed it," Richard said. "Now hit the goddamn brake and turn around!"

"I can't make a U-turn in the middle of a main street."

"Just do it before I shove you out of the car and do it myself."

"Listen to me." Tapping the brake, Ken pulled to the curb. "You've got to calm down. Won't do Katy any good, the way you're carrying on."

Richard pushed back his dark curly hair. "You're right. I know." He released a breath. "It's just that Katy's… There's got to be something… What am I going to do if she…? How can I…?" He slouched in the bucket seat.

"I know, kiddo, I know. But she's not gone yet." Ken hoped it were true.

Like a marathon runner who'd gotten a second wind, Richard jerked forward. "Okay, I'm calm. Now move this damn car. I've got to get to her."

Pulling into and out of the deserted golf course driveway, Ken retraced their path. After a few turns, the Jaguar slid into a pile of snow that had been plowed to the curb in front of the Niagara Inn. When they burst into the house, Ronnie ran to Ken. Wrapped in his arms, head on his chest, she looked over at Richard. "I'm so sorry," she cried.

From Ronnie's uncontrolled tears and the way she clung to her husband, Richard thought I was already dead. His face dropped. He doubled over as if he'd been punched. "Where is she?" he demanded.

Ronnie buried her face in Ken's chest.

Andrea O'Rourke told him, "Upstairs. The… the doctor's with her."

"Oh, Richard…" Ronnie moaned. She reached for his hand.

He jerked back. Andrea and the Hoffmanns trailed behind him as his long legs took the stairs three at a time. Ken steadied him when he skidded on the polished floor and smacked into the upstairs wall as he tried to make the turn around the banister.

Dr. Early was standing over the bed when they entered the room. Finished with his latest examination, he put his stethoscope into his bag. Mrs. Hughes stood nearby.

Ken rested his hand on Richard's shoulder. "Don't know what to say."

Richard looked down at the bed. He saw my hair fanned over the pillow. "I never told her how the feel of it against my face makes me tremble with joy. God, there's so much I haven't told her!" His voice broke as he asked, "Is… is she gone?"

"Not yet," Dr. Early answered.

"What's wrong with her?"

The doctor wiped his glasses on his tie. "Best the lab can figure out, she's got viral cardiomyopathy—that's the medical term for it. It means some kind of virus is attacking her heart."

"What can we do about it?" Richard said. "Doctor, money's no concern. Spend anything you have to. If I don't have enough, I'll borrow more. Just make her well."

"Heart transplant's the only thing that would help." Dr. Early shook his head. "Even if we could locate a donor immediately, her immune system is so compromised it's much too late to consider a transplant."

Richard sniffed back tears, caught his breath and pushed his face close to the doctor's.

***

Abigail gazed through the window, as if she still watched for Will's return. "When he fell, it was the end," she said. Wiping away a tear, she turned to me. "But at the same time, it wasn't."

I saw her search my eyes for a flicker of comprehension.

I had no idea what she meant.

Her cheek resting against a windowpane, she said, "I've seen my Will over the years, you see, walking along the street to the beach. Sometimes he's on that corner, staring at this window with the most darling expression on his face. It's like there's something up here he should remember. One time I saw him in this room—" She stopped for a brief moment. "That was hardest for me, because he lay in our bed with someone else."

"How could that be?" I asked.

As Abigail began to explain, I got distracted by something pulling at me. I brushed at it, as a mother might absently chase a child who yanked her skirt. I felt another tug. This time I slapped hard.

Abigail's lips turned up in a smile that didn't reach her eyes. "What makes you think slapping will do any good?"

"It's annoying," I complained.

"I'd be glad at being bothered in such way."

"What way?"

She pointed to the bed by raising her chin.

I glanced over to see Andrea, Ken, and the innkeeper gathered around me. Ronnie sat on the bed, rubbing my hand. She pulled at my nightgown to straighten it. Across the room I felt the tug.

"Why do I feel that?"

Abigail shrugged. From the look on her face I thought she knew the answer but wouldn't tell.

Before I could press the matter, she pointed to a corner of the room where Richard spoke animatedly to Dr. Early. His face showed wide-eyed, all-color-drained terror. "Do something!" he shouted.

The doctor replied so softly I couldn't make out his words.

Richard glared at him and gesticulated wildly. "Dammit, you quack, if you won't do anything, I'll find someone who will!"

I turned to Abigail. "That's Richard. He's my—"

"I know who he is."

"There isn't much about me you don't know, is there?"

"I can't say why I do."

Again, from her expression I thought she did know. In our time together I'd learned it was pointless to push her for answers, so I attacked it another way. "You also seem to know what's going on in my mind before I do."

"I can't tell you the why of that, either."

My eyes locked on her face, annoyed, I muttered, "Okay, then. If you're determined to be—"

"Mysterious about it? I'm not being that," she said, "You'd not believe me if I told you. Not without knowing more than I should say."

I was about to argue when Abigail looked squarely at me, and said, "You have to trust me in this, Kaitlyn. By our friendship, I promise I'd not deceive you."

She'd been open with me about everything else—well, mostly—so I figured there must be a good reason she held back now. *She'll tell me when she's ready*, I thought, and turned to what was happening in the room. "When—"

"Did Richard get here?" Like a very old friend, she now finished my sentences.

I gritted my teeth.

"I'm sorry. I'll try not to do that anymore. But to answer your question, he came in while we were seeing Corporal Beeber tell how my Will died. And before you ask, I don't know how long ago that was. Time, you see, doesn't mean anything where I am. Leastwise, other than in memories of what happened while I lived."

I felt lightheaded. Abigail knew my mind, everything about me. She saw the past and present as a single moment. If I were ever to understand what was happening, I'd need help from somebody much smarter than I.

"Richard," I called out.

His face pressed close to Dr. Early's, he didn't react.

"Richard, I need you!" I called again.

"What makes you think he can hear you?" Abigail asked.

"I was able to hear *you* moving around, and I heard you talk to me and Leah."

"Haven't I explained already?"

I looked at her blankly.

With a sigh that conveyed exasperation over the dullness of my memory, she said, "You could hear me because you needed to."

We were back to this thing about *needing*, and I still didn't understand. "Doesn't Richard need *me*?"

"He certainly does," she said. "But it never occurs to him to say so. Never used to occur to you either, from all I've seen—leastwise, not in a way anyone could hear." She went on before I could argue. "Besides, when you heard me you were there, and I talked to you from here."

"It's the same thing," I insisted. "Richard's there and I'm where you are." I held my head in both hands to stop the reeling dizziness I felt from the circles Abigail led me in.

"It's not the same," she told me.

Frustrated, I said, "I don't see the difference. Richard's where I was—"

"Yes."

"—and I'm where you are."

Abigail smiled. "Ah, that's where you've gone wrong. It's neither there nor here you are, it's someplace 'twixt the two."

Richard's raised voice stopped me from considering what she said. I heard him scream at Dr. Early, "It's only a matter of time? Don't tell me she's dying and you don't know how to help her!" His face was bright red.

Ken Hoffmann stepped between them. "It isn't his fault."

White spittle on his lips, Richard leaned past Ken to grab the doctor's collar.

"Hey, this isn't helping Katy!" Ronnie said. She rushed over and whispered to the men.

Richard's shoulders slumped. He rubbed his hands on his coat, pulled at his shirt.

Shaking my head, I gave a laugh that wasn't quite one. "The man prides himself on his dispassion and control. Look at him, he's completely lost both. No calm reasoning, no logic. Not even a single literary quote to use as a metaphor."

"He's always been this way," Abigail said. "You wanted him reserved, not making demands on you, so he never let you see."

"He… did that for me?"

The way she rolled her eyes, what I said might have been the stupidest thing she had ever heard.

Now Richard paced rapidly in front of the fireplace, muttering to himself while Ken spoke to the doctor. Back at my bed, Ronnie leaned over me. "Fight, Katy, fight," she said. "I know you can do it. Get mad at me. Holler. Dammit, don't leave me!" She sank to her knees and stroked my forehead.

On the window seat ten feet away, I felt her touch. "Stop doing that," I whined.

Abigail snickered.

"Why's she bothering me?" It seemed that when Ronnie gently caressed my body's face, her touch translated into a tug. I felt as though she were trying hard to pull me someplace I had no intention of going.

Abigail's face brightened. She took both my hands. "It's good you can feel your friend's touch—you've not given up the attachment to your body yet, you see. It means there's still time."

"Time?" I said. "Didn't you just tell me time has no meaning here?"

"Och, must you take everything so literally?"

I held up a hand. "Okay, okay, time as an abstract, then. But time for what?"

"To finish telling what you need to know so you can decide."

"Decide what?" I groaned.

She closed her eyes and took a deep breath. "What you need to. Didn't I just tell you that?"

"I know, I know," I said. "The answer to everything is in what happened to you."

Once more I looked at Richard. He slumped against

the fireplace, clutching the mantel as if he might topple over if he let go. I looked at Ken with his arms around Ronnie, who again was crying against his chest. The others stood a silent death-vigil by my bed. Each sob felt like a needle prick on my chest. I rubbed where it stung. "If it'll make this stop, please tell me the rest."

Abigail leaned back in the nook. "I hesitate to. For when I have, you'll be gone from here—from me—no matter what it is you decide. I'll miss you, Kaitlyn, truly I will. But I understand that fate, not me, holds the thread of your life. Still, it hurts so, and I can't yet bring myself to let go."

Words I desperately wanted to say to my new friend caught in my throat.

She reached for me across the window seat. "I know you feel it, too. And I swear by all I hold dear—by Will, and my Ma and Da, by Mother and Father Bender, and Brinny—I'll find a way to ne'er be far from you." She wiped away what I thought might be a tear for one more friend she would soon lose. She touched her heart, then mine, and began to tell me the last chapter of her tale.

Chapter Thirty-Six
Abigail's End

For two days after Nathan Kinsley and Henry Beeber visited, Mary sat beside her daughter, holding tight to Abbie's hand. All the while Abbie stared at the street from her second story window, refusing to either eat or move from the window seat, even to sleep. She no longer wept, but neither did she speak except to periodically whisper Will's name.

"It's better this than hysterical," her father remarked when the vigil stretched into a third day.

"Aye, it is. But more fearsome yet," Mary said. "Look at her, Sean. She's turned away from all she knows."

He knelt before Mary. "You must get some rest, wife. It'll do neither of us good if you fall ill. Lay down, love. I'll sit with the girl."

She shook her head. "I'll not leave her. And if we're to eat, you must go back to fishing with Brian. The lad can't do it himself."

Sean hesitated.

"It's all right," Mary assured him. She placed a hand on her daughter's shoulder. "Tell your Da it's all right."

Abbie turned her head slowly, and said, "Go on, Da. I'm okay now."

Mary's eyes opened wide. She hugged her daughter. "You see, Sean? It's what I've been telling you. It was only time the lass needed. You heard what she said. Go on now, get back to your fishing. Abbie and me will be fine here."

He looked uncertain, but left after his daughter once again said she was all right.

Abbie leaned out the window. Below, her father

turned and looked up at her. She waved to him. He nodded, then lowering his head he walked down the street toward the beach.

As soon as he passed from sight, she closed the window. "I'd like something to eat, Ma," she said.

Mary's face lit. "Come downstairs. I'll fix you anything you'd like."

Half-risen from the window seat, Abbie slipped back. "My bones are a bit stiff from sitting here. Go ahead to the kitchen. Fix something nice for the both of us. I'll get myself straightened out and be down after a while."

"You should wash yourself. Change your clothes too, while you're about it. You'll feel better for doing that."

Abbie smiled at her. "It's a fine idea, Ma. A beautiful morning like this calls for something bright to wear."

With a sigh of relief, Mary left the room. But a finger of doubt must have touched her. At the bottom of the stairs she stopped, and called, "Abbie?"

"I'm fine, Ma."

Mary entered the kitchen. Soon, her humming mixed into the rattle of pans. Shortly afterward, the aroma of fish and eggs frying in butter floated through the house. Fear that something might be terribly wrong broke through again as she turned the food in the pan. She heard no sound of footsteps overhead. She ran to the bottom of the stairs, calling, "Abbie?"

She received no reply.

"Abigail Bender, are you coming down, child?"

Still, there was no answer.

With what had to be growing trepidation, Mary tore up the stairs. She stopped short with a gasp when she looked into her daughter's room. The child for whom she had such high hopes lay on the bed, neatly arranged in the bright frock she had saved for the day Will would return. Her lips had a blue tinge and turned up in a contented smile. Her face had a deathly pallor, her chest barely rose and fell. The remaining doses of Dr. Bernard's laudanum powder were unwrapped, the empty packets neatly stacked on the table.

"Oh, my poor girl, what've you done?" Mary moaned as she gathered her daughter in her arms.

Abbie Bender took a thin breath—not much more than a sigh—and opened her green eyes that were pale now as the need for sight left them. "I swore to Will I'd not stay here as his widow," she said with her last breath.

***

Abigail leaned into a corner of the window nook as she recalled her last moments of life. Her cheek against a frosted pane, she said, "Poor Ma. There was nothing she could do. I knew it would be that way when I sent Da off. No one was in the house but the two of us, so Ma could either stay with me while I died or run for Dr. Bernard. Of course, by the time she fetched him, I'd have been gone. I'm truly sorry to have put Ma through the pain of seeing me die, but with her insisting on being with me every minute, there was naught else I could do."

From the way Abigail sighed, I understood that reliving the pain love had brought to her and those she cared for had been an arduous task. She stared through the window into the dark sky. "It's all been told now," she said at last.

I should have found soothing words to say, something, *anything* to let her know I truly empathized. But just then I felt anger at what she had done. How dare she rob herself—rob me—of her life. It sounds irrational, but we'd shared so much I forgot she would have been long dead before I was born. So, instead of comforting her, I said, "It's all been told? How can you say that when you left your mother to pay the emotional price for letting you take your own life?"

A puzzled expression grew on Abigail's face. "Emotional price?"

"Yeah, you know, carry the guilt?"

She still looked as though I had spoken in a foreign language.

I sucked in my lip. "Okay, I'll rephrase it," I said rather harshly. "Didn't you think your mother would suffer, watching you die? She could have taken the laudanum away. Didn't you consider for a minute what it would be like for her to live with the knowledge she might have stopped you?"

Abigail gave me a wry smile. "You mean the same way your friends feel, standing by your bed while you decide to do the same as I did?"

"I got sick, I didn't kill myself! It's not the same thing."

She raised an eyebrow. "Oh, isn't it now? Haven't you been running from life all these years? In the end, isn't that what I did?"

I opened my mouth to answer, then stopped short and laughed. "Clever girl," I said, "I didn't see that coming. I'm glad I didn't meet you as an opposing attorney in court."

Abigail bowed her head. "Thank you, but I wasn't setting you a trap. It's you, Kaitlyn, who hides behind the trick of fancy words—did you think I wouldn't see that in this time we've had? More important, did you truly think living apart from your feelings would keep you from pain? So now you know, what'll you do with the knowledge?"

"What'll I *do*?" I glanced at the bed. "What *can* I do?"

"Ah, I wish I could help you. I gladly would if I could." She looked pained.

I touched her hand. "I believe you would. And I remember you said I'd have to help myself. But since I don't know how to get back into my body, I guess it's too late for anything but regrets—" Abruptly I looked up. "Wait a minute. You told me the answer is in your story. What your dying did to your mother is part of it, so there has to be more."

Her head cocked, Abigail seemed to search through her life and death for the promised answer. After a minute, she said, "I surely was sad at leaving Ma that way. I've paid a dear price for what I did—isn't that part of the reason I've been here all these years and not allowed to move on?"

"Why are you asking me?"

She skewed her eyes. "I wasn't asking. The answer's one of the few things I know. It's a rule of living and dying. Deciding to take your own life is against the rules God wrote down when He started this world. I think that's because He wants it to be fate's job to have its way with us. So I've calculated that because I did what I did, I have to stay in this room while people who die other ways get to come back."

"You started to say that before. You told me you'd seen Will on the street." My voice lifted with hope. Perhaps what I needed to know might be hidden there.

Abigail looked back at me. "Yes, it's true. I've seen Will since I died. Sometimes he's short, other times his hair's dark. But I know him just the same. He's drawn to this house, you see. Maybe it's part of my punishment—seeing him and not being able to be with him. I'm thinking he keeps coming by without knowing why, because his soul recalls being happy here. Still, seeing him pass in the street isn't the hardest part. No, hardest was seeing him awake in that bed long after his wife was asleep, and not being able to comfort him or even let him know I was here."

Tears now ran freely down her cheeks. "Oh, how I hurt for him, knowing never in any lifetime would my Will be happy again."

"Not happy? He was reincarnated."

Abigail stared at me.

"He came back for another life. Since he had no memory of you, it follows he would have been able to find happiness in love and marriage."

"My Will did love and marry," Abigail said with a sigh. "When I saw him here, he was making love to his wife."

"Okay, so how can you say he'll never be happy again?"

"It's another of the rules I know. There's one person fate means you to be with over and over. For me it's Will and I'm his. But as long as I'm forbidden to leave this room, he'll not find me again."

I understood what she meant. I began to repeat a story Richard once told me—an oriental myth about how a soul, a single entity in heaven, gets split into a man and woman and the two pieces are sent to earth. There, each searches relentlessly for its mate, finding no peace until they're reunited. But a more urgent thought stopped me in mid-breath. "You mean, because you killed yourself, you're stuck here forever? One mistake, that's it?" Overwhelmed by the unfairness of such an outcome, I demanded, "There's no chance of parole, no pardon… or whatever they call it here?"

Abigail shrugged. "I've not been told."

My years of legal training caused me to bristle at her situation. Images of *The Devil and Daniel Webster* flashing in my mind, I said, "Wait a minute. Who's telling you or not telling you these things? Give me his name. I'll write a letter. Better still, maybe a writ of *habeas corpus* is in order. That ought to get someone's attention. Then I could negotiate—"

Abigail raised her hand. "Things don't work in such a way here. It's not like a prison where somebody tells you what you can and can't do. It's worse, because the only rules I know are those coming into my head and I know they're true when I think them."

Once more my heart felt as though it would break for her. "Then… there's nothing I can do to help you?"

She favored me with a look of friendship so vast it filled my heart. "Ah, there's naught you can do," she said. "Still, I truly thank you for wanting to. Not many have been as kind. But it's *me* that's supposed to help *you*."

"How?"

"By having told you my story."

I leaned from the window nook. My friends still stood in a death-watch around me. Abigail Bender's story had been told, but nothing was changed. "So that's it? That's everything?"

"It is." She again thought for a minute. "Except that soon after I was gone, Mother Bender had a fit of her own. She broke into tears and wouldn't stop. She insisted it was Father Bender's fault for making her move here. She swore if he hadn't, she wouldn't have seen two children buried. Father Bender couldn't comfort her. In the end, he sent her back to her family in Erie. I'm thinking he wasn't able to face the people back there, so he moped around Niagara-on-the-Lake a year before moving to Toronto."

"What about your parents? And Brian?"

Again, Abigail showed her wistful smile. "Fate didn't grant Brinny's wish to sail off to the west on a great schooner. After your American war ended, he married a girl from the Dock and took a job with Mr. Burke. A few years later, Mr. Burke sent him off to open an office in New York City. I can't say what happened after that. Ma and Da were stronger than anyone. They were sad at losing me, but they had enough love between them that they stayed together till God took them. They're buried side-by-side in the yard of the church where Minister Cox preached."

"So that's everything?"

"As much as I can tell."

Lost in my dilemma, I missed the second meaning

of the words she used. "Okay, what happens now?" I asked.

She shrugged.

There seemed to be nothing else to say, so we sat in silence for a long while—Abigail, gazing through her window, me, gently rocking the baby in my arms until, as if the sun had broken through dark clouds, I felt bathed in light. Everything she had said and done had meaning—like bulbs in an electric sign, each was intended to illuminate part of what I needed to know.

"You haven't told it all," I said.

She looked a question at me.

I held out the infant. "You haven't told me the part about Jeremiah."

A gleam in her eyes, Abigail said, "I can't tell you about him."

"Why not? Is he another secret?"

"He's no secret. I can't tell you because he's part of *your* story."

Gripped by a sudden chill, I stammered, "*M-my*... story?"

No change in Abigail's expression, she said, "After holding him all this time, have you not felt a connection to his soul? Do you still not realize Jeremiah is the babe you carried?"

In a flash, I recalled what I had pushed so far from memory nothing before would bring it back. Jeremiah. My baby. *I* had named him—not Barry, who'd been so withdrawn he wasn't even a presence in the birth and death of our son. Jeremiah I had called him so he could be christened before they locked him in his tiny white coffin.

"My... precious baby."

Rocking back and forth, I cradled him tightly against my breasts. With Jeremiah in my arms and his small face lit with joy at my touch, I felt filled with a bliss I had never known. I rested my head against the window. When I did, the dark outside became daylight. Instead of viewing Abigail's memories through the frosted panes, I saw what might have been. Jeremiah was there, and I stood beside him while he grew tall and strong. I saw him at play, heard his childish laughter. I saw him walk out my door, a young man entering the world. I saw the woman he married, the children they had. There was someone with us. His back turned, I couldn't see who he was. It didn't matter. My eyes returned to the images of my son.

The scenes faded when Abigail reached for Jeremiah. "It's time now," she said.

I jerked away. "No! I won't give him up!"

"You must." She stared into the shadows of her room. When she turned back, she said, "Do you not see the choice you have?"

Panicked at the threat of once again losing my child, I demanded, "What choice?"

"Whether to let fate have its way with you and your wee babe or refuse as I did. So ask yourself, Kaitlyn Novacs, will you condemn Jeremiah to remain here as I have—and yourself as well—or will you go back? It's whether to live your life as fate demands or die you have to choose. But before you decide rashly, remember all we've talked of."

Abigail looked toward at Richard. I did, too, then jumped back, startled by what I saw. Only his right half was solid, the rest just a vague outline.

"What's happing to him?" I asked.

"The same as is happening this very minute to you."

I glanced down. My left side had faded into a mist-like aura.

Abigail said, "It's as I knew it would be from the first. Like me and Will, the two of you cannot be whole apart. It's that, Kaitlyn, you've needed to know all your life."

Chapter Thirty-Seven
Remembrance

Richard knelt beside my bed. He pulled my hand from beneath the quilt and held it. His head bowed, he whispered a prayer—something I'd never heard him do. When he finished, he kissed my hand and brushed it against his cheek. First Ronnie, then Ken rubbed his shoulders and back. He shrugged them off.

Ken tried to lead him away.

"It's just a matter of time," Dr. Early said. "Let him stay with her."

"That's right," Richard said. "Let me be! The rest of you get out. Leave me alone with her."

Drying their tears, Ronnie and Andrea left the room. Ken, Mrs. Hughes and the doctor followed them. When they were gone, Richard kissed my forehead, cheek and ear.

"When a man's crazy with grief, it's better to do what he wants than argue with him, huh, Katy?" he whispered. "Who said that? Someone must have. But, you know, I really don't give a damn. Funny, huh? Richard Slattery, the man who knows a million quotes, can't think of—"

He laid his head on my chest and wept.

Sometime later, he pulled the covers down and slipped into the bed. He cradled me against his chest. "I never told you how lost I feel when you're not with me," he said. "I never told you that having you beside me makes me believe living is worthwhile, or that nothing I'll ever do means a damn if you aren't with me. What's wrong with me that I couldn't say those things? And the way I proposed, as if it were a business arrangement— Oh, Katy,

I'm so sorry. But you're so damn independent. I thought I had to be also in order to keep you. Yes, I know, you'd say it's an admission against my interests, but… Dammit, dammit, dammit to hell! Katy, please…"

Ronnie Hoffman poked her head into the room. Very softly, she said, "Richard, we have to let her go."

He held me tighter. "I can't. I won't!"

Dr. Early came in to take my pulse. Richard let him. It wouldn't make a difference, he said. He intended to stay beside me even after my heart stopped beating.

In the middle of the night, he sat up and peered into the shadows near the window. As if he saw something move, he caught his breath. He looked harder.

"Just the moon crossing the horizon, Katy," he said. "The cloud cover's finally broken. It'll be a beautiful night. Please, open your eyes, look at it. What use is beauty if you're not here to see it with me?"

My breathing became shallower. Soft clicks came from my throat. Richard must have known the end had come, because he cursed the clouds for separating to let God reach down and take me.

A short time later he again sat up and looked to the window seat. From the way he listened, I thought he must be able to hear Abigail and me talking.

***

Richard might have heard Abigail saying, "—like me and Will, the two of you can't be whole apart."

Her words rang in my ears like the bell of truth. I understood that, just as Abigail Bender chose to die when Will did, I had chosen to die with my Jeremiah. There was a difference, though. While Abigail had been condemned by unseen hands to haunt her room, my punishment was self-inflicted. I had condemned myself to a dark emotional chamber of my own design. Unlike Abigail, I had been free to leave my chamber at any time but refused.

From my mother and father I'd learned the bitterness of a loveless marriage. Barry stole my childhood fantasy of a better life. Jeremiah was the only real love I had known. I cherished the thought of him from the moment I saw the positive symbol on my pregnancy test. He died because I broke inside. His funeral was simple, short—what could a minister say of a life taken before it began? The words he spoke to ease my pain, to tell me I had to accept my loss, sounded as though he'd said them a hundred times. 'Jeremiah's soul is with the angels.' What did the minister know of loss? What did I care about angels? I only knew Jeremiah wasn't where he belonged, with me. The small chapel at the cemetery was cold, unadorned. No flowers, one candle smelling of incense. On a hard bench, Ronnie's arm around me, I knew this was really *my* funeral. My heart had been nailed inside the tiny white casket the minister spoke over. At the gravesite I collapsed in tears, a clump of dirt in my trembling hand. I tried to climb into the grave. Ken grabbed my arms, held me back. Only my heart was interred, buried in a grave so deep Richard couldn't dig it out no matter how hard he tried. Whose fault was that? Everyone's. No one's. My own! That's why I needed to see Abigail, needed to hear why she chose to die and what her death had cost. Yet, knowing the moral to the parable of her life and death and the consequences attached to the choice laid before me, I refused to surrender my son a second time.

Once again Abigail nodded into the distance. "You have to decide quickly," she said.

I glanced heavenward, desperate, and railed against God for the dubious gift of free will. "Why quickly? I want time with my baby."

She shook her head. Urgency in her voice, she said, "Have you not paid attention to what's happening to you? The wee babe and me, seeing us, touching and talking to us is draining the life from you. It started when we first met.

It's why you've grown so weak. It's why your heart is failing. Look at you on the bed. If you tarry here longer, your connection to your body will be broken. So you must decide if you'll trap yourself and Jeremiah here forever whilst your friends mourn the loss of you or go back. Look into your child's eyes. He's waiting to be born again now that you've recognized the other half of yourself."

I held Jeremiah's little hand and stared at the bed. Richard had me clutched in his arms while he cried and rocked back and forth. "How can I think of what to do when he won't leave me alone," I said.

"Leave you alone?" Abigail gave a thin laugh. "It's many I've seen through the years who'd be glad of knowing this kind of love. Will you risk everything for a chance of the joys, and yes, the hurts being one with another brings or keep running from it? You've got to choose."

"I won't!" I closed my eyes tight to block out everything but me and my son.

"Not choosing is the same as choosing to stay here. He's a good man, Kaitlyn, and strong. He's fighting hard for you. Your heart wasn't buried with Jeremiah. Listen to it for once…"

Abigail's sorrowful tone mixed into Richard's moans, and she faded into the shadows.

***

As the moon slid from its apogee, Richard dozed off. He stirred when he felt me snuggle into the crook of his shoulder. His eyes snapped open and he yelled, "Doctor, get in here!"

Ronnie tore into the room, Ken and Andrea close at her heels. "Is she—"

Richard laughed uncontrollably. "No, no. Listen to her breathe," he said. "Isn't it wonderful? Call the damn doctor."

Within moments Dr. Early stood at my bedside. He took my pulse. "Uh-huh, uh-huh." He reached for his stethoscope. "Uh-huh." He stood back. "I, uh, don't understand this," he mumbled. "In all my years of practicing medicine— No, I surely don't understand."

Richard looked down at me—I know he did because I saw him. My eyes were just slits, but they were open.

"Why won't you stop pulling at me?" I whispered.

"Because I love you, dammit, that's why!"

He silenced me with a kiss.

Chapter Thirty-Eight
Epilogue

A week later I had recovered enough strength to return to Richard's East Side apartment. When I walked into his kitchen that morning, my eyes went wide. I saw on the dinette table a book, open and turned down, as if someone had been reading it and gone off to tend to something. My hand trembling, I picked up the book and looked at the spine. *Anna Karenina*. My jaw dropped. This was the book Abigail had been reading! I hadn't taken it with me when I left the Niagara Inn. How had it gotten here? I opened the book to the title page and saw written in a flowing script, *Thank you.* No signature, just the capital letter *A*.

Instantly, my heart filled with joy. I knew what this meant and who had written it. At least I thought I did. In freeing me from my prison, Abigail had freed herself from hers.

I'll find a way to ne'er be far from you, she had promised me. By leaving this book she had kept that promise. She would forever be in my life.

Still feeling the joy, while I sat over coffee, I twisted the engagement ring now so loose on my finger I could easily remove it. I no longer wanted to.

Richard came up behind me. He lifted my hair and kissed my neck.

I latched onto his hands and pulled him close.

He glanced at the book, then at me and smiled. "Do you want to talk about it now," he said, "or should we just go back to bed?"

I hadn't told him what I'd experienced at the Niagara Inn—hadn't told anyone for fear they'd call me delusional and say I should be immediately returned to the asylum. Trust didn't come easy to me. Still—

I kissed his hand then picked up Abigail's book. "I'm ready to talk about it, Richard," I said, and held out the book. "This is part of it."

He poured a cup of coffee, refilled my cup and moved a chair close to mine.

Haltingly, hesitating often, I told him everything: the three days I spent with a ghost, how I held my baby and saw his future. When I finished, I said, "I know it must sound like a hallucination caused by my being so ill, but Richard, I swear to you it happened just the way I—"

He put a finger on my lips. "Katy, the only ghosts I know are literary ones. I can't know if all this really happened to you, but I'll swear with my dying breath it's true, and I'll believe it without question because you do."

I took his hand, kissed his palm, then held it to my cheek. Tears filled my eyes. Never had I received a greater gift.

Our wedding was a plain affair with no embroidered wedding gown or tuxedos. I did, however, wear a woven tiara of daisies in my hair. "To remind me of Abigail," I told Richard.

His parents and a small group of friends and colleagues attended the ceremony at the church. Ken Hoffmann was Richard's best man, Ronnie my matron of honor. Phillip Cowen, who had started everything by ordering me to have dinner with a new client, gave the bride away. All day I called him Mr. Burke and laughed, but I refused to explain when he questioned me about it.

In the evening we gathered for a celebratory dinner at SPQR—Richard had bought out the restaurant for the night. Just before the meal was served, I heard laughter behind me, more a trill than the deep rasp I had learned to expect. Still, I caught my breath and glanced quickly over my shoulder.

I saw Ronnie laughing at something Ken had told her.

"Guess it's going to take a little time for me to stop being afraid," I said.

Richard leaned over and kissed me. "Take all the time you need—even if it's a lifetime. I'll always be here to hold you when you're afraid."

From the way he'd fought death for me at the Niagara Inn, I had no doubt he would keep his promise. I closed my eyes to let my love for him radiate through me in the same way Abigail had felt love for Will Bender in every pore. After a minute I dug into my purse.

"What have you got there?" Richard asked.

I showed him a reproduction of an old sepia photograph. In it, a woman in a lace wedding gown with daisies in her hair stood near the door to a wooden church.

"The other day I surfed the net looking for any mention of the people and places Abigail showed me. I found this on the Niagara-on-the-Lake Historical Society's page. When I called to ask about it, the man I spoke with said he didn't know who she was, but I recognized her. Richard, this is Abigail's wedding portrait." I stroked the picture. With a self-conscious laugh, I stood it against the flower arrangement in the center of our table. "It's silly, I guess—it cost a lot of money to have them copy the picture and overnight it to me. But, well, I wanted Abbie to share tonight with us."

Richard's mother came up behind me. She bent and kissed my cheek. "I know I'm a little looped from all the wine," she said, "but I've got to tell you how happy I am to have you in the family."

Richard gave her a one-eyed stare. "Mother, it's the fifth time you've said that tonight. Have another drink."

She stuck out her tongue at him.

I slapped his hand. "I appreciate it, Mother Slattery, even if this thankless son of yours doesn't."

"See, I knew I loved this girl for a reason." Again Richard's mother bent to kiss my cheek. When she leaned over she noticed the photograph in the center of the table. "What an interesting picture." She picked it up and examined it. "Who is this?"

"Uh…" I immediately got stuck. Would my new mother-in-law welcome me so warmly if I told her a ghost was my friend?

Richard rode to the rescue. "This is a photograph of a woman in the new story I'm writing. I got it for inspiration."

"She's pretty," his mother said. "*Hmmm*, she looks familiar. I'm sure I've seen this picture before. Where have I seen it?" Her brow knitted, she beckoned to her husband. "Howard, come here a moment, would you? Look at this. Where have I seen this picture?"

He laughed. "Wherever did you find this? Of course you've seen it, Sarah. It's a copy of a picture in my family album. This woman was the sister of my great, great grandfather. When I was young and my grandmother babysat for me, she'd take it out and tell me about the woman's adventures on the Underground Railroad."

"I remember now. Your grandmother told me about her the night we got engaged."

Howard Slattery brushed his wife's cheek. "You recall that?"

"Of course I do, dear. I remember every moment we've spent together." Richard's mother turned to me. "The woman in this picture is something of a Slattery family legend, a very tragic story. Remind me to tell you kids about it sometime. Her name was Abigail Bender."

I can't tell you why I know these things, Abigail's voice whispered in my memory. *You won't believe it without knowing more.*

I thought I might faint.

About Susan Lynn Solomon

Susan Lynn Solomon is the facilitator of the Buffalo Writer's Critique Group which is co-sponsored by the Buffalo Central Library and Just Buffalo Literary Center.

She is the author short stories that have appeared in numerous literary journals. These include, Abigail Bender (awarded an Honorable Mention in a Writers Journal short romance competition), Ginger Man, Elvira, The Memory Tree, Going Home, Yesterday's Wings, Smoker's Lament, Kaddish, and Sabbath (nominated for the 2013 Best of the Net and winner of second place in the 2017 Word Weaver Writing Competition). A collection of her short stories, Voices In My Head, has been released by Solstice Publishing.

Ms. Solomon is also the author of the Emlyn Goode Mysteries. A finalist in M&M's Chanticleer's Mystery & Mayhem Novel Contest, and a finalist for the 2016 Book Excellence Award, her first Emlyn Goode Mystery novel, The Magic of Murder, has received rave reviews, as have the novelettes, Bella Vita, The Day the Music Died, A Shot in the Woods, and 'Twas the Season. The second Emlyn Goode novel, Dead Again, was a finalist for both the 2017 McGrath House Indie Book of the Year and the 2018 Book Excellent Award. Writing is Murder, the third Emlyn Goode novel follows this tradition.

Stepping aside from mysteries, Abigail's Window, Ms. Solomon's latest novel, traces two fate-driven romances—one, that of a woman fearful of love's cost, the other, that of a ghost that pulls at her at a quaint Canadian inn.

Social Media

Facebook: http://www.facebook.com/susanlynnsolomon

LinkedIn: https://www.linkedin.com/in/susansolomon-8183b129

Website: http://www.susanlynnsolomon.com

Twitter: https://twitter.com/susanlynnsolom
@susanlynnsolom1

Acknowledgements

As always I thank Solstice Publishing, Kathi Sprayberry, Melissa Miller, and Kate Collins for believing in a story that is so different from those I've previously written. Also, a big thank you to Anthony Kohler, a magnificent editor who crawled into my characters' minds and ensured that their voices and actions remained consistently true to the story. Thank you also to the members of Writers' Refuge—Chera Thompson, Lou Rara, Eileen Werbisky, Michael Marrone, and Geoge Morse—wonderful writers who worked with me on the development of Abigail's Window. I thank my sister, Robin Krasny, for constantly pushing me to write. Finally, I thank my friend Krista Gottlieb who read an early draft of this novel, and insisted it's a story worth telling. I also must thank Michele DeLuca and *the Niagara Gazette* for the wonder photograph on the back cover.

If you enjoyed this story, check out these other Solstice Publishing books by Susan Lynn Solomon:

The Magic of Murder

When his partner is discovered in a frozen alley with eight bullets in his chest, Niagara Falls Police Detective Roger Frey swears vengeance. But Detective Chief Woodward has forbidden him or anyone else on the detective squad to work the case. Emlyn Goode knows Roger will disobey his boss, which will cost him his job and his freedom. Because she cares for him more than she'll admit, she needs to stop him. Desperate, she can think of but one way.

Emlyn recently learned she's a direct descendant of a woman hanged as a witch in 1692. She has a book filled with arcane recipes and chants passed down through her family. Possessed of, or perhaps by a vivid imagination, she intends to use these to solve Jimmy's murder before Roger takes revenge on the killer. But she's new to this "witch thing," and needs help from her friend Rebecca Nurse, whose ancestor also took a short drop from a Salem tree. Rebecca's not much better at deciphering the ancient directions, and while the women stumble over spell after spell, the number possible killers grow. When Chief Woodward's wife is shot and a bottle bomb bursts through Emlyn's window, it becomes clear she's next on the killer's list.

https://bookgoodies.com/a/B015OQO5LO

Dead Again

When Emlyn Goode's mother returns to Niagara Falls for a high school reunion, so does murder. During the reunion, a woman's body is found in the ladies room. Is this killing connected to one that occurred 40 years before in the woods below the town of Lewiston? Harry Woodward, a young police officer working his first murder case suspected Emlyn's mother of the crime, although there wasn't enough evidence to arrest her.

Home from a year-long leave, Harry—now the Niagara Falls Chief of Detectives— together with Emlyn's friend, Detective Roger Frey, investigates the latest killing. Distraught over indications her mother might have been involved in both murders, Emlyn, with her cohort, Rebecca Nurse, sets out to prove otherwise. But, danger lurks in the shadows when amateurs—even ones with witchy skills—get involved with murder.

https://bookgoodies.com/a/B01N0OA1IV

Bella Vita

A car burns in the parking lot behind Bella Vita Hair Salon. The corpse in the front seat has a short sword pushed into his ribs. Beneath the car is a cast-iron cauldron filled with flowers. This seems to be a sacrificial rite Rebecca Nurse had been teaching Emlyn Goode. But is it? The corpse has been identified as George Malone, and earlier on this summer solstice day, he and his wife had severe argument. Could it be that Angela Malone has murdered her husband? Prodded by Elvira, an overly-large albino cat that wants the case solved so she can get some sleep, to Rebecca's dismay Emlyn again dips into her ancient relatives Book of

Shadows to find the answer before her friend and neighbor, Detective Roger Fry, can.

http://bookgoodies.com/a/B01I01WEWW

The Day the Music Died

A rock star's murder leaves Emlyn Goode questioning everything she knows about herself.

Amanda Stone, a rock and roll icon who vanished at the peak of her career in 1986, has returned to her hometown of Niagara Falls. She brings with her a message that causes Emlyn Goode to question everything she knows about herself. When Stone is murdered, Emlyn must use the craft her ancient relative wrote of in a Book of Shadows to solve the crime. If she fails, she'll never know if what Stone told her is true.

https://bookgoodies.com/a/B0747V1DPT

Writing is Murder

Cursed by a Native American, the Bennet House is one of the most haunted locations in Niagara Falls. This is where Emlyn Goode and all but one member of her writers' group hunt for ghosts on Halloween. What they find in the house, isn't a ghost, though. It's the body of Daniel Bennet, the missing group member.

A few days earlier, Daniel had shown Emlyn a document he'd found in the Bennet House, and told her it would anger people if made public. When the body is found, the document is missing. Accused of Daniel's murder, Emlyn is certain that document will identify the true killer. But her search for it becomes dangerous when her lover, police detective Roger Frey is shot in the Bennet House, and then the killer comes after her. Without Roger's protection, can anything written in her ancient relative's Book of Shadows save Emlyn this time?

https://www.amazon.com/Writing-Murder-Emlyn-Goode-Mystery/dp/1625267916

A Shot in the Woods

Turkey hunting season in Western New York, and a short, round woman walking her dog in the woods, blends in with the trees. A shot rings out. The police call Claire Finch's fate a tragic accident, but Roger Frey's family insists otherwise. Emlyn Goode steps in with her witchy ways to learn the truth, only to find the hunter might now see her as his prey.

https://www.amazon.com/Shot-Woods-Susan-Lynn-Solomon/dp/171802438X

'Twas the Season

"How do I get involved in these things?" Emlyn Goode asks.

It's Christmas Eve. Instead of singing carols around a fire, Emlyn and Roger Frey are at the historic Echo Club for the Niagara Falls police precinct's annual holiday celebration. Tonight there will be good food, dancing, and time with friends. A joyous night—that is, until the body of a man Emlyn knows too well is found in the Club's stairwell.

Now she refuses to rest until she figures out who killed him, and why.

But, each time Emlyn's gotten involved in a murder, the killer has come after her. Can she find a clue in her ancient relative's *Book of Shadows* before that happens again?

44584491R00175

Made in the USA
Middletown, DE
09 May 2019